THE
BLACK
SNOW

ALSO BY PAUL LYNCH

Red Sky in Morning

PAUL LYNCH

THE BLACK SNOW

Quercus

First published in Great Britain in 2014 by

Quercus Editions Ltd
55 Baker Street
7th Floor, South Block
London
W1U 8EW

A CIP catalogue record for this book is available
from the British Library

ISBN 978 1 78206 204 2 (HB)
ISBN 978 1 78206 205 9 (TPB)
ISBN 978 1 78206 206 6 (EBOOK)

10 9 8 7 6 5 4 3 2 1

Typeset by Ellipsis Digital Ltd, Glasgow

Printed and bound in Great Britain by Clays Ltd, St Ives plc

For Anna Taylor

Who shall remember my house, where shall live my children's children
When the time of sorrow is come?

T. S. Eliot

Because the known and the unknown
Touch

George Oppen

Part I

I T WAS THE BEGINNING of darkness when Matthew Peoples saw it first. The thick shape of him upright in the field half-turning to scratch a nick at his shoulder. He stood there stripped to his grey vest unwashed and puzzled quietly upon what he saw — a thin cat's tail curling grey into the sky, some kind of smoke that mingled easy with the cloud's pewter. Evening was pressing down gentle and in the way the light fell he could have missed it, a yellowing that shook upon the fading day and cast the fields of Carnarvan in a flaxen glow. Three human shapes in that field and a triplicate of shadows winnowing long beside them. The bay horse for a moment easy.

Hardly a word was Matthew Peoples' style until the work was done and maybe then he'd say a few words, a suck on his pipe and he would lean back and crack a joke quietly. He cleared his voice now and when he spoke he found himself unheard. He bent again to the work, the hair on his hands white to match the white shadow of his jaw, and he bore old-man eyes that sat deep in his skull, marked him out as older than he was. His hands red and spading at rocks that had sat for who knows how long in compact tight with the earth, lay orphaned now by the side of the field.

Matthew Peoples was following behind the horse. Eight years

old she was and there was something unsettled about her. He had led her out from the stable that morning but she balked in the yard, tried to back up away from him, snouting the air with intransigence. Hold it easy there you. He thought he could smell an anxiety, something quavery beneath the skin, and he stared at her and took in the dark glass of her eye and saw in her the lengthening warp of himself. She blinked heavy a few times, turned her gaze towards the ground like she was in reverie about something and he watched her then lift a knee as if he had dreamed the disagreement. He was no expert with horses but he'd told Barnabas Kane about it and the man's mouth made for a smile that did not reach the smiling place of his eyes.

When she's not right she'll as good as tell you, he said.

Well maybe she did.

Matthew pulled from the earth a stone shaped strange and he stopped and rubbed at its muck. A quality to it he saw and he spat on it and wiped it on his trousers. The stone was discoid-shaped like some neolithic tool he had once seen pulled out of a field, and he wondered if it was — the item smooth and flat and moulded by ancient hands he guessed as near a perfect thing. He looked towards Barnabas's son Billy and held it up for him to see but the boy stood staring into his own thoughts. He was beside the horse, cradling his hand in his shirt, having scratched it earlier off a snarl of old bottle sticking out of the earth. He turned from the boy and pocketed the stone. The blue rope he used as a belt had come soft and he redid the knot and bent again to the work. A feeling then began to worry at him, like some strange tongue that came from a place felt but unformed, and he looked up the field towards Barnabas who had stopped to adjust the horse's hitching. A gleam of power in the way Barnabas stood, squat and coiled under the muck-stained shirt. The stance of a man who was generally agitated. A man prone to thoughts of deeper things but awkward to mention it. The growing lank of Billy beside him, fourteen years old with a pussing face.

In her ears the music of bees and then the silence of the house. Eskra Kane stood thin in the hallway in a blue smock that near matched her eyes. Her brunette hair slid into her face as she took off her bonnet, the bee-veil draped bridely over it, and she placed it on the bannister's snub-nose. The living room was held bright beside her by the yellowing light and it shone upon the dark of the piano. She sighed. Days like these dried the damp in your bones, set loose the heart from the hasp of winter. When she came to Donegal with Barnabas, the boy Billy was learning to speak. The locals watched them with wary eyes and the wind burled and sank its teeth. Only Barnabas knew the talk. She saw the country as wild and poor, a vision darker than the dream spun by her emigrant parents, Tyrone folk who took the boat for New York and built for themselves what they could. Here she saw damp and desolation, a gnawing you had to fight against that was relentless. Those first nights she would lie awake beside Barnabas and listen to the rain and the wind and then nights when the weather seemed to cease altogether and she heard in that silence the opening of a void. This place her husband had been sent away from as an orphaned boy. She had learned to find comfort in rare evenings such as this, drew solace watching the boy grow up natural in a country that was by rights his home.

In the kitchen she found the stove ticking. Must of turf and the savour of cooking stew. Lavender on the air lightly. A storm of crumbs as usual about the place where Matthew Peoples had sat down to eat, big slow hands reaching for the black bread and pulling at it. She wiped the deal table and saw they were near out of loaf. Time soon enough to light the lamps. Around the room the gloaming bore its shadows that stretched like a circus of dark animals waking.

The field was an uneven hummocked thing long unused, lay like a withered leg alongside wider pasture made separate by trees. It was of no use other than as a dumping ground. At the start of February Barnabas had stood knuckling his cheek and said he was sick of looking at the place. A funny few days of warm weather. We'll plough it up and get the rocks out of it and manure it to fuck and let's see. They stood looking over it. Swathes of the field nettle-fleshed that roiled when the wind rose up a wild sea. Half-hid amidst them was the wreck of an old grubber spored with rust. They had to drag it out using the horse and left the old implement tensed and gnarled in a hollow by the trees. The field cornered with bunching blackthorns and Matthew Peoples went at them flashing smiles with a billhook.

The horse was giving Barnabas trouble and Billy stepped in to lead it by the harness. Barnabas looked at the boy and walked over to him, took his hand in his own. Go back to the house would you and get that tended to by your mother. He let go the boy's wrist and pinched him softly in the ribs and Billy shrank away from him. Leave off will you. He stood there looping the end of his shirt around his hand ignoring the instruction.

Barnabas sighed. You'll ruin that shirt.

Shirt's old as fuck anyhow so it is. I can fix the horse.

The horse doesn't need no help.

Billy leaned in to examine her. A coin-sized patch of hair missing just behind the harness and he walked around and saw the same on the off side.

She's going raw so she is.

I doubt that.

Maybe we should rest her.

Barnabas laughed. That horse's been on her holidays, lying in field and stable all week.

Billy soothed the horse's muzzle, looked into the dark of her eyes as if he could transmit some feeling or intention into her.

Matthew Peoples stretched his back and he heard then the distant sound of the byred cattle. Lowing like a sour wind. What in the hell's up with them? The damned rope-belt had come loose again and he fixed it tight and felt some queer thought nicking at him and he turned and caught sight then of the smoke, saw how the curling cat's tail had thickened into a spiral of dark slate. He watched how it folded upon itself and in an instant seemed to increase twofold and he looked across to the others, felt something flutter inside him. His voice in his throat tight and his mind seized upon words and made them concrete.

Hey boys, he said.

Billy's mongrel, Cyclop, had appeared in the field beside him, stood watching fierce-gazed with his orange eye unblinking. The dog with a mind of his own, a lordly indifference to the call of anybody and he turned and woofed toward the trees. Barnabas stood wondering. Maybe the horse was getting old or maybe there was something wrong with her like Matthew Peoples said but he couldn't see what it was. Never a bother before. And that boy needs to get that hand of his sorted. His face was hot and he was itching under his shirt and he waved at a fly buzzing by the horse's withers. He turned to his son.

Would ye go and get that hand seen to. You'll get it infected so you will.

The boy looked down at the hand and the blood on the shirt and he addressed the ground as he spoke.

I'm all right so I am.

Go on and get the rod for the horse then.

Barnabas bent and grabbed a rock shaped like the tooth of some old animal that had fallen there to die under the wheel of an ancient sun, and perhaps that may have been, but as he tossed it lazy towards the ditch Matthew Peoples took a step forward and cleared his throat again. Jesus Christ, boys. They took no notice of him or perhaps they didn't hear, for later in their memories what each of them heard was the dull sound of Matthew Peoples' boots thudding up the field. Not a word from the man and something comic about the way he moved with his limbs all thickly, like he was set to stumble and hit the ground at the knees, fall without his hands into the dirt face-forward, break apart into his constituent elements. But they'd never seen him move quicker, his hands balled like stones and the whites of ankles winking at them through the rise and fall of his slacks. And if Matthew Peoples had known what he was running towards he might have stopped right there, turned instead for the road gated at the far side of the field. Barnabas wondering what was up with the man when he heard him bellow belatedly, a single word that came backwards over the man like a lobbed stone. Had to hear it twice in his mind till his eyes travelled to a place above the trees where he saw the swirl blackly, a shimmy of smoke that seemed to do a bow just for him.

Fire.

A skim of starlings in the sky above Carnarvan seemed to mirror the rising wreath of drift smoke. The murmuration swung in unison like minds entwined, weaved the sky with giant breathing until the dusk pulsed like a lung. The group inverted and swirled, caught the light and bent it, swung again into a strip of infinite looping, nature's way of mocking perhaps what was playing out below, or more likely the birds were oblivious, locked into their own state of being. The boy saw the display above the townland but did not register it in his mind, watched instead his father run blind up the field, looked towards the darkening trees. Like a visitant, something passed through him cold.

Barnabas's mind staring over an abyss he could not see. He followed Matthew up the field, a drunkenness in his legs as if apprehension had become a fluid thing administered into his blood, and then he managed himself into a run.

Not the house, please be. Oh, Eskra.

The narrow field and the stretch of it endlessly and then he saw Matthew Peoples disappear into the trees. He followed, trees of oak and sycamore and a wizened beech that remained with fingers pointed to the sky as if trying to beseech some urgent claim upon life. The path worn through. He met relief in the shape of Eskra running towards them, her skirt hitched, her elbows flaring, flour on her hands. Never more fully alive in the way he saw her, her two cheeks burning. He saw Matthew Peoples stalling for a moment to listen to her, the man bent on his knees to catch his breath, and then he was off at a run. Barnabas caught up and stopped for her and she took his wrist in her floured hand white as if the blood had drained out of it. Sweat filming her high forehead and her breath jagging at the air like a knife, jagging at his eyes. She tightened her grip, tried to catch her breath. What he saw in her eyes near defeated him before she spoke, and when she did so, a sheaf of hair fell loose across her face.

The byre's burning, she said.

She swiped quick at her hair and put upon her cheek a line of flour as if she had been marked.

Go shout for the boy, he said.

An imprint of her face upon his mind as he ran. His world narrowing down into a different kind of seeing.

The byre stood right-angled to the house, a building made of stone that was upon the land when he bought it. In length it was some fifty feet with pens for cattle now housed for the winter. Fodder in the loft under old oak beams. The byre had red double doors at the front that were not built wide enough for big cattle to walk through shoulder to shoulder, made it slow-going to move them in and out. His mind went over what he expected would meet him. Why now to fuck in February when they weren't yet in the fields? Another few months and they would be passed it. He could hear Cyclop panting behind him, strained his eyes beyond the trees but could see nothing but what was before him, tree shadow serpentine on the track as if he had stepped into an unreality that annulled all time and rewrote all laws indifferently.

He came upon the pasture field and what he saw was a helix of black smoke that hid the house, spread like squid ink in water.

The west end of the byre's roof was blazing. Smoke sidled from its windows like water streaming backwards over rocks, curled towards the roof where it made with darker smoke a sickening union. He ran into the yard and saw Matthew Peoples working the long handle of the pump. The huge tree arms on him. A bucket slung over the pump's snout and water sloshing in. Matthew Peoples turned with his face lit as if by rage and he began at a run towards the fire, swung the bucket back and pitched into the air a river. The water travelled for a moment glittering and strangely beautiful until it fell dimly upon the roof like a stone met with an ocean. Barnabas ran to him, grabbed at his shoulder. Fuck that, he said. He pulled him by the arm and pointed. They ran to the byre's double doors and stood facing them, a wraith of smoke sly through the cracks as if the fire were but a small thing. Matthew Peoples' eyes widened, took the look of a man who can't swim being asked into water. He shook his head at Barnabas who stood squinting at the door. A pleading in Matthew Peoples' eyes that went unseen and Barnabas stood watching the smoking door, felt for a moment his legs weaken, forty-three cows inside, and he took a breath, saw Eskra and the boy approaching the gate from the field, and it was then he put a hand to Matthew Peoples' back and pushed him towards the door.

Perhaps the jambs had buckled in the spreading heat for the doors shook but wouldn't give. Matthew Peoples pressed down the latch and he kicked at the wood and it met his advance with a judder that was made mute by the fire's roar. Faintly they heard the voices of Billy and Eskra. Matthew Peoples took a step backwards and he looked nervously for the sky hooding slowly with evening and saw it instead made naught by smoke, and then he bulled towards the door and the door sucked open into a strange dark that swallowed the man in his entirety, Barnabas running in after him with his shirt hitched to his mouth.

The different smells of the barn wiped out like nothing in it had existed. The catalogue of smells – the way grass and dung and feed knit into an odour of their own making. The weighted must of hay. The damp smell of an aged building. Now just the rank smell of burning and the air smoked to the nullity of a dream. What terrified the two men most was the sound of the animal's frantic thunder. The cattle locked in their pens clamouring on top of one another to get out. One dark autumn day Barnabas had seen them rattled and stampede as if they were a single thinking thing, fleeing towards the byre during a break of thunder under clouds that had come down to meet them. Now they gave off a dismal bellowing that no person would want to hear. He felt Matthew Peoples' arm upon his shoulder but could not see him, felt the arm let go, the impress of the man's hand still upon him. The faint outline of things, his eyes rawing to the smoke, his breathing shallowed as if he had taken a kick to the belly. He coughed and bent to his knees, and what he heard then was the issuing of the fire's own sounds, the deep purring of contentment, as if fire was something that sat compact and waiting in a coiled malevolence and revelled being let out. He had to replay in his mind the layout of a byre he knew backwards but wherever he crawled he could not find the pens, could find nothing at all, his hands upon the ground yet the surface yielding no clues to him, no marks nor points of reference, as if what had been was erased, and when he tried then to find the door nothing at all was visible, not the walls nor the light from outside nor the man who went in with him, and he called out to Matthew Peoples, could barely hear his own voice as if he had been wadded at the mouth, and the panic then that seized him was like the bursting of light in his mind.

A pair of hands huge on him. A hank of his shirt noosed about his neck and he felt himself being pulled backwards, out the byre door and then into the yard where he was laid upon his back. His eyes stung shut from the smoke and the daybright hurt his eyes to see it. He lay there on the flagstones with his head turned dumbly and slowly he began to see, the world a thin blear, a patch of sky empty as a vale of snow until he saw it stain with dark smoke. The weft and warp of his breathing undone to a ragged stitching.

He looked up towards Matthew Peoples to thank him but who he saw was another. The hard-nugget eyes of his neighbour, Peter McDaid, one strabismus eye upon him and the other staring past his head as if he saw the shade of another there to disturb him. The laughter lines that made a marionette of his mouth had collapsed now altogether and a terrible frown was etched into his forehead with smokedirt in the creases of it. He began to shake Barnabas. Are ye kilt? Are ye kilt? Eskra leaning over him and then she helped Barnabas to sit up. The air was rank and yet in that moment he caught a linger of soft and ordinary smells off her, jasmine in her hair, a trace of the lavender she liked to place about the house in small bottles salvaged from the garden, flour dust from the hand she placed upon his cheek, and in that moment though he could not speak it he felt for her an eruption of no greater love and gratitude. And then as his eyes took full view of the byre he could smell nothing else but the smell of the world corrupted. He saw McDaid run towards the byre and saw him beaten back by smoke that corkscrewed towards him, the man going at it again and standing at the door helpless with his hands to his head. When he turned around Barnabas saw in McDaid a childishness that spoke of the man being stripped of all action and power in the quickening then of what was. The struggling of Barnabas's tongue and he leaned over and tried to spit, his voice scratching out of his throat as if the greater part of it had been ripped out and left behind in the byre, a scream upon the floor shapeless and mute. Trying to sound the words to them.

Matthew Peoples.

What kind of day it was afterwards those who talked about it hardly remembered. A temperate yellow evening with no rain was made forgettable. The fire had forged its own weather, wind-smoke that burled and circled like demons unleashed, one woman said. The way the evening heated up seemed as if the fire had boiled the air. Soot softly like snow that fell a brittle powder to the skin. The event impressed itself so strongly it consumed them like a folktale. The sound of the fire's hunger was like some enormous force let loose upon the world – an epic thing that held within its violence the fierce, rolling energy of the sea. Human shapes rising up against it, their smallness pressing forward in waves only to be beaten back. Later, Barnabas could not even remember the difficulty they had with the horse. Or the things he had done that morning – the egg with the two yolks he had cracked open into a bowl and noted how it had happened twice that same week. And when darkness had sooted all but the smouldering byre's embers, he did not remember about the horse that had been left hitched in the field until Billy reminded him of it. Must have stood for hours in discomfort. Sent the boy out to get it, an oil lamp bleary against the swamping darkness and then that warped communion of shadows coming back in.

In the space of a few minutes neighbours came to help. Three McLaughlin brothers running through riven fields, the three of them near-alike. They charged like racehorses with their chests out and their shoulders backwards slung, chestnut hair fluttering behind their ears. Shadows from the failing light made stern countenances of their sloping hard faces and they came to the house with their clothes thorned and burred like men who had climbed through all of nature to get there. One of them scratched red from the wrist all the way to his rolled sleeves. They saw Barnabas lying foetal in the yard, Eskra bending over him helping him to sit up. Peter McDaid standing there helpless with his hands to his head. The boy skulking back by the house like some animal wild-eyed and confused trying to remain hid. They saw too Peter McDaid's bicycle where he had dropped it in the yard, the back wheel spinning slowly to a stop like a rickety wheel.

Soon more people came. A neighbouring farmer called Fran Glacken appeared stout-faced from an adjoining field with his two grown sons beside him, their wine-bald heads wet with sweat. Later, the wives and children who made their way to the farm began clutching at each other's arms as if upon each other they could find resilience. How they stood together like a fortress.

Eskra ran about the yard but her mind in its violent thinking would not allow her to see. Fran Glacken grabbed a hold of her shoulder and shouted at her, his face held inches from hers and his eyes fit to bursting. Woman. Where are the buckets? The man before her an ageless beast, hairless and red like he had been skinned raw by weather after years of service to it and was left hardened like a lobster. She pointed towards the byre and froze till Glacken shook her again. She turned towards the stable and said you'll find some more in there, swiped at the hair on her face that fell upon her vision like a curtain. Glacken moved towards it with his feet hid by smoke, a huge-limbed gliding thing, and he came out with buckets and went to the pump. He began to work its gasping mouth and nodded for one of the McLaughlin brothers to give the bucket to the men lining up in file. Saw Billy beside him wearing a look of confusion. Billy saw how the man's face was smoked and his eyes were burning as if some kind of lunacy was let loose in them and perhaps it was, for Glacken reached out then with the flat spade of his hand and struck the boy in the face. Wake up there, he shouted. He sent Billy into the house for towels and the boy ran stunned into the kitchen. He stopped at the window to look, saw his father broken in the yard, three clocks ticking and then the slow lolling sound as each one belled five o'clock. He went upstairs to the cupboard and tumbled everything out and it came upon him then what it was and it shook itself loose, a great heaving thing inside him, and he became helpless to its forces. He stood staring at the wall and took a deep breath, took a heap of towels and went to the hall mirror and rubbed his eyes dry until it looked like he had not been crying.

Smoke lingered in the kitchen and nestled catly in the corners. It thickened the air of the back yard like a wall. He pushed through it towards the pump where he saw the outline of Glacken as if the man was half-being and he came close and wary and saw the man's forehead split by a swollen vein. Glacken took the towels without looking at him and sluiced them and passed them up the line telling the others to tie them about their faces. Eskra came alongside him then, tried to push him without a word away from the pump. He moved her away with one arm and a shout. Yer not strong enough woman. He saw igneous in her eye and outstared her, thrust into her hand a full bucket. You'd be better off, Eskra, if you were passing buckets in the line.

Nobody saw Goat McLaughlin appear in the yard, the father of the three McLaughlin brothers. He sidled through the smoke with quick small steps, a prophet face fiercely bearded save for brilliant blue eyes that shone out of him as if he carried within him a conviction more righteous than all others. His muscles were waste on his bones and dewlaps of skin hung off his sinew and his quick-seeing eyes picked out Fran Glacken at the pump. He stepped silently into the chain and pushed one of his sons to the front so now there were three men throwing buckets of water upon the roof, water coursing into the air and firewind spraying some of it back upon the yard and upon their faces, a lurching carousel of limbs that began and circled back to Fran Glacken.

Barnabas sat on his haunches with his head in his hands, his breath a ruined thing. He looked across the yard and met the eyes for a moment of his wife, the woman swivelling her hips to pass backwards an empty bucket, wasn't sure she even saw him, her hair now hanging loose over her face like she did not give a damn to see. He eyed the burning door of the byre and could hear the dying of his animals. The body of Matthew Peoples in amongst them. Jesus fuck. What have I done? In his mind he saw Matthew Peoples reaching out for the pens, blind and grasping through smoke as if you could get a handle on such a thing, the smoke scattering in his hand like dream dust. A big man like that brought down. He could see him lying there, his lungs full as if he were drowning. Matthew Peoples' mute face. He felt then an urge to run back in for the man even though by now Matthew Peoples would be dead, thought again of that smoke welling in his own lungs, and it brought to him a perfect terror.

At first, stunned word went through the line that Matthew Peoples had not come out of the byre, but then they grew quiet, wore it in their faces. It was if they were afraid of acknowledging it to one another, a glance told that would speak of some communal guilt that only one man amongst them had gone into the fire and he could only bring one man back out. They knew too the dangers without having to talk about them. The way the buildings were laid out. The new shed fattened with hay. A small mountain of turf under a tarpaulin. The way the firewind made towards the house. They wondered if the fire would reach it, saw the way the smoke mapped the wind's movement so that the shape of it became visible, a calligraphy of violence that rewrote itself with a capacity endless for its own pleasure. Peter McDaid dropped out of the line and ran to the turf and began to move what he could but the heat became too much for him. He swatted at it as if it were a horsefly bothering him, held his elbow up beside his face until he was forced to turn. The chickens long scattered from the yard to the back fields while Cyclop ran about the yard barking at the commotion and then he turned and retreated to the back step.

Goat McLaughlin saw a drop in the wind and told his eldest the weather was granting favour. The house will be saved, he said. He pronounced it like a sage and the son turned and spoke behind him to his brother. The fire humming with its own satisfaction while every person there blocked from their mind the noise of the cattle – the mournful slow sounds of their dying that cut through the air like bassoons.

Nobody saw Barnabas as he leaned himself up and began to walk slowly towards the house, a dread thing with torn breathing. A wheezing in his chest as if something had nested itself inside him. He noticed how smoke had pressed into the house so that everything stank of it and he went to the kitchen cupboard and took down a box of cartridges. He walked slowly towards the door and took the break-action shotgun that leaned behind it, a twelve-gauge Browning, and sat down on the chair with a slump. He put the gun flat on his lap and hinged it open and fumbled with a shaking hand for the cartridges, fed them into the gun's mouth. He stood and filled his pockets with the remaining cartridges and held onto the deal table, sucked air through a rasp in his chest as if he had been holed by the gun, saw through the window the way the smoke had unmade the farm into the remainder of some dim dream.

Nobody saw him drift up the yard, the way he walked slowly like a man footing thick sand. At the west end of the byre the heat was less intense. They heard the sound of two gunshots and some of them thought it was an explosion. Then Peter McDaid saw Barnabas by the side of the byre trying to reload the shotgun. He ran towards him and Barnabas raised the gun and aimed it through the window. McDaid ducked when he heard the third shot and he saw Barnabas squaring to fire another. McDaid upon him then, seizing the gun. Jesus Christ, Barnabas.

Eskra came running towards them with her hands hid by her sleeves. Her lips parted when she saw the shotgun. They propped him under each arm and walked him through the yard and she saw the look Glacken gave them, a look of pure disgust. A car came into the yard as they walked towards the house. Out of it stepped Doctor Leonard, the old man tall and stooped with a thicket of greying yellow hair. He came towards them with his bag and a cigarette perched at the end of long brown fingers. He smoked undeterred, smoked as if to seal his lungs from what plumed around him, looked with concern at Barnabas, saw he was infirm and reached for him under the elbow but Barnabas weakly shook himself free. Naw, he said.

The doctor took hold of him again. Come inside now, Barnabas. I need to be out with them.

The doctor walked him in. He pulled up a chair at the table and sat him down, saw amidst sweat and smokedirt the man's frightened crying eyes, could hear his rent breathing. He leaned his cigarette in an ashtray on the table and helped Barnabas out of his shirt, put a stethoscope to the squall of greying hair on his chest and listened to the storm amplified. Eskra stood fidgeting and angry behind them. What were you doing with the gun, Barnabas? she said.

A knife-edge in her voice brought out the foreign notes in her accent and the doctor gave her a long look to leave the man alone. He nodded to her hands. I see your eczema had broken out again. Barnabas looked up at the outline of his wife, his eyes half closed, and he smiled at her a look she saw as blank and bovine. Leave him be for now, Mrs Kane. He's taken in a lot of smoke.

Eskra dropped onto her knees, her hair loose about her eyes,

and she grabbed Barnabas by the hand, spoke to him sadly. Tell
me what you were doing with the gun.

Barnabas continued his strange smile and then he let the
smile fall and began to whisper to her but she couldn't hear
through his breathing. She leaned in closer.

I wanted to give them all a clean death.

Nothing they could do could stop the byre burning down, though
the wind with a mind of its own turned before the fire reached
the house. No one spoke about the dying sound of the animals
and they kept silent to themselves the thought that a man's
bones were mixed up in it. The burning made the darkness that
fell around them more compact and as the dark deepened the
sounds of the animals quietened. The men began to stand in the
comfort of women. Somebody made tea and steaming cups were
passed around. The men slaked from the cups and wiped dirt-
sweat from their eyes with blackened towels. Eskra encircled.
Barnabas kept in the kitchen by the doctor, who sat with him.
Everybody heard the sound of the collapsing byre like the last
rattling breath from something huge now spent of its life force.
Whatever beam was left standing collapsed with a shudder and
that was it. It made a shiver of dark smoke and a glittering of
sparks shot terrible amber into the sky that burned itself out
into black snow. They heard what they guessed was the sound
of a wall caving in and they took a step back and some of them
gasped. Christ, a man said. The others followed to look. Every
person had assumed that no animals could have survived, but
they were met by the vision of dark shapes emerging from the
byre, shapes indistinct but for the flaming that consumed them
and turned them into ghastly silhouettes, the voices of the

animals weirdly silenced. Barnabas struggled past the doctor and came out of the house to watch. He saw whatever was left living of the cattle come pouring out through the broken wall, some of them tottering and then falling, others running blind, living things it seemed that had become the separate parts of some sort of slow explosion that sent them in different directions through the night. The flaming cattle ran into walls with a pathetic dull thud or came with a silent end upon a tree. Another cow collapsed upon a whin bush and the bush took light and winked at them an eerie yellow purple and when the bush burned itself out the animal still sedately flamed, while some of the animals did not run at all but dropped down under the silent sky, lay there with their burning hides. Barnabas turning around to the doctor, trying to speak, clutching at his arm. He whispered the words out of him. As if the black gates of hell have been cast open.

Part II

THE AIR NOW WAS not air. To him it had changed, the shape of it made different. He saw atoms bent out of shape, tarred and burdened with weight and smell, nature a great violence wreaked upon itself. The smell sat about the farm too heavy to be displaced, sat about all sloth a tight and bitter stench. The place had become warped with it and he thought he could smell it as if what had occurred had become a part of him, seamed itself into his skin, living inside him like an infection. The great morning silence a cavernous thing to a mind that once woke with the animals, a mind that heard now the echo of its thoughts more shrilly. It heard too the silence left by the cockerel that had not been seen since the fire, a tattered old rust-feathered bird with a sickle of black plumage and perhaps cockerels too are affected by such things.

Barnabas could hardly draw himself out of bed and missed Matthew Peoples' wake. He sent Eskra and the boy to the widow's house instead. Eskra stood silent in the bedroom when he told her he wouldn't go. She was bending upwards from a drawer and froze in the dresser mirror, a wan ribbon of light between the curtains catching her whitely on the neck. Just that long reverse look she gave him in the mirror and then she turned and combed over her shoulders her long hair in straight drifts, tied it into a bun. She came over to him and smoothed his cheek and he coughed phlegm all colours of the bog into his hand to prove it. But he knew she could read him through.

I know you're sick but I still think you should go, she said.

Tell them I'm still recovering, he said.

Matthew's face. Not his features in particular, though those he tried to see and found he could not, the man's face like a dream of sand. He could see parts but not the whole and began to wonder if he'd ever truly looked at him. A face like a lived-in map. The high terrain of his cheekbones and the spread of red veins on the pads of his cheeks like great rivers were written on him. Skin grooved by the wind. The way he'd half look at you. Those dopey blue eyes and thickened eyelids that hung heavy making him look half asleep, and the clod heavy foot and his hair gone white, a look that made it seem he was a man of slow reaction. As if you were bothering him from a dream. He could picture the settle of Matthew Peoples in a room, the hunch of him in the seat at the table, the hunger always as he leaned over the lunch plate shovelling hot spuds with his hands. Chewing quietly with a steady efficiency all sleepy eyes, and when the plate was clean the way he would lean out over the table all jaw for a second helping. But of the definite thing that was the man's face he could not see. Just the nature of a look, a glimmer of something in his eyes — the man's thoughts, perhaps. How the man shook his head not wanting to go in.

The weight of his hand upon Matthew Peoples' back.

What remained of Matthew Peoples was put into the ground on a day of cold weather. An assembly of bones they thought to be the man but mixed up too with the bones of the cattle he died with, bones charred and warped by heat. The coroner who did the work was a drinker and his nerves were shot and he just wanted done with it. Jesus fuck, he said when he saw it, and he looked away and folded his hands.

A late frost two days previous had iced the earth with a weave almost spectral and put a reverse on spring. It sleeved the buds on the trees and made the plot resistant like rock, the hardest grave dug that year. The two gravediggers who shovelled it worked their way through another pouch of tobacco. They breathed smoke like dragons, cursed the dead man with their slate-blue faces for the bother he brought to them, though in their quiet way each man remembered him fondly. Matthew Peoples, the big slow man who sat in the corner with Ted Neal, the two of them easy drinkers. Just the tops of the gravediggers' hats visible as they dug deeper into the earth while cigarette smoke would sidle upwards like phantoms cut loose from the grave.

He sat beside Billy and Eskra with his hands balled. Whatever heat there was from those assembled in the church was cast out of them, fled into the granite walls and was made waste by the fleeting down-draughts that came upon them as if to flay them cold for their sins. Peter McDaid arriving late for the Mass, drew up alongside the pew opposite and genuflected, the man mucked to the knees in his welly boots and Barnabas looked at Eskra and nodded towards McDaid. Would you look at him, he said. She stared ahead into the pillared shadows that leaned solemn upon the tiled floor and swallowed the light that came pale through the windows.

That thing nesting in Barnabas's chest had settled inside like blight. It rawed the back of his throat and hollowed him brittle and he coughed through the sermon like a man carved out, as if a great wind were rattling his bones and they would have to carry him out in such pieces. The sound of his coughing echoed off the stone walls and was amplified into a coven for the sick that drowned out the sibilant words of the priest. In person he had smelled out the priest's uncertainty, had met him once or twice in McElheny's pub where he took a drink and eye to eye it was the priest who was hesitant. Wax-paper cheeks on the young priest and the word of God wet on his lips. The earth and the sky fled from his presence and there was no place for them. I saw the dead, the great and the lowly, standing before the throne, and scrolls were opened. Hearing those words Barnabas ground down on his teeth. The earth and the sky to fuck. He saw the world for how old it was stretching back in geological time that was for the most part without human beings on it at all and he saw Matthew Peoples' life as a flickering instant of light burnt out. No fucking scrolls. No judgement on this here earth but our own.

Eskra turned when she heard Barnabas muttering and he turned from her, watched McDaid across the aisle, saw how he prayed a litany of supplementary words, worked his hands as if he could mould penance. He could hear Billy crying. Eskra weeping openly with her hands hid. The skin broken out bad again. She must have fed the dead man three thousand dinners.

They walked solemn up the long line of people to offer their condolences, their hands clasped in front while a guttering candle snorted. Matthew Peoples was a childless man and his brothers and sisters were lined alongside his wife, five siblings, all of them bearing some resemblance to him but for a youngest brother who Barnabas looked at and saw wasn't right at all. A face frozen in youth and hitched into a permanent smile as if nothing could deter him from finding all that he met in the world beautiful. The man shook everybody's hand with a buoyant two-handed hello while the rest of them were quiet. Barnabas shook each person's hand and said he was sorry and none of them knew who he was and he saw in their faces variations of Matthew Peoples, Matthew as a more elderly man with a similar terrain, those red-rivered cheeks and a mountain-peaked nose. Matthew's eyes in a woman with hands a soft mink and her eyes alert to what she could see inside him. Matthew incarnate with no hair at all, the same eyes all rheumy and eyebrows thickened like slugs, and he tried to picture these together into an image of the dead man. When he came to Matthew Peoples' wife, Baba, she bore him no face at all, stared right through him as if he were invisible. His hand unmet before her and faltering while the word sorry sat frozen on his lips. The woman was diminutive, like a little girl that never grew up and had begun twisting into old age with a face like bad fruit, her breath soured long ago from whiskey. She worked sometimes as a seamstress and was losing her hair and wore the remainder of it long and grey like a schoolgirl that came early to decrepitude. Matthew never spoke of her and Barnabas could not picture together the two of them, and though a gentle soul Matthew was he knew that it was she who doled out plentiful the hurt. He stared at the sheen of her scalp, a bad job she made at hiding it and he wondered why she was balding, and he thought of how stupid he looked with the hand outstretched and then Eskra came alongside him with her sore hands open to the world and she took in both of them the woman's hand wholly.

*

The air outside bore the same chill as the church and the dimmed sun not even a smouldering coin. The mourners travelled on foot to the graveyard on a road that slanted southwards from the church, passed under a poplar tree that trembled as if it had a memory of leaves. They walked behind a carriage led by solemn stallions, the two horses risen out of slicks of oil all dark majesty with their black coats gleaming and their heads held haughty beneath a fan of raven plumage. Behind them on high sat two undertakers and they bore a solemn bearing more upright than Christian crosses and Barnabas watched them until he saw one of them lean over and sneeze. Eskra walking beside him red-eyed holding tightly onto Billy's arm, the boy strapped with a sullen face. The wheezing in Barnabas's chest had settled as if the creature inside him had gone mute and lay hunched, waiting. The dull music of shuffling feet and the brighter percussion of horse hooves ringing the silence while the wind blustered about them like an animal craving affection. Barnabas buttoned up his coat. People on the street stopped and stood with their heads bowed as the procession went through the town though the world went on as it was – a column of choughs in from the sea made aerobatic shapes above for anybody to watch, while a motorcar made a distant but purposeful whirr. From a room above the street could be heard a radio with a song and then a voice that had news of the war in Europe, news that seemed to every person there an event that was more rumour than truth, and the radio was switched off and then the bells of the church began to ring to the silence, sounded to him as if they were straining to be heard over an impossible distance, as if they were pealing to make sound to the dead.

*

Later, some people stood near the graveside speaking quietly while others drifted away and Barnabas met in passing Fran Glacken who stopped and searched him with his shooting red eyes, searched the man as if he were seeing over one of his animals. I see yer fixed up then, Barney. He turned to his two sons and motioned for them to follow. I must be heading on, he said. He called to his sister, Pat Glacken, who stood talking to Eskra. Pat was square and sexless, a spinster with a density about her frame as if her bones were made of thick wood and that density reached as far as her face. It knit her small eyes together behind glasses that slid down her nose. She was nodding solemnly to Eskra, while Eskra's eyes flitted to watch Billy who was with some girl.

Barnabas turned and stood a minute watching the sky laid out in white cold sheets and the way of the swallowed sun and he saw there was no promise of the day warming. He heard someone step towards him and he turned and saw Goat McLaughlin resting his fierce eyes upon him as he approached rolling one of his talon hands through his beard. He dropped the hand out of the white floss and proffered it towards Barnabas and Barnabas took it and felt the skin like old wax paper.

Yes, Barnabas.

Yes, Goat.

The old man stood looking up at Barnabas and Barnabas reached into his coat and produced a rolled cigarette and Goat watched him take a soak of it, watched Barnabas cough and catch his breath again, and Barnabas watched him watching. Goat looked to the sky and nodded. Tis a cold day for it.

A heap of shit so it is.

Yer back up on your feet.

Someways.

Have you figured out yet what caused that fire?

Barnabas shook his head. Naw. I just canny figure it. Canny figure it at all.

You're lucky that house of yours didn't catch. The Lord in heaven in his mercy choose to spare you that.

Barnabas sucked on his cigarette and held inside him a cough, eyed the old man long, the rivering beard and the pink shine of bald head glimpsed under his cap. The Lord in heaven in all his mercy thought it just fine to kill all my livestock and take away my living and me with a family to feed. God of mercy and all that, he said.

The old man pulled at his white beard as if he was working free further thoughts for consideration and the corner of his small mouth tightened. And the life of Matthew Peoples, he said.

Barnabas glared.

Goat continued. There is a time in our lives Barnabas when all of us are tested, he said.

He leaned towards Barnabas and took a pinch of his coat and pulled him closer, leaned up to put a quiet word in his ear.

We all saw what Baba Peoples did to you up there.

Aye. What of it?

Well. I'm told to tell ye that the affair afterwards is a private house as far as it concerns you.

Barnabas straightened up and smiled but the smile was false and then it fell away again. The old man still held onto his coat. What kind of joke is that you're saying to me?

I reckon you understand what I'm saying to ye. I'm told Eskra and the boy can go.

Barnabas pulled his arm free of the man's grasp and stood to his full height.

But I was a friend of the man. His employer.

This is what I'm told. To tell you. That is all.

A crow alighted on the cemetery wall and tested the air with a quick fan of its wings. Out of its black-feathered coat it flashed metallic blues that shimmered spectrally, as if it bore other colours from an incorporeal part of its being. The bird turned and faced the crowd and cawed to them its birdspeak message but the thoughts of it were not heeded nor understood and with that the bird took wing. Barnabas cut the Goat a mean look like he wanted to skin him, parade around in that skin and then cut out of it with a knife. He sucked on his cigarette and drew it down into him harder and Goat watched as whatever it was housed inside Barnabas awoke and asserted itself with a movement that shook vex in his lungs and sent Barnabas violently to coughing. Barnabas saw the look of curiosity on Goat's face and it was then that Billy appeared beside them, his skinny arms held loose. Jeez, I'm wild hungry so I am, he said. Barnabas hinged himself up out of the cough and glared at his son and tossed the cigarette, held himself still a moment as he summoned his words, and he leaned in to Goat and took two sniffs of air. Jesus, Goat, there's a wild awful stink off you of pig shit.

Billy's mouth dropped open as if the jawstrings had been cut. Goat turned in temper and began to step away and then he turned back quick and spoke. She says she couldn't wash him, Barnabas. She says she couldn't wash him.

He lay in bed curled sideways and nursed a cough and let his mind roam back to his earlier life. How he was one of the few who had returned from America, the void that swallowed them whole. Bucked against the movement of history. Had returned aged thirty-three with a wife and child and the hard light of knowing in his eyes. Twelve years ago now that was. He knew then everything about steel but what he knew about farming was little but he had ideals and yearning and that was enough. To live again in this place that was once home. To build something up of this new country as he had done in New York. He took the boat to America as a youth cut off from all that he knew, carried great dark eyes that marked his face. You could catch in a rare moment a startle fixed permanent in his soul, a look he kept guarded, and perhaps what people saw in his eyes was the mark of grief. His mother succumbing first and then his father to tuberculosis. No brothers or sisters and when he was orphaned he was taken in by a childless sister of his mother's who resented the intrusion. He didn't last long, was sent to America on a boat with a letter addressed to a cousin, the year 1915, a time when some boys he knew not much older than him were travelling east across the water to fight the Hun. He lived with a cousin in Brooklyn who was a stranger to him and was put to work shouldering slack until his hands lost their white and he could not wash the dirt from his face and all he could do was sleep. And then the dark morning when he was sixteen and he rose silently to meet the shadows of the streets that did not return him.

He asked her how there could have been a fire, and she said, I do not know. And he said, these things don't just happen, do they? There was nothing at all to start it. I just don't understand. He was silent for a while and she watched him as he walked about the kitchen knuckling at his cheek and taking alternate sucks of his cigarette. How in the hell can a fire like that take out a whole byre, kill off every living thing we own? All of our cattle? He clicked his fingers. Just like that. What did we do to deserve it? I did everything right so I did. I did what they told me to do for safety. I even moved that lime outside, that heap of it that I'd left in the byre. Matthew Peoples told me that under certain conditions it was combustible. The fucking joker. It's lying there now up by the haggard cool and wet as mud. It weren't dry enough for the hay to tinder. There wasn't a bolt of lightning in that sky for I was out in it all day.

I don't know, Barnabas. I just don't know. It seems obvious to me it was some sort of accident. But there is no point thinking about it. What's done is done. There is nothing we can do but move on.

He started coughing and when he stopped he continued and he said somebody must have started it, I just know.

She said, stop this now, Barnabas. You're getting daft. What's all this based on? She sighed. Barnabas, there's nothing we can do to change this. As she looked at him she felt a tightness in her throat. We'll make a claim for the insurance and we'll build it all back again and it will be better than it was before.

He turned quickly to her. That thing with my not being invited back to the house, Eskra. After the funeral. You should have gone, Eskra, with the boy.

Not, Barnabas, after the way they treated you.

He stood staring at the wall for a moment as if it had opened before him to reveal some shining truth. Eskra, he said. They all think that I killed him.

The days wore on, the familiar noises of the farm playing only in their minds like the ghost of a thing they tried not to hear. Just the wind that blew as if it had won its freedom to streel about the yard, a lazy drawl that skittered the dust on the flagstones and ruffled the feathers of the remaining chickens. Into the air went the black dust, catching on the breeze and flung blindly, onto the field, black spots cancerous on green that made the grass seem sick. Or it caught in the sills and put a smear on the glass obscuring the view so that looking out the kitchen window became a moment of memory, the day sliding back to the evening they kept trying to forget. Eskra staring out of the window with a crease in her brow. She took a bucket and filled it with soap and hot water from the kettle and washed the windows until they squeaked. She frowned as she worked, kept stopping to fix the drifts of hair that fell loose in her face, noticed how the water softened the scabs on her fingers. When she was done she took a newspaper and balled it and streaked it angrily across the window. Two days later the rims of the windows were dark again.

Every morning she would rise amidst the farm's silence and leave him lying there in bed a sack shape. She would go to the fire and stir the coals awake beneath their ashy palls. Breakfast then and tea on the stove and she would resume cleaning. The more she cleaned the more she felt that what had been made unreal to her could be forced back into its old shape.

In the field beside the byre, dark birds swooped and settled. A black-dressed parade that made circles above the field incessant. She saw carrion birds thicken the scene, not living things at all but dark smudges as if what was yielded by the flames in some dream had become animate. When the daylight began to fade, the birds seemed to swell in their hundreds, made their scratchy meat-hungry song that sounded to her like the tearing of sinew. The cattle had begun to rot where they had fallen dumbly in the fields, propped strangely on the grass at the unusual angles of their dying, the rib bones of one animal beginning to show like a swell of teeth. The birds feasting. She watched them from the window, told herself it was only nature, but looking at them she could not escape the hand of horror in her belly.

The plough still in the tapered field, poised with the lean of an animal in the moment before attack, its teeth bared waiting to tear at the neck of the earth, but it sat with a dog's patience through days of raw cold and then rain and he had not the strength to go back to it. In those days after the fire the sun would climb up to its highest resting place before Barnabas would get out of bed and emerge downstairs coughing. He paced about the house and paced about the yard, Cyclop with one-eyed curiosity watching the directionless pattern of his footsteps, and Barnabas stared into the sloping face of the horse with its dark glass eyes and saw just himself reflected back as if he had been hammered out of shape.

He watched Eskra scrubbing the windows. Eskra washing the white gable wall of its smokedirt. Eskra sweeping soot from the yard. Eskra placing lavender about the house that to him had no effect, no colour, no smell. This place that was dead. He just stood around, smoked like he hated it, the fag between finger and thumb and his unshaven face puckering up as he sucked, his lungs sending to him short sharp messages of resentment. The smoke burned into him, seared him afresh, and when he was done with one fag and heeling it into the yard he had already withdrawn his tobacco tin from the shirt pocket and was rolling another. Eskra calling out to him to stop smoking. A suck and a grimace as he moved about the place, kicked the dog out of the way, sat on the step, stood up again coughing. Eskra watching him from the window as he walked under his own cloud like the man's thoughts had become manifest, disappearing into himself beneath it, away into his own darkness where even she could not reach. And when she worked the long tear-handled arm of the pump in the yard and the pump yawned and began to mouth water, he didn't see her at all as she stood watching him, and when she closed the door she began to cry, saw then how everything could be lost.

I could hear the old man shouting at me from the byre that he needed help with the cattle but the Christmas market was on so I sneaked past him as if I were not there. I'm up the town then nosing about the stalls when I get talking to John the Masher, fucking pain in the hole so it was — there was me having a smoke thinking no one would give a shit and then someone comes behind me and yanks me by the lughole. It was that bastard teacher Broc so it was and he takes the fag out of me mouth and squashes it with his boot and then he lets me off giving me ear a twist. The Masher was watching the whole time and when teacher lets off The Masher sidles up and produces a fag for me from behind his ear. Hey sir he says. I'd heard The Masher was a bit funny in the head and there was an old story about him that when he were a squirt he took his wee infant sister for a walk and he let go of the pram and the pram went into the river and she were drowned. And he were never right in the head again. And when I asked the auld doll about that she said it weren't true but that he probably went funny when his mammy died wild young and that his father was difficult. He seemed fine enough to me no smell of crazy off him at all but for his eyes one of which was flecked with a different colour of grey that did make him look a bit strange. And he didn't really seem to be four year older. We went down the back lane and he climbs up over a wall and disappears into the back yard of Doherty's Hotel never minding the dog that was in it and he comes back over with two bottles of Guinness.

We drank the two of them and the taste was bitter like bog water so it was but I kinda liked it made my head all dreamy. We got the giggles wild bad and then he says to me did you know we're neighbours and then he calls me Billygoat and then he burps right after it. He starts to laugh and the way he laughs was like he was gurgling. His hair was curling wild like dark ferns off his head and his eyes could never settle on anything for a minute. I says to him aye Billygoat surely and I kick like one too. He didn't seem to give a fuck about anything and straight off I knew he was more interesting than those other bucks my own age and he was able to get drink wild easy. Then the other day he calls around to the house and the auld doll has her hands in a bowl making the Christmas pudding and she looks at him like he were a dunty calf, gives me a pointed look when I went outside with him. Fuck her anyways the auld bitch. I can hear the old man in the byre shouting to the cattle and Big Matty Peoples is coming out the byre door and I put my finger to my lips to tell him to shush and run off quick before the old man sees me. We fucked off down to the Glenny river and I took Cyclop with us on a rope. Masher, he produces this big fuck-off knife a six-incher all curving like it were from an exotic storybook and he lets me hold it and I get my initials good into a tree. I ask him where he got it but he wouldna tell me and then he begins to dam up the river. It were only a stream really and he stands above it like he were lord and all over it and he slaps down moss-slimed stones and one of em falls out of his hands and splashes him. He rubs his hands dry on his trousers and leaves streaks of muck on em and leans back and laughs. He were off then and I followed and I took to wearing a fag in me ear like he were doing. I ask him where we were going and he just laughs again and says take the dog with us. I says that dog sure in hell will come with us anyway like it or not. We went off across the fields and the sky was growing dark and I kept Cyclop on the rope beside me. It were strange going up into the hills in the purpling light and I kept looking at the sky.

If you looked at the clouds a certain way they became like islands all misted and far away at sea and I imagined I was the captain of a ship travelling on a voyage towards them on an adventure. There was an auld twisty dirt track and we followed it and saw the darkening shape of a house just off it, I think it mighta been McClure's place but wasna sure and there was a dog barking from the place but no lamplight to be seen. Cyclop going mad on the rope and The Masher leans over and takes the dog off me. We stay clear of that place anyhow, the pair of us blowing smoke towards those islands in the sky. The bog is so different at night. No fields at all just the roam of the land like no one ever set foot upon it and we got high enough to look down on all below, Carnarvan getting darker and the town far off and the last light on the bay. I'd heard there were old caves up there used by moonshiners and I wondered if that were where we were going. There was an energy off The Masher like something was wound up inside of him, like he could do anything and then he just starts shouting, roaring out curses at the sky and I begin to roar out too until he starts making up curses that make no sense at all and I tell him so and then we just laugh our holes off. Our voices rose upwards into the sky and for a moment we owned all what was of the world and took for ourselves purple heaven and its stars and when we stopped we heard how our voices were swallowed up by a silence that was total as if we never were. We walked on and then we came upon them. Fucking stupid things and in the light there were a kind of indigo and I could see Cyclop begin to change, sharpened up then like a wolf on the end of a rope, like he were awakening to a deeper nature. I seen him draw back his lips to reveal his teeth and the dog became a fuckin beast. The Masher lets go of the rope and shouts to the dog to go and get em and Cyclop goes off like a shot as if he didn't need fuckin telling. It were hilarious watching the sheep stand there all stupid watching us and then scattering the way they did with the sweet fucking Jesus scared out of them. There was a sound like low thunder made by their hooves on the heather and Cyclop goes after one of them and then begins making zigzags as though he needs the other eye he's missing to help him make up his mind. The Masher ran after the dog shouting and hollering and the way he ran made his legs look like loose hinges without a door, and he were roaring and laughing the whole time. The dog snaps at the heels of a sheep and then turns for another and I was laughing at the mad sight of it and then the dog swings for one that came straight at him confused and he leaps at it and pulls it to the ground by the neck. The Masher came running with his arms flapping and he came up behind the dog and he made that big wobbling laugh like gurgling. There was more wind up where we were and when the scattered sheep stopped to watch us from a distance you could hear the wind whistling softly. That dog a yours is half blind but he's a right wolf so he is says The Masher and he lets out into the air a great whoop. I realize then The Masher ain't sick in the way they were saying he were sick, he is just wild as the wind is all. He has no stones tied to his feet like most others do. And I went up to the sheep to have a look and then wild quick I felt funny about her, the way she was lying there tamed and her eyes looking up at me like sometimes you see in a dog that's cowering after a beating but I knew that sheep was dying for the throat was got out of her. And I went down low to her I donny know why but I put my hand on her belly. This one's pregnant I said. I felt a sudden feeling sink inside me and saw Cyclop had lost interest and was walking about in circles sniffing at the air a true beast of the wild and not the plain dog at all we thought he was. The darkness now was more complete and the atmosphere of the place had changed to us. The Masher's face was hid in the dark and when he came towards me I was wondering if he felt the same as I did but when I saw him up close I saw the same spirit in him pure as the dog. Just hunger in his eyes for more wildness. C'mon he says, let's do it again and I says naw, I have to go home for my tea or the auld doll will kill me. We stayed there a while all quiet. The sheep lying there being blown by the wind that gave it the appearance of shivering and I turned and saw then The Masher had started talking to himself real fast and I begin to wonder what the fuck is wrong with him and I canny make out a word he is sayin and next thing he just tears off running at full pelt. I stand up and look at him running down the hill and realize then he isn't right in the head one bit and I turn and take another look at the animal, saw the way she was lying there useless with the throat torn out, the weirded angle of her head and her eyes lookin at me as if she were asking me for something, some kind of grace in her dying moment that I could not give her, and I could see her blood souse darkly the moss. The wee lamb inside her I nearly saw. I figure when I'm an old man I'll read this here story I wrote and laugh at all the stupid things I done.

H OURS WERE MADE LONG by the void of empty days. He sloped about the yard like a man not bothering to look busy, so lost inside himself he no longer heard the farm, what was emptied out to silence, nor did he heed the weather that passed over it – the dry spell that stretched unusual for days making the ground firm and then the rain that came a dull sadness. And when he walked amongst his empty fields he was numbed to the changes around them, the spurting green that softened the crooks of the trees, nature a slow shifting thing heaving into spring. How the grass was greening and would grow unkempt without the mouths of cattle to feed on it. Just the goings on in his mind, trying to undo the knot of a long thread that led to dormant anger. A feeling in his mind he had been cheated. He wandered about by the blackened byre half seeing it or he went inside it and kicked through the tangled remains, looking for clues amongst the pen metal, some of them twisted like question marks to torment him.

Too many days he sat slumped in the kitchen chair drifting into the mesh of memory or shifting in unsettled sleep. She watched him doze with his mouth open, watched his face at peace and saw him different, how what was held tense in his face fell away from him weightless. She wanted to speak. A butterfly of light from the hall caressing his stubbled cheek and she saw him young and how he was. How he began working as a youth of sixteen in high steel, hazardous work, like some kind of man-god he was, but he didn't know it, took to it like a natural. Raw and dumb to the work and he worked with the Mohawks the most fearless of men and Irish who were foolhardy enough. The skyscraper boom of New York. They reshaped the sky with their steel, walked girders like gulls. New York below them like a pop-up picture book you could close with your hands. He would listen to the sky's hush through the din of steel, the sibilant forces of the wind as if the sky was breathing. The clouds mute and drifting to lay their shadow slabs upon the city. The men worked like perilous angels and the sound they made was incarnate of hell, reached towards heaven a fiendish thing that warped the structure of the air, crazed even the birds. Gulls leaned against the wind to watch these strange creatures stride on narrow beams, or work in teams foursquare on scaffold strips sized hardly for two of them. He used to talk her through the movements, how a heater man put coal into a tiny forge and withdrew the steaming rivets, the man's face scrunched against the heat, tossing the blushing steel into the air to be caught by another in a tin can while the third man pulled out the temporary rivet. The waiting beam with its eyehole gaping, waiting to be scalded shut. The hissing rivet pinched with tongs and inserted into the hole. How he worked relentless with a pneumatic drill, the rivet soft from the heat, turning the stem squat into a button. Kneeling over the earth like he owned it.

He awoke with red eyes and saw her looking at him. Jesus, can a man not get a nap in peace. Her mouth fell open but no words came out and she retreated from the room silent. He leaned forward and stood up and walked about the kitchen and stopped and put his hands over the stove. He went into the living room to the cabinet, took out a bottle of whiskey and reached for a glass and the floorboard behind him squeaked. He felt the boring of her eyes into him as she stood at the door and he turned and put the bottle back.

The way you scared me when I awoke, that's what I meant, he said. Standing over me like that you gave me a fright.

She turned without a word and went back to the kitchen. He stepped into the hall and took his coat. I need to go for a walk, he said.

The night was cold and dark and in the harsh winter of his mind wolves roamed openly the frozen tracks.

The day bright and she stood glad under it and she saw the horse in the field. The animal came towards her, canted her head and took last autumn's wrinkled red apple from the flat of Eskra's hand and listened to the woman's words and nodded sagely as if the tone the woman took impressed some horse meaning. Eskra left the field in dew-kissed shoes while the horse walked over to the trough that held upon its rainwater a cylinder of light and when the horse dipped its head into that light it seemed to drink directly the sun's luminance.

She went for the laundry basket and walked to the washing line where she put her hand to the dry fibres of the towels that lay slabbed upon it. She unpegged them and broke their stiffness with her hands and folded them. She began to walk with the basket at her hip as if she could have been any woman from any of the past ages bearing what it is a woman abides and she saw herself as ancient and soul woman. She took the basket up the stairs and went to the press and began to fold the towels and place them inside when she stopped. At the back of the press she saw heaped in a ball the white sheets that were hanging out the day of the fire. They were stuffed in carelessly on top of the folded sheets and when she opened them out she saw they were ruined with smoke. She scratched her head in wonder. She put her nose to the sheets and what came to meet her was the smell of corruption. She took the sheets outside, held them to the light and saw how they had absorbed the fire's smoke as if they had taken an imprint of the day, a stripe of dark on one of them beside a stripe of near white, as if the wind had folded the sheet over to protect some part of it. She looked at one sheet more closely and paled at what she thought she saw, a face she thought she imagined, her mind seeing the outline of Matthew Peoples and his wide lips and the broad nose and the lined mark of a forehead. She dropped the sheet to the flagstones and went inside and swore at her herself for having such thoughts but later that morning when she saw the sheets on the ground she bent and picked them up and held them out. Saw again the face of him.

She took the sheets to the washboard outside and filled a bucket with hot water and added soap. When she filled the tub she leaned over the washboard, wondered again who had taken the sheets down in the first place, put them into the press like that, maybe it was one of the neighbours, that day all chaos and who was to know what went on. She abraded the sheets off the washboard's corrugations until the skin on her hands from the water began to pleat and her scabs were softened and sore, worked until the sinews in her hands had stiffened and the water turned a grey grease. And when she took the last sheet out and held it to the light she saw that the smoke still inhabited it in a way that could not be washed out, neither altered nor erased, and that the sheet she looked at still bore the face of Matthew Peoples.

A night like most other nights and he could sleep only in short drifts that dreamed up for him a howling dark that gave him images of fire. The shapes of flaming cattle. His arms reaching into a void of smoke. When he awoke his mind was bleared from sleep fog and he lay with his knees tucked to his chest and the blankets tight to his neck. A long while just thinking. He kicked a leg back to Eskra's side of the bed, found it a lonely cold and sat up and saw the bedside clock. Ten past ten in the morning and the boy gone hours ago to school. When he left the bed he doused his face cold with the jug water and stared into the mirror dead-eyed, saw the sacks under his eyes pooling with storm grey and he sniffed dream-smell about him still, a thick lingering reek of smoke.

He put on his shirt and trousers and fixed loosely his tie and went downstairs in his socks. No sign of Eskra and he saw porridge left out for him in a bowl. He poured honey on top and watched it pool a golden ooze and he sat to the table, ate it cold looking out the window. The fleet shape of Cyclop across the front yard. He sat there thinking of thoughts he could not shake from the night's dreaming, the way Matthew Peoples had morphed into somebody else, a man tormenting him now in the guise of a stranger, some dark-faced young man leering at him with features wild and full of perversion, an incarnation of Satan perhaps, if he had believed in such things. The notion he could not shake was the strange feeling he'd killed somebody else he did not know about and that his dreams were awakening him to this fact and making him account for it.

He stared blankly at the day outside, a timid flat light and the trees wagging in modest conversation, and then what he thought he saw drew him from inattention. The shape of Baba Peoples. She stood half hid on the road watching the house between the trees, and when he slid the chair back and stood and leaned to see better through the glare of the window she was gone. He kept looking but could only see the communing of trees and he could not even be sure of what he saw. He went to the front door and watched the road but saw nobody on it and he cursed to himself his tiredness. He stood in the hall and rubbed his eyes and noticed then the smell about him still, how he could catch it when he went back into the room, the smell no longer part of his lingering dream but a thing that was surely manifest, a defiance of some kind. He rose out of his chair to meet it, put his shirt sleeve to his nose and sniffed it and found the fire's smell was waiting for him in its fibres. He pulled at his tie and yanked the shirt over his head and balled it towards the floor. Outside the high yap of the dog and the stable door closing.

He lifted his vest to his nose and could smell the fire in it too, ripped it off and bent down to take a sniff of his trouser leg. He unleashed the belt and it came loose into the room a snake's testing tongue and he kicked out of his trousers, threw them across the room towards the other clothes, goddamn nothing fucking clean in this house, and then he was moving certain, the curtains now in his sight and he could smell in them too the burning, the curtains that were the first thing Eskra had made when they moved into the house, a deep red velvet he tore down ripping the railing out of the wall and he hurled them towards his clothes. He put his face then to the wall and could smell the burning in the wallpaper, scratched at it with his nails, turned around and went to the dresser drawer and removed from it a knife. He daggered it and began to cut at the seam of the wallpaper, watched it come loose in strips that fell to the floor a sad thing with the taut life force gone out of it, and then behind him he heard Eskra's shout. She stood by the door, saw he had gone mindless, the man near naked and a lunacy in his manner she had never seen, and when he turned to look at her she saw his eyes had narrowed down into a look of unseeing, saw the knife in his hand, and she went to him and reached out and took the knife from him, and it seemed to her then he awoke from some dream, began moving towards her, fell like a child into her arms.

She held him and brushed her hand through his wire-dark hair and saw in him the little boy she was holding, saw full and clear the measure of his distress. When his breathing had calmed she led him upstairs and sat him on the bed and watched him curl childly, went to the curtains and closed them. His voice small in the room. I'm just so tired, he said. She sat on the chair and watched him fall asleep, daylight pressing through a gap in the curtains to light a daguerreotype jellyfish upon the wall, while the rest of the room became an ocean of unlit depths, like the inscape of his mind she was fearful for. How he had aged this past while she saw, the dark of his hair beginning to whiten at the sides and it seemed to her that life had worried more lines into his eyes. Before she left the room she leaned over him and saw in that dim light those lines now smoothed as if only in sleep he could find repose.

Later, the sun hid while a marble-grey sky let loose rain with insistence. She saw the rain speckle and leap from the flagstones, saw through the cataract of rain towards the mountains where a wash of light had brazened itself and made everything that was dim and dun under it brilliant. She brought him vegetable soup and tea and he sat up with the pillow to the small of his back. She drew open the curtains and settled on the bed, saw a rare look in his eye. He leaned towards her and coughed. I didn't mean to, he said.

We should take you to the doctor.

I could still smell it, Eskra.

Smell what, Barnabas?

The fire.

Barnabas, the smell is all gone. There's nothing left of it. I've been cleaning like a char woman. The wind took the smell all away.

I could smell it in my clothes. Buried in the fibres. I want all them clothes tossed out, Eskra.

Those clothes have been washed pure clean. You didn't smell it yesterday in the same clothes when you were wearing them. Where do we have the money now to get new ones?

He sipped on his tea and grimaced.

What's wrong with you now? she said.

This tea is only lukewarm.

She shook her head at him as she spoke. It might help if you got yourself busy, Barnabas. Get yourself ready for when the insurance comes in. Get you out of your funk. It's natural so it is for a man to feel down on himself after what's happened. But there's so many things that need doing around the place. You need to get going again.

He said nothing and shifted and gathered a heap of blanket in his fist. Then he looked at her, those blue eyes that had their vice-hold on him. Eskra, he said, but she began to talk over him and what he heard sounded like bone in her voice, as if she had grown new strength having to bear up the extra weight of what was for all of them. You need to start fixing up outside, she said. That byre needs to be cleared out and made ready for the rebuilding. There are broken walls that need fixing. The farm is going to waste. The fields are a disgrace. The land needs to be maintained till we get it to rights again. It is time now for you to put your mind to it. And don't worry about the vegetables. The early cabbages are near ready and I've already planted the rest.

Eskra.

Do you hear me now, Barnabas?

He sighed. Aye. All right.

And, Barnabas.

What?

I can't look any more at those dead animals.

He had come to her, he used to say, like an angel from the clouds. Saw you first from five-hundred feet in the air. Through the noise of riveting steel that could bend the sky out of shape. I watched you above that bellyache of traffic. Heard on the concrete the press of your footsteps. From that height you develop eyes for seeing. You stood out from the crowd. Your eyes glittering up at me. The swan sheen of your neck. I was only waitin for you.

It was impossible, of course, but Eskra liked the story. You latch onto small details and from them write the book of your life. Before she had met him she had been watching the skyscraper go up between Nassau and William Street, would walk around the block from the typists' shop where she worked to spend part of her lunch at the barricade. She would squint her eyes and imagine the men on top and could not grasp in her mind such daring. One evening she stood behind Barnabas in line at a cobbler's shop, saw him peering into a book while eating a sandwich, and she just knew he was a steelworker. She followed him up the street. Excuse me, she said. I'm sorry, but you are one of them steelworkers, aren't you? He turned around and eyed her sly-smiling. Aye, he said. He held aloft a pair of ragged resoled boots. The one thing you need the most working high steel is good shoes. A pair that fit you just right and the soles all properly on them. You want those shoes to feel like your own feet. I never spend money on hardly anything but drink and good boots. A gleam of mania in the way he laughed and his face stained with grease and the ivory of those eyes in the look that held her. She had to ask what it was like up there, if there was a danger he could fall, and he met her question with a hurt look as if he had never considered it. He pointed towards the sky. We're up so high I swear to you now I could reach the clouds, but I never look down. And it was then she bade him a smile. My parents are Irish too, she said. What county are you from?

He saw the way she hid her hands, fingers curled like a bird's beak hid up cardigan sleeves that were pulled out of shape. Saw how her hands were rashed red and scabbed in places and that she hid them because she might be ashamed of them. She saw when he talked how he liked to use his hands, a gesticulator, moving the air with knowledgeable movements like he was working metal, pushing and pounding at the air, heaving huge girders or hammering rivets. She had learned to speak with her fingers hid and relied more on her eyes to do her bidding, but when she forgot her embarrassment and used her hands to speak, she drew the air before him with gossamer, gestures soft and diaphanous like spiderwebs.

Barnabas put on his coat and slapped on his cap and stepped out into the yard. From the haggart, Cyclop spied on him like a sniper, his nose barrelled between his forepaws. A single squinting eye that watched Barnabas walk out the gate and then the dog stood and yawned, a great silent saurian roar all fanged pearls so that it seemed the animal's entire nature in that moment changed, took the spirit of some kind of ferocious bawling beast, and then the shape-shifter's mouth returned the animal to its tamer form. The dog followed the man out the gate, giddied after a bird with a wag of his tail and made zags in the hedgegrass following his nose. Barnabas heard the rustle of the dog and he stood and called for Cyclop to come along but the dog paid him no heed, followed a trail that took him into a ditch and disappeared. Barnabas shook his head and shouted after him and heard emptiness after his own voice. Stupid fuckdog.

Peter McDaid's house was a five-minute walk beyond the curve of the road and the air here was different to him, unsullied, met his nose a sharp, clean thing that held what he remembered to be pure. The route sided with hedgerow trees of willow and oak and between them sat hawthorn and holly. He saw a robin trail the air, a brisk and flitting red that shot into the trees. McDaid had built a flat-roofed brick shed across the road from his house so that his yard was the narrow lane itself. His dog, Queenie, made the middle of that lane her kingdom and sat now upon a throne of high shadow, a mongrel with a regal, long face and in her look was a register of suffering that could be read almost as human. Come here to me you, Barnabas said. She rose up and came a distance towards Barnabas and sat and waited for him to ruffle her ears and then with a red-stubbled tongue she licked the hand of her subject. McDaid appeared on the front step bare-chested, his short legs in his welly boots. He hawked up phlegm and spat it into the yard and watched the way it bubbled.

Yes, Barney.

Yes, Peter.

McDaid put his hands on his hips. Did ye hear about Ruddy up in Birdhill? Buck eejit. A heap of his cattle escaped onto the road and roamed their way into the grounds of Glebe house. Trampled the living shite out of the lawns. Went at it like they were squashing grapes, making holy wine for the priest. Devaney must have thought it was Hitler invading if the Jerry weren't already on their way back to Berlin. Ruddy had to spend the next two days filling in all the holes in the grass, a terrible mess they made. Going around the place with a bucket and shovel. As McDaid spoke, the claws around his eyes tightened and the lines around his mouth made a puppet of his lips, and then he leaned back and laughed a whoop skywards. When he saw Barnabas was not even smiling he stopped and shook his head. Since when did you become such a dryballs?

Fuck knows.

That's wild funny so it is.

Aye.

Going around the place, a bucket and shovel. Like he was at the fucking seaside. McDaid slapped his belly and began to whoop again.

Barnabas rubbed his cheek with his knuckles. Peter, I need a wee bit of help.

Let me guess. You want help clearing up that field?

Are you a mindreader or what?

Eskra might have come to see me yesterday so she did. Mentioned it to me.

Did she now.

Aye. Sure she can't be waiting for you to yank yer socks up.

Go in then and put on your flitterjigs.

McDaid stepped into the house and began to curse and knock things about and he came back out with a dirty vest in his fist. He stood looking at the dog and then he necked through the vest and nodded up the road scratching an armpit. What tools have we got? Let me bring my hooring shovel just in case.

They went to the field with their tools slung like rifles over their shoulders and they stood wary at the perimeter taking in what they saw. Carrion birds circling and making terrible noises in the sky like warnings. The men swung their shovels down and leaned against them and McDaid spat venomously. He looked at Barnabas. Would ye not heap them up and burn them proper instead?

Maybe I don't want to smell again the stink of their dying.

Arrah fuck.

Barnabas began to walk forward into the field and he stopped and kicked the half-burnt corpse of a cow. Fuckdog, he said.

They walked to the bottom of the field and stood in the shadow limbs of the trees and started. The pitch and slice of spade into sod and they turned the grass, put it face down on the field, bared the raw earth to them. They began to dig their way down and the ground was soft and then two feet deeper they began to meet stones that screeched in protest when the shovels struck.

They dug around them and pulled them free with their hands and Peter McDaid rubbed the muck off some and said these'll do surely for a wall when yer stuck. Every once in a while Barnabas fell to coughing and McDaid watched him suck on his fag as if the cigarette and his lungs were unrelated things and he shook his head in wonder. Jesus, Barney, do you want us to stop for another day?

In the field the sun spun shadow clocks around the bones. The men began to disappear down into the earth and the smoke from Barnabas's fags clung to the interior. McDaid took off his vest and threw it out of the hole, stood bare-chested to the work like some misshapen vision of a warrior red-faced, swarded upon the shoulders with black matted hair that he would use to wipe the sweat of his forehead. They dug the hole down to the height of their chests and stood in it ten feet long and then Barnabas climbed up out of it, put a hand down to pull McDaid up. They sat for a few minutes smoking on the old stone wall and when they were finished they began to walk through the field.

Nothing left of some of the burnt animals but heads and hooves that looked as if they had been discarded by itinerant folk who just picked up after a huge feed and left. Darkened rib cages pointed at them like petrified fingers. Flies fed upon the corpses and the sound of their buzzing thickened the air and McDaid carried his vest hitched to his nose. The corvids pitched upon the trees and the perimeter walls to watch with their mechanical heads or they circled beady-eyed and raucous. The men walked about the field surveying the mess, over by the stone wall where one of the cows had collided with it, sent the top rim of stones sprawling, and they travelled around by the old oak that stood sentry over the fields some two hundred years but had never been witness to anything like this.

Barnabas went back to the yard and fetched some rope and looped it around the shanks of the lesser-sized animals and they began to drag them towards the pit. Some of the cattle were too big to move by themselves and they left them as they were to be dragged by the horse. One cow had the throat burned out of it but for the muscle of tongue that lay exposed and cooked as if ready to be eaten. They stood over another that lay near intact in the middle of the field, its front legs curled delicate as if it had been sleeping. The way its head rested belied the violence of its death, the skin flayed into a charred leather that lay pleated like finger folds at its rear and the sheen off it like new shoes. McDaid rested his foot upon it and put on his vest. Get me a knife and I'll cut you a pair of brogues, he said.

Barnabas was silent.

Arrah, Barney, the big serious head on ye.

The birds had been to work on the carcass, took the sweet eye jelly from the sockets while the ridges of the animal's back were burned black as if the fire had only licked up its spine and left the rest to brown in the heat. They walked up the low rise of the field and at the crest they saw one cow lying on its back as if it had been stunned by a blow. Barnabas stared at it. God damn, he said. The legs of the cow were starred to the skies in a salted biblical manner, its head stretched back and its body stiff as stone. They looped rope around the shanks and tried to pull the animal but the dead beast was stubborn to them, as if it had enough of what already was and it flashed fire-browned teeth at them in defiance. Barnabas went for the bay horse.

A lemon sun swung pale arcs of light that shined the horse's flanks and made her fawn. She flicked her dark tail as she sauntered. Barnabas rubbed the dark poll hair and began to talk to her. Rotten business here old one. Hope you don't mind looking at it. Just do like me and hold your nose. He ambled the horse through the gate and saw McDaid standing bent at the edge of the pit. Barnabas looked at the corpse and wondered if the horse had any sense of it. Aren't these your brethren? he said. The horse breathed easy and stared superior into the distance, the darkening fuzz of head hair to match the colour of the hills watching down on them. Barnabas lined up the horse and tied the rope to the harness and got her to pull and the slack rope stretched taut until the carcass was dragged into the hole. McDaid kicked dirt after it and shook his head. Jesus Christ, sir, he said. That's some lot of beef.

Barnabas reached into his pocket and began to roll two fags and he lit them both in his mouth and proffered one to McDaid. The man took the fag and grimaced as he sucked on it.

You know what bothers me, Peter?

What, sir?

When you pulled me out. I have no memory of it.

Arrah, Barnabas.

I canny stop thinking about it. That I might as well have been dead. His voice trailed off. I'm wondering if that is what it was like for Matthew Peoples. Quick, like.

McDaid chugged on his cigarette and blew it out good and messy. He began to pull up his vest and revealed over his hip a scar with a star-shape. When I was fifteen I got gored by a dunty bull. Knocked me clean into another field. One minute I was awake hearing some vague shouting not wondering that all the blather was directed at me and then the next minute I wasn't.

Out like a lamp. When I came to I was in a kitchen. The great black in between, Barnabas, and I reckon that's the way of it. One minute you're here and the other you're not and you won't know nothing of it. That, at least, is what I hope.

Barnabas mussed the air with smoke. It's strange all right. When they carried you to the kitchen you might as well have been dead for all you remember of it. The thing is, when you took me out of that fire, Peter, there was a minute there where I was a fucking ragdoll too. That's what I canny stop thinking about. That I was half dead and now I am not but I did not know it. That I had no knowledge of it. I cannot decide if that should be a comfort. That I've had some experience of what dying might be like.

McDaid snorted smoke out his nose. Fuckin bog philosopher, he said. You weren't a ragdoll. You were a heavy-arsed cunt that nearly broke me back and you were still breathing when I had ye. And you're the same heavy-arsed cunt now, just look at ye. He winced on his fag and took a deep last drag and flicked it into the pit.

At the far side of the field the corpse of one cow remained and they let the horse wander as they walked towards it. The carcass lay as if dropped by the jaws of some darkling tide. McDaid looped the rope around the shanks and Barnabas went for the horse that stood hinged upon herself to nuzzle at her flanks. When they had dragged the last carcass into the pit each man took his shovel to the earth that sat in two high mounds either side of it. The dead animals all in a stinking limb sprawl that hurt the eyes to see it and Barnabas had to turn away, stare towards the trees, the swaying yellow of distant whin, a cloud shape over the hills a mutant triangular fish. He drove the shovel into the earth, sent the dark dust down on top of the animals.

When the pit was filled and the ground heaped over, that lemon sun had swung low for the afternoon. McDaid stood over the pit smiling and began to make the sign of the cross. *In nomine patris et filii et spiritus sancti.*

Amen to that.

They began across the field to the horse and Barnabas spoke. Don't you think it strange, Peter? That somebody someday will be lifting you about. In my case, Eskra. Washing my body. Dressing me for a funeral. Combing my hair. Putting me in a wooden box. Carting me about the place then on a carriage horse and me having no say in it. You know, he said, because of what you did, whenever it is my time to go, Eskra can hold me and wash me. That's something I canny say for Matthew Peoples.

The men were silent. Barnabas looked up through the trees towards the tapered field and saw in his memory Matthew Peoples standing in it, the man's big-boned shuffle. The slow blink of his eyelids. He began to roll another two cigarettes but McDaid put up his hand to say he'd had enough and Barnabas continued with just the one and smoked it. As he did so a blackbird swung down and hitched a ride on the horse. It paraded its amber beak as if it had dipped to drink in a Christmas orange and what it drank filled its eyes with rings of coloured juice. The watching carrion birds had scattered and Barnabas looked up and saw two rooks linger on the wall talking noisily till both of them agreed on some point of conversation and took off. The horse turned and the way the sun's shadow fell upon her cast the blackbird like a pterodactyl. It stretched its wings on the horse's flank hugely. The ground full of dark lesions as the men began to walk from the field and Peter McDaid spoke. Eskra says there's insurance due in. How long have ye to wait?

Barnabas shook his head. That woman.

He stood silent for a moment. Will you come in for a wee sup?

I would but I've a huge shite in me that's dying to get out and I donny want to do it in your outhouse. You'd need a bucket of Jeyes.

The big dirty hole on you.

The men laughed. Barnabas called out to Cyclop and saw the dog ignoring him. He turned and pointed. That useless fuckdog. Never does what he's told. McDaid squinted, saw the dog snouting the field under a burst of ragwort yellow, and he turned and began to walk off. Barnabas called out thanks and McDaid waved a big dirty hand into the air as if the work meant nothing. He slung the shovel over his shoulder and began to march leg-high like a soldier. I'm off to take Berlin, he roared out, pulled the shovel off his shoulder and began to fire it like a gun. Barnabas roared out. Say hi to the Jerry for me. He turned and went back into the field and walked towards Cyclop, saw the dog holding something in his mouth. Come here to me, you, he said. The dog in plain sight ignoring him. Saw when he came up close what Cyclop held in his mouth was a cattle bone.

Through the window she saw them. Three shapes roaming the yard, two men and a boy. The men were strange-looking, grey and hard as if they had stepped out of hills formed by intense heat and pressure, and when they began rummaging through the byre an invisible hand tightened around her heart. One of the men stood so tall and gaunt she saw something in the way he held himself that evoked in her an ineffable sadness. He moved through the rubble with his long arms swinging sadly, went at the stones as if his hands contained teeth, could have been some kind of peculiar ruminant, rummaging the byre's remains for food. The other man was steady and stout, wore a porkpie hat, moved about the place with the quick feet of a goat.

She called out to Barnabas upstairs but he made no answer and she shouted again and then she opened the back door and stepped out. She went towards them hesitant, each hand beaked birdly up her sleeves. Dark rust of hair on the boy and she saw he whispered something quick to the others when he saw her. The stout man turned, made a step towards her, took off his black-brim hat that wore an emerald feather clean as a blade. His voice was hoarse, came at her in strange, fast-talking cadences she could barely understand. No trouble at all meant to you missus just looking for some scraps from the burning, wild bad so it is. She heard in his voice notes of foreignness and colour. What she saw in his eyes was earnestness, and something else, a quality as if he was bearing up with fighting shoulders some ancient curse or weariness. Thick lips as he spoke and the flash of yellow teeth and the stubble on his face was dark and almost bearded. As he spoke the tall man turned around to look, held draped in his hand a piece of warped metal like a wilted flower that had died to his touch.

Sure you know how it is missus, my own missus isn't well and please be to God she'll get better and we got through the winter tough as it was with God's help and thank goodness for the spring, anything at all now from the burning might help us you're very kind. Suddenly he produced a smile that reached up gibbous. The tall man kept his quiet and averted his eyes to the ground when she looked at him. The boy stood where he was and she found herself looking at him, saw that his clothes were threadbare like those of the others. The boy pure of face with crooked yellow teeth gapped widely, freckles that shone from his face like inverse stars. She saw a change come quick in the boy's countenance, a worried look that flashed in his eyes and she heard Barnabas before she turned, saw him storming past her towards them with his arms rolling boulders. The short man rose a hand up in hello and went to speak, got the words out of him, howareya sir we meant no harm, but Barnabas was already upon them. Get to fuck off my land, he said.

Eskra saw the boy and what was pure of spirit became a darkening thing as if he had witnessed the blooming of evil. She turned to Barnabas and cast him a look he read from her as a warning to back down, but he took no heed, and he said to the strangers, go on, get, pointing towards the gate. Eskra's voice fell away from her. The men lowered their heads and the boy cast Barnabas a petrified look and the gaunt man began towards their horse and cart on the road. The stout man began talking. We meant you no harm so we didn't no harm at all sir praise God and may the Lord look after your house and everyone in it, may there be a year's blessing upon it and no harm meant to yous at all God bless.

Later, she stood over the sink and noticed her hands were shaking. Through the bluing glass of sundown she saw the remains of the byre that sat to her like some kind of depravity. She let drop a cup into the water. When she spoke her voice came loose, a coiled spring that stung him where he sat. I did not marry the bastard you're becoming, Barnabas Kane.

Barnabas in the range chair straightened up, folded over the paper, did not answer, did not look at her either.

They were only good people. Poor is all. Tinker folk. What did you have to do that for? she said.

She turned and faced him and he stood and turned his head as if he planned to leave the room but then his head snapped around to her, the look in his eye measuring the fight left in her. Them people? he said.

There's nothing out there but scraps of wood and metal and cracked stones. What would you be wanting with them? That thing staring down at us every day. An abomination. Why wouldn't you want to get rid of it?

Their kind are good for nothing, Eskra. They roam around living off others. These are lean times. We need what we have round here. That's all there is to it.

Why couldn't you let them take what they need? That byre will be rebuilt without any of what's there. Why did you have to be so rude to them?

I'll tell you why, Eskra. It's because they're insects. Parasites is what they are. None of them ever work. I'm sick of them traipsing around the countryside eating up everything with their eyes. Should be rounded up the lot of them. The smell off them.

Eskra's shook her head in disbelief. Many's the time I talked to Matthew Peoples about them and he had great time for them. Said they were full of uses.

Matthew Peoples was a half-baked fool.

He saw her mouth and eyes open as if to let in more light against the darkness that came from his mouth. What do you mean by that? she said.

That's not what I meant.

What did you mean then? He saw her eyes set down to disdain. Do not speak ill of the dead like that. Weren't you the one after all who sent him in?

Barnabas's mouth opened like his tongue had been yanked

out of him. Billy came into the room and asked what time it was and began to saw at the bread. Barnabas tried to speak, shook his head violently. After all the work I done yesterday burying them cows. You think that was easy? He pulled at the back door and left her standing, went up to the byre and took the snake-twisted metal that had been left lying on the ground by the gaunt stranger and threw it off the wall. The metal pinged a brief high note that rose into the evening silence and then dulled fast like it never was.

He stepped out of the house and could not read the sky. The weather withdrawn into a nilness that was wan and made him tense with unknowing. Everywhere he saw foreshadows of rain and opposing signs of sun held in slivers and when he looked again towards what he thought were such signs, everything he saw could be read otherwise. Eskra was still sullen with him. She spoke one thing, told him to take the car on account of his lungs. He walked towards the Austin and saw the breeze dance detritus and dust at his feet in leaps little like a child's playing. He drove determinedly, choked the car's gears, leaned over the wheel into his thoughts, followed the main road in the direction towards the town for a half mile. The road skirted patchwork fields of cattle and sheep he saw if only by his refusal to acknowledge them. It seemed to him that spring should not keep.

Strange these days to see a car on the road on account of the petrol rationing, and walkers or those in the fields turned to see who it was. They saw him hunched over the wheel and he wagged unseeing a finger at them. He took a turn-off where the land leaned down lazy like a barren afternoon and he turned then onto a lane. Gravel muttering under his wheels and he followed the way made dark by deciduous trees until the doctor's house loomed before him. A two-storey house with a small extension that led to the doctor's surgery. He parked in the lee of the gable wall, sat in the car and did not get out. Sat there and looked up at the wall. Upon it a tree made a shadow drama of lightning invert that fired darkly without sparks towards the roof. He looked for his tobacco and rolled a cigarette, coned the smoke out his nose without coughing. Took another drag and noticed the settle in his lungs. There you go, doctor. Not a bother on me. He rolled down the window and flicked the butt out onto the stones and watched it snuff out, heard the surgery door open. He started the car quickly, clanked the gears into reverse. An old woman bending over a boy came out the door.

He drove towards the town that rose greyly into a ragged shape upon a hill. Two-storey houses lined each side of the road in rising uniform fashion. He made his way to the centre of the town and parked where the streets converged into the shape of a warped cross. He walked past the hardware store where an old man nodded to him, the fellow sitting on a chair with his legs spread out like he had groin pain, nursing in his mouth a limp unlit cigarette. Barnabas stopped and lit it for him, stepped into the post office, fished from his pocket a letter from Eskra addressed to her mother in New York. The small black script neat as calligraphy had smudged. Would be opened no doubt by the sister. He posted it and went towards the butcher's, stopped outside, heard the bone-snap of a cleaver, stepped in. Gag of meat smell that hit him. He stared at the floral tiles on the wall and made his order and tried not to breathe for the meat smell that persisted and wove into him its reminder of death.

He went back to the car and put the meat on the seat and

rolled down the window. As he reversed the car, rain came with a sudden temper and he looked at the window and left it open. As he drove the rain sprayed his face and put a slick upon the road. Soon the surface shined and made the reflection of the car passing over it a sleek tremulous thing, the shadow of an animal fleeing half seen. In the film of rain everything that was held in it shimmered as if the shadow image of things were themselves alive — solid-stiff trees made trembling and buildings quivering as if that which was solid of the earth was not solid any more.

He took the turn off the main road and followed the track for the half mile towards his house, parked and put on his cap and got out. He stood under the rain and listened to it make music with his hat. His eye followed the downpour towards the mountains and he saw their dark countenances near hid behind cloud. He reached into the front seat and took out the grease-paper with the meat cuttings inside and stepped into the house. He did not note the strange settle of the place, how the radio that usually hummed with music or chatter was hushed, how even the clocks seemed careful. He hung his coat on the coatrack's curling tongue and his hat on a hook. As he lifted the package off the bureau he noticed a trickle of thinning meat blood leak towards the floor. Fuckdog, he said. He hurried with it into the kitchen and walked past the shape of Eskra in the range chair, put the meat into the Belfast sink. Said to her, the meat's leaking all over the place, goan get the mop for me.

She did not answer, sat where she was. He saw she was sitting with her hands flat on her thighs, the way she was staring blankly at the wall. What's the matter? he said. No answer came and she did not move her head to meet his eyes and he wondered then if she knew he had not visited the doctor. Billy not yet back from school. What's the matter? he said again. He walked towards her but she averted her eyes from him and pointed. He looked towards the deal table and saw on it a letter opened, knew then what it was, felt his stomach sicken and the veer of an abyss unseen came suddenly towards him. He stood looking at the letter as if by not moving he could put a hold on time and the event in the room that was unfolding, but the mantel clock took opposition to that thought and began to unfold the mechanism for the bell that would chime for quarter past, a preparatory stretching sound and then it clicked and the clock made note of the time passing, and he knew he would have to say something.

She spoke then. I wrote to them not knowing. Asking them for the forms. Writing to them all kindly like some kind of stupid woman I am. They must have laughed at that letter all right. Must have passed it around in there. Laughed at me like I was a fool.

Eskra—

You cancelled the insurance last year without telling me.

His legs grew heavy like he was stood in manure to the waist and he turned slowly on the ball of his foot and his chest began to tighten, could feel the manure pooling towards his throat. He took a deep breath and his mind roamed but was unmet with answers and his eyes swung wildly to the brown-tiled floor, to a fly resting still against the window, to the place that was newly wallpapered, anything but the shape of her. The shriek of her eyes. He tried to speak and he had to clear his throat and then the words turned solid and he spoke. I never thought we would need it so I cancelled it. It was a waste of money at the time. We needed it for other things.

And then she was coming at him out of the chair and he stood and met it, the flat of her hand that caught him on the cheek and the slap made his eyes water, could feel the sting as if her hand had been left in the fire to brand him. She took off out of the room but her voice reached him bitter as she mounted the stairs.

You thought everything could be good for ever. That you were made now, Mr Big Shoes. That all the work was done. In your mind nobody dies and nobody grows old and there is no sign of winter. What in your stupidity have you done to us?

He stood looking at the door, blinked dumbly. A door slammed upstairs. In the sink a trickle of blood threaded slowly across the white enamel, made a small bubble, slicked across the metal flange and slipped slowly, silent down the dark drainhole.

He slept self-imposed that night in the car and in the dream from which he has awakened he is asleep still in the Austin. He is parked somewhere he does not know for the windows are smeared against the greased light of the morning and he lies across the two front seats somewhat foetal, his knees tucked under the steering wheel and silence but for the leather that complains beneath him when he begins to sit up, his breath frosting the air, his arms tucked about his body for the cold has nestled into him while he was asleep and he can feel it now in his bones – old-man cold like a body about to be beaten – the window rivered with condensation so that he cannot see out and that smothering of grey light and something beneath it, distant like dark mountains, and he tries to start the car but it will not catch – the engine coughing like it is sick and then with a rattle it cuts silent – and he tries it again but this time it is dead and he decides to get out, see where the hell this place is, and he goes to open the door and pulls at the handle but the door does not open, puts his shoulder to it but it will not budge, and the door on the other side proves the same, the car then feeling very small, feels as if it is cramping in upon him – and he sees then the far off dark and distant thing is not distant at all but upon him, upon the car and blanketing upon the windscreen, upon everything – and the door is stuck with it, and the sight of it sucks the breath from his chest and he starts coughing, finds he cannot breathe, clamours towards the window and wipes at the moisture furiously – the sky so thick with it, it seems like no sky at all – the car half buried – falling listlessly like a gentle thing to form drifts deep all around, burying him and everything around it – a black snow.

Down Tully hill I was speeding hard as fuck and then I'm free-wheeling, round the twisty bend into the long drop down to the road. At the bottom I see somebody watching me. The bike rattling like it was set to fall apart and I'm nearing the bottom and I see the figure with the eyes fixed on me is The Masher. He looks with his tongue out like a dog leaning over a bicycle. Jesus you're some buck Billygoat he says to me when I pull up. He pulls a shoulder of poitín from his pocket and passes it to me and I take a swig and it near tears a hole out of me throat. Like drinking pure heat and him laughing at me. Jesus the wooze in my head straightaway I was all fired up and he says to me c'mon we'll go for a spin. I followed him down the road and took a turn that took us up into Treanfasy. There's a house settled quiet in amongst some trees and he goes to the front door and knocks. Whose is this place I ask and he says it belongs to a cousin Burt Ruddy and there's no answer at the door so he strides up all brazen to the car out the front, a 1936 Austin 10 Sherbourne, and he squares up to it with an air of certainty like he'd been driving all his life. I could tell it were all show, something about him putting on an air of danger all the time but I could sense something else off him too, a fear to him like he was used all the time to being hit. Get in he says. The key's in it already when I get in and he's taking another slug and passing it to me every drink an act of violence upon myself but I pretend I'm used to it. What about your cousin I ask and he says that Ruddy Arsecheeks owns the car but he never uses it cause he canny drive, leaves the key in for the neighbour to borrow. Won the car years ago in a raffle. The Masher couldna drive at all neither. The car jerking about the place like it were having a fit. We took it down the road and steered it into a field and began to rally her about making slow circles and trying to spin her but couldna get enough speed and then we got the car stuck in a mushy part at the end of the field. I get out and stand slushed to me ankles and start tryin to push and he gets hold of a stone and puts it on the pedal and the two of us start to heave. What happens then but the car frees up and takes away like it has a mind of its own, away like some headless person were driving it. Oh for a moment it were the funniest thing I ever seen only for the horror quick to sink in. The car is bouncing forward on the grass with the door hanging open and we run like fuck after it, The Masher catching up with it, his big long legs hinging up behind him and he jumps in, and I don't know what he was doing but he couldn't seem to lift the stone or maybe it were something else because next thing the car veers off rightwards as it nears the far end of the field and drives itself down into the ditch. The rear bucking up into the air like a horse, the two back wheels spinning muck about the place and the engine making a straining sound like a frightened animal. The door still open and I see him get out holding onto his head and he walks wobbling across the field and then he sits down and when I get up near him he is just laughing even though his head is cut. Big fucking whoops out of him. Ye stupid cunt ye I says, what the fuck now are we going to do with the car? And he just laughs, fuckin leave it he says. That Ruddy Arsecheeks will hardly notice. We leave the field and we grab our bikes from the ditch up the road and I says to him what are ye getting for Christmas, and he says to me, fuck all, and then who sees us as we're startin to go down the road but wee Molly the Moss, and she stands at the side of the road the wee hussy that she is smiling at us as if she knows rightly what we just done and I start then to get the fear wild bad she would go and tell on us. The Masher stares at her and I roar out at her, ye dirty wee bitch, and then I cycle off, take the long way around to get home to make it seem I were coming from another place. Afterwards I could hardly sleep. I imagined the auld bastard Ruddy going mad about the place and rightly so, for a few days later Sergeant Porter was up at our place asking questions saying somebody seen me on my bicycle up in the townland but I flat out denied it to him and I'm wondering if it was that wee hussy that told. The auld doll gives me the longest look afterwards like she seen right through me into the part of my mind that held quivering the lie but I held the look back at her. The thing is I don't even know why we were doing it we were just doing it I suppose.

THE SILENCE OF THE farm spread malignant into the house, laid itself upon everything a dense weight. In the evenings the gas lamps flickered and reached for the dark but could not light what gathered between them all that went unsaid. The clacking-tongued clocks commenting on the passing silence. Billy watching the distance thickening between his parents, watched the way his mother walled up her words, sat glazed over her food, left the dinner table early, did her chores with a distant stare. His father quiet about the place or grumbling to himself, a gliding shadowed thing that seemed happier outdoors.

Eskra rose daily at sunrise and went as usual about her work. She fetched the water and mucked out the horse and fed the animals and the remaining chickens. At the start of the week she baked the rationed black bread. But something within her had changed. A wheel in the middle of her being was pulling tighter the strings that held every part of her, and she stared out the kitchen window and imagined what it would be like to let that wheel loose, to let the parts of her be flung upon the wind that came down wild off the mountains a hunter of souls. Billy ghosting about the far field of her vision and she did not have the energy for him. She noticed the settle within her bones of rancour.

For days she could not look at Barnabas and then when his back was turned she began in her mind to speak to him. Just you turn around now you son of a gun. Talk to me and tell me how we are to survive. Let me hear it from your lips. You big lug you. How many fields we are to sell. If we are to give up this damned place. You and your big ideas. She watched him slope about the yard a stupid beast afraid of her, doing nothing at all now but making his clouds of cigarette smoke or carrying about a hammer and hitting things with it absentmindedly. The way he ignored the dormant farm as if pretending to himself things were otherwise. The dog ambling about the yard with his own concerns, lying out bold in the weak sun chewing cattle bones from the field, Barnabas roaring at the dog each time and pulling the bones out of the dog's mouth as if the pair of them were stars in some futile comedy and the dog watching on with what could have been amusement as the man muttering to himself reburied the bones in the field. At times, too, the dog could be seen watching one-eyed the sward, as if he was looking for something or someone to arrive, for Matthew Peoples perhaps to come sauntering all slow and big boned.

Dull-weather days put a hold on time and brought them neither wind nor rain and when the storm came Eskra was glad for it. She stood in the yard and watched the evening sky change – an angry bluff of cloud that rolled in low over a blood horizon. What came from the sea unmade the sinking sun and pulsed with distant flickers of lightning and she saw in its dark swell an inevitability of other things. She hutched the hens and put stones upon the lids of her hive. Took down the clothes from the washing line and walked with them heaped towards the house. The rain began to fall before she reached the back door and she looked up surprised, saw the darkening scrim had yet to reach overhead and that the rain was falling from white. Billy came running from the fields and stood in the kitchen soaking, his panting breath bellowing the secret reek of cigarette smoke. He stood over the stove warming his hands in his jumper and shorts. Eskra scolded at him. Would you look at you.

The boy shrugged.

You'll catch your death of cold. Where's your coat? she said.

The world dimmed suddenly through the window, the yard and the fields and what lay as far as the hills, as if a pall had been strewn. He looked at her and pulled a face, chewed on his lower lip. I donny know, he said.

Is it upstairs?

Naw.

Is it lost?

I might have left it some place.

Eskra's voice rose. That was a new coat we bought you. How dare you lose it like that.

I didn't mean to loss it. I'm all right anyhow.

Lose it not loss it. We won't be able to get another one with the rations. Wait till I speak to your father.

The boy stood silent a moment and then he raised his head and cast her a look of defiance. Goan and tell him then.

The way his words leapt across the room caught Eskra by the tongue and she turned away from him, began to tidy the table. You'll have to use for now your father's old coat on the back door, she said.

That auld fuckin thing.

A look from his mother that could hurl stones.

*

The dark of the ceiling and all night Barnabas lay sleepless listening to the storm. Rain upon the window like the fingernails of some termagant prying the glass to get in. A voice in the sad skirling wind that could speak for his mourning. He lay thinking about the grim wind that had struck, the farm and the death of Matthew Peoples a total loss that had emptied him out, wondered what does a man do to deserve such a fate. Nothing but hard work and now ruin. His mind ruminating upon how the fire could have started and he could think of nothing else. He heard something smack upon the yard and he sat up in bed. The sound continued, a rolling clatter, and he swung out of bed into the icy room. He reached for his dressing gown, a slumped shape upon the door, and put his feet into the cold mouth of his slippers. He felt his way down the stairs and into the kitchen and lit a lamp. When he opened the back door wind-cold rushed past him like a wild animal seeking heat. The night was sealed black and he stepped out into it, a zone of dense and hidden forces, and he could not map the order of the winds. The pale spill of the lamp faltering and his cheeks stung by the raw-cold rain and he could see nothing at all through squinting eyes, could not see what damage had been done. Just his own wild imaginings of the wind as it blew around him and he stood for a moment and watched the sky, saw the moon had been cast out, that the stars were all voided and all to see was the world without form.

He went inside and stood shivering, opened the stove door and rested his hands above the dimmed coals. A scant heat and he closed the stove door and poured himself a dram of whiskey. When he went upstairs his side of the bed was cold. He lay down afraid to turn into her, listened to her breathing. He could sense something wakeful about her, as if her mind was alert and roaming the room, and he could not help himself and he leaned in and whispered to her. I went out to look but it was too dark to see anything. I didn't know what I was looking for.

What he heard heave was the deep breath of sleep.

In the morning nature ruled its fixed compass. The sky distant and inert and its lungs blown out. He saw all over the yard the debris of hay and twigs, found a dead sparrow lying on its back by the wall. How it looked asleep and so restful, the straight fix of the eye glassed dark, the regal drape of its wing as if in death it had dressed itself in its own dun colours. And he saw it asleep to the night in its nest, shook out of its tree, thrown about in fright by that death wind until it met its end on the wall. He scooped the broken sparrow onto a spade and slid it into a ditch. Further up the yard he saw what had made the commotion. A sheet of corrugated iron blown loose from the new shed roof. He took the ladder and climbed up to look and saw three sheets were lifted. Fuckdog, he said. He searched about and found one sheet aslant a whin bush in a field and the other behind the barn napping. He went for his tools and heaved up the iron and hammered them into place. He stood then lordly on the roof and surveyed this kingdom. It was as if the night's disorder had been dreamed of, the mountains serene and the bog spread below them in its timeless nature and draped now in cloud shadow that drifted upon the heather as if some kind of behemoth animals were grazing. In a hollow in the pasture field he saw a newly formed pool of water and a broken tree limb sprawled there as if dumped by some person, wondered what strength of wind was needed to carry it there. Eskra pumping water in the yard. Without thought he waved at her and she did not look at him and he watched her go around the side of the house. Through the tops of the trees he could see McDaid's farmstead. Saw the distant shape of the man in a far field bent to his fencing. He turned around and found himself looking at the house of another, a white building isolate against the distant bay, the long stretch of fields from his farm leaning down to it, the view clearly visible through the trees. The house owned by Pat the Masher. He recalled the bother they had with The Masher's son a few months ago just before Christmas. Fucking crazy-eyed kid. He saw smoke drift from the chimney and the way then he saw the house unlocked something in his mind, an unthought thing that moved forward into thinking.

She was working water from the pump when she saw bird shadow fleet upon the flagstones, looked up and saw a big bird glide real low. The bird was solitary and flapped hugely to take rest upon the fence ten feet away, a creature with large dark eyes and a curving beak. A raptor of some kind she did not recognize and rare to these parts she guessed. It was the kind of bird that owned the air, took other creatures in its talons like skyhooks. Must have got lost in the winds. She watched the mechanical action in the way it bobbed its head, wondered if it was a falcon, and then the bird took wing. She tried to follow its flight path but her view was blocked by the house. She left the pump and walked around the corner to watch it further and she remembered then about the bees, walked over to the hive and saw they had been sheltered sufficient by the wall and the juniper trees.

She dressed in her protective sleevelets and wore her bee-veil bonnet and lit the rotten wood in the tin cylinder of her smoker. To the bees she brought the opium of smoke and poured them some sweetened water. In her mind she saw the way they awoke energetic to the spring each year as the purest kind of purpose, an intensity of living without any awareness of such a thing. The wind sloped the tips of the grass and a curl of smoke drifted up over the hive, swung back towards the junipers. It took for a moment the shape of a coil and then untwisted, mapped out peculiar forms. What she saw then was a shadow on the grass leaning towards her. A person. It stopped in her mind the hum of a song and she watched the shadow shape into a steeple. She would not turn around for him. The wind took the drifting smoke and swirled it into her eyes but she kept her back turned, would give him no satisfaction. The shadow lingered, grew taller as it came then towards her, and when she snapped around what she saw was the face of another in smoke half hid, the face of Baba Peoples. The woman wearing widow black and her face under her shawl was starched and hairless as if she had been sloughed of her sex. Baba moved her baby feet towards Eskra, the air around her thick with bees, waved her hand for Eskra to come to her. Eskra made a gentle motion for the woman to step back, spoke to her. Don't go waving your hands like that or the bees will go for you.

Baba continued to walk forward. I wouldn't feel nothin of it, she said.

Eskra stepped forward and took the woman by her elbow light in her hand as a bird's wing, began to guide her away from the hive, but Baba shook the grip off, stood defiant. Show me your eyes, Eskra Kane, she said. Eskra sighed and undid the safety pins that held the veil to her coat and rolled it up her face. Not yet ten o'clock in the morning and she could smell drink off Baba, leaned back to get away from her rank breath, that husband of hers was so simple and sweet and this here woman shameless and sluiced with the drink.

How are you doing, Baba?

The woman looked at her through yellowing orbs that were shot with spicules of red and her mouth pulled a smile that was dead on her face as soon as it was upon it. And then the light in her eyes seemed to brighten, a strange kind of pleading look she gave Eskra but there was something false about it and Eskra saw something flash in the woman's eyes before the woman was able to conceal it, a note of contempt. The woman tiny before her yet Baba placed her hand on Eskra's wrist, began to hold it tight as if to impress greater meaning to what she said. Her voice scratched and childish.

Isn't this a lovely place you've got here, Mrs Kane? You've got it well kept. Aye, you with your foreign ways, your bees and all, and I suppose you be making honey with it too to sell. Aye, you've a good place going, good land and you did well of it. And how's your boy? Matthew was very fond of him so he was, talked about him all the time like he was his own. And that was it, Mrs Kane, we were never able to have any of our own. The bonesetter said I wasn't fixed for it. No weans at all in the world so we had and you can imagine now what a time I'm having of it left on my own.

Eskra felt the woman's grip tighten.

Aye, God rest his soul, Matthew Peoples, there never was a kinder man, nor more hard-working neither. And he was a kindly soul to the boy and a dedicated man to that husband of yours – I will not say his name.

The woman leaned over and made a dead tree of her face to hawk tobacco spit.

Aye. I'll tell you it was that man who left me with nothing

in this world, Mrs Kane. Took from me everything I had in it that you have here. No husband now and nothing coming in to help me mind myself. And it was that man who made my husband go in. I know it. My Matthew would not have gone in there of his own accord, twas not the like of him. He wasn't that stupid.

She looked at Eskra as if daring her to look away and Eskra flinched and held the look before shaking her wrist free. She rubbed the place on her wrist where the woman's phantom grip remained.

You know I'm sorry to hear that, Baba. Truly I am. But I won't hear of you talk about my husband that way. What happened was beyond terrible, it was a tragedy. It has affected badly everybody here—

I can tell it in your eyes you're sorry, Mrs Kane. Such kindly eyes you have. What I'm wondering here and now is what you want to do about it. To make things better for me.

A bee curved the air between them and swung to land on Baba's cheek, began to walk brazen, came up near her eye, and Baba did not blink with it. Eskra waved the bee away and looked nervously at the hive and rolled the veil back down her face.

Baba. We lost everything, all our cattle. We don't know how the fire started and we don't know how we'll get the farm back. I just found out we had no insurance. I married a man, Baba, who thought all his battles were won, that nothing bad could ever go wrong. He wasn't prepared for it. I don't know what we are going to do.

As she spoke, her voice dropped down to a whisper and she glanced over her shoulder. Listen, Baba. I gave you money for your husband's funeral. It was the least we could do. But now all our money's gone, Baba. I have enough savings to put food on the table to last us for a while and that's about it.

The woman slowly swivelled her head, took a long look at the house and its adjoining fields, and then her lips wore that dead smile again. That being what it is, Mrs Kane, how can all this be nothing?

Eskra sighed loudly. A soft stamp of her foot. That's the way it is, Baba Peoples.

The older woman bore upon her a look of judgement, held it unblinking until Eskra turned away for relief and in the silence that fell between them Eskra heard carry on the wind sharp peals – hammer blows on metal that came from Peter McDaid's farm. She counted seven soundings before Baba took a step towards her and held her with her yellowed eyes, shook slowly again her head before making a quick half smile.

That is a wild shame, she said.

A piece of turf in her hand baked dry by the wheel of fifty suns and she laid it on the fire. The cheek of that woman. How brazen coming around here asking for more money and the trouble we're in as if she didn't know anything about it. Speaking of Barnabas like that an absolute disgrace. She climbed up off her knees and dusted angrily her smock and her gaze fell upon their wedding photo crooked on the wall. She leaned her hand against the chair to straighten it, saw it momentarily as if she did not recognize herself or Barnabas, the way she was sat with her hair fashionably short and Barnabas plain and strong beside her. The man's striking youth. Those thick-fingered hands spread on his lap and in his eyes a faint look of incomprehension, as if the photograph had been a surprise to him. A cow-lick of dark hair over his forehead. She tried to recall the room or the face of the photographer but was met with an empty space of mind until she recalled the smell of fresh lacquer on the stairway.

She stood by the kitchen window later and caught sight of Barnabas, the man standing in the yard staring at the byre as if he saw in it something other than what it was. The way he turned in profile and for the first time she saw his stoop, a faint bend in the back as if he had taken upon him fully the weight of recent events, and she saw in her mind Barnabas as he was at the time of the photo. The full blaze of him. His pure physicality. Teaching him to dance in her mother's front room in Vinegar Hill with the street light reaching in to couple with the yellowing of the lamps, guiding him around the room in the space between the pushed-back furniture – the old horsehair couch, a tray-top table – and the man in her arms stiff as the table's cabriole legs, his inner workings as ornate as its carved putti if she could only work him out. Barnabas exhausted but making the effort. In the stiffness of his arms she could sense all that power coiled within him while her mother pretended not to watch through the half-open door to the bedroom. Duke Ellington on the record player. She would listen for the hobnail thunder of him climbing the stairs and then she would make him dance in his socks. The stink of your feet. The state of you. This man who could work all day on a tiny piece of plank with barely nothing beneath him but the drop to his own death and the fall in her own belly just to think of it. And here he was now stumbling nervous in her arms as if he could fall any moment. You can dance the sky, she said, but down here you're all left feet. The big brute hands on you.

The newness of another body in the plain sight of an evening. And the things you lose later on – the sense of space between bodies. How aware she was of the spaces between them – at the other side of the room by the table pouring tea. One cushion apart on the sofa. Dancing, the heat of her palm pressed against his. Eye to eye so close she could just about see herself in the dark centre of his pupil, a shadowy thing trying to find form within him. And the way his tanned skin gleamed in that fading light was still impressed upon her as if that moment of him had been conserved in perfect form within her not subject to time or forgetting. And as she saw him now in the yard with his stoop it came to her in a vision, the span of his entire life before her, and she saw in that moment the coming of his old age, his fading splendour, and what she felt then came up out of her unexpected, a surge of pity strong and true, and something else, a moment of white love that escaped from her like a bird.

He stood in his own dark, the night sky cloudless and bright with the distant beauty of stars that shone for him a measure of time impossible for his mind to see. To get away from all things. To slide out from under what was and disappear into the cool of the dark, reach the place of sound receding a soft and distant ping. The Austin was low on petrol but he took it anyway and drove it into town, parked it outside the saddler's shop. Stood out of the car buckled darkly against the glass. Inhale of shoe leather and crinkled echoes of laughter from up the street. As he turned he saw a man coalesce slowly from a lane, the figure lopsided and coming towards him inebriate, some slop form of human that turned out to be the saddler. He watched the man come to a stop looking down upon his huge waist, trying slowly to belt his trousers. The leather long enough for four widths of him and Barnabas watched him in wonder, saw how he had to loop the belt around his girth twice and then the long struggle to buckle it, the saddler making a low groaning sound all the while as if this single moment was not a man at his most ordinary but the lowest of him.

A chalk-dust moon lay scattered upon the street and Barnabas made towards The Bridge bar, heard rise from it an assault of loud laughter, knew it to be Fran Glacken. Three youths that hovered by the doorway looked at him. They held cupped in each hand a fag and their faces were hid under their caps. One of them spoke. Yes, sir.

Yes, boys, he said.

The youth stepped forward. Ye wouldn't go in would ye and get us a wee naggin? He held out a note.

Barnabas shook his head. What makes you think I'm going in?

He walked past them up the street until he came to the door of another public house, a place called Tully's. He stood and listened to its quiet for a moment. The place was crouched and dark and the air hung with turf must. In the corner glowed a sunken fire. As he came towards the counter a fat yellow candle guttered at him, stood in a solid pool of its own waste. There was standing room for no more than ten men and he saw two youngsters at the bar near hid in their own smoke. They talked quietly between themselves and he did not know their faces, figured them for farm labourers. The wooden stool complained when he drew it back and he nodded to the barkeep. Yes, Annie, he said. The old woman eyed him without smiling. He saw in her face an appointment with death, the impress of her skull through paper skin, cheeks like sundered sails from the loss of her teeth. Safeguarded in her eyes though was a fighting spirit. She slid off a stool to fix him a pint and watched him slake it in two long drinks. He wiped his chin with his sleeve and looked at her. She took the glass and refilled it and put it back in front of him, took a chequered towel and began to dry glasses. When she was done she sat back down on the stool and hung a pipe from the wrinkles of her mouth. A side door opened and an old man slid out. His ears were red seashells and his chin bore sprouts of thick whiskers and he carried in his hand a hatchet. He stood to the far end of the counter that had a hole in it the width of a man as if something had risen to bite a piece out of it. He swung at the hollow with his hatchet and the grinning blade bit the wood with a wallop and Barnabas flinched. He watched the old man collect the flitches of counter wood and go back out the door. Barnabas sucked on the pint and lit a pre-rolled cigarette, blew a draft of smoke towards the low ceiling that hung there in slow turmoil. He looked at the old woman and nodded towards the counter.

I can see that being a problem down the line, he said.

Annie Tully lit him with a glare. Mind yer own business, Barnabas.

Her face changed as soon as she spoke and she leaned in towards him. I'm sorry, Barnabas. I didn't mean that. It was a terrible thing happened to yous.

What's that you're talking about now, Annie?

She saw something in the look he gave her had the smell of trouble off it.

What happened up on the farm.

Oh that, he said.

He screwed his eyes at her and let her talk and as she talked he saw clearly the ancient scores in her skin as if she had been marked up in her old age for some benediction. Her throat a cross-hatch of lines and the wrinkles around her mouth held within them the shadows of the pub.

And never mind what people are saying about ye. This town. People jabber on just to make sound for their ears. They're always at it. I don't pay them any heed. And neither should you.

He concentrated on her words and his breathing slowed up in accordance and he leaned in towards her, trussed her up good where she stood with his eyes. And tell me now, Annie. What is it people are saying about me?

She tried to retreat, found she couldn't and he took a read of her face, saw she knew she had gone too far. She shrugged, withdrew back to her chair. You know how it is, she said.

I don't, Annie. Goan tell me.

Annie picked up the towel again and began to fumble with it till she hitched up her voice. I don't like your tone.

He leaned into her and his voice rose up like he didn't give a damn. Is it that they're saying I'm responsible for a man's death? Is that it? Is that what they think? That I went out and deliberately killed a man? Sent him in to do my dirty work? That I stood there like some cunt and sent Matthew Peoples into the fire? I was in there too you know. I went in there after him. I was nearly kilt by it too only for Peter McDaid. That man just about got me out so he did and he didn't make no decision about who he was choosing for there were no choices to be made. That smoke in there was thicker than hell. I might as well have died, Annie, because I lost it in there and went black.

The young men to his side began to look around and the old woman cut them a dangerous look. She relit her pipe and was silent a while as she toked on it and then she spoke. How is Eskra taking it?

Barnabas took a long drink. I'm beginning to think that fire was started deliberate. Things like that just don't start on their own.

The old woman eyed him and shook her head, turned to the stall of drinks and poured a glass of whiskey. She put it down softly in front of him. Hearken to me here now, Barnabas. This one's on the house. I know you're down on yourself but there ain't no point trying to blame others for what happened even though it's natural. What's done is done. It happened the way it did even if you don't know what caused it. If I were you I'd be careful of trying to find blame for things for I know only too well it can lead you up the wrong path.

She sucked on her pipe and saw it had gone out again, leaned forward and sparked a match to it. If there's one thing I know from my long years on this here earth it is that people can't stop making up stories about things. We are natural speculators. We dream stories in our dreams and are convinced there is meaning there for us. We see our own lives as something from a book with beginnings and endings. We tell ourselves that everything that happens to us is part of our story. It's a devil in us, this making things up. All the time people don't know what causes things but we go on as if we do. And here's the thing, Barnabas, we don't even know we are doing it. Ask yourself, how often when you were sick did you tell yourself with certainty what caused it? Or where you picked it up? Or who gave it to you? As if you are privy to such information.

She watched him staring at her. All this jumping to conclusions is dangerous business if you ask me. I've seen so many times that there are things in this life that are outside our purview. Yet that doesn't stop us reaching into the dark for answers and telling ourselves they are true. You'd be better off, Barnabas, staying away from that kind of thinking. It'll lead to nothing but trouble so it will. Ask yourself, how many times have you been totally wrong about something? How many times? All the time, I'm sure, and yet I'll bet you don't remember. I'll bet you only remember the times you were right. But a stopped clock gets the time right twice a day too.

She took a suck of her pipe.

If I'd known I was going to get a lecture, he said.

Unless you have hard information before you, Barnabas, there is no point trying to pin the cause of that fire on people, or ghosts, or any other things. It can only lead to pure trouble so it will.

Barnabas sat there eyeing her intensely, but behind his tight lips he was grinding on his teeth. Oh right, he said. You're saying just to forget about the burning down of my livelihood. That it was some sort of accident was it? And leave it at that? An act of God? Nature's diddling thing?

He took the glass and swirled it until it stormed circular and he sunk it whole and put the glass back down. He leaned slowly towards her, scald of whiskey down the back of his throat, and he held her eye until he saw the melt of her hard stare and in the folds of her neck a quiver.

Let me tell you, Annie. You can tell a wild lot, a wild lot from people. The way they behave. Or the way they don't behave. It's in the not behaving when things are going on around them that is telling. Isn't it? Don't you think that's so?

The old woman stared at him and blinked.

All I know is there's some cunts behaving what I'd call strange. And there were people who didn't come to help put out that fire even though they could see it good and rightly. People who would have good reason to hurt me so they would.

The woman kept her silence and Barnabas stood suddenly. He shook his head and put coins on the counter. I've had enough for tonight, he said. I'm going home to me wife.

She travelled the yard with her arms to her chest, her fingers smelling of apples. He did not hear her come behind him when she cornered him at the new shed, spun around to meet her as if she were the bearer of malice. She saw how he tensed and his breathing tightened, his eyes fixed quick to the points of a knife.

You and me need to talk, she said.

Her words sounded out of her with the relief of hemmed-in animals let loose. His brows leaned down to meet his eyelashes.

You're talking to me now again?

A dour light trapped everything in that yard and he stood where he was in the shadow of her voice, heard in it a quaver of sadness, the skyfall of a child's small kite.

What I want to know, Barnabas. How you could have kept that quiet from me about the insurance? All that time? When you could have said something? And all the times I mentioned it?

She shook her head as she spoke and he found himself staring at patterns of shadow on the ground as he listened to her, the imbricate of all things vertical from the sun to the dust. He began to knuckle his cheek, looked towards the sleep-slumped dog by the back door. In that moment she saw what was held tight in his face fall and a long breath came out of him.

I didn't know how to tell you, Eskra. I thought you were sore enough. I didn't want to hurt you. He turned then to face her. Honestly, love. I was trying to figure out something. I don't know. At the time nothin could be done so what was the difference?

She shook her head again at him. We are going to have to sell up some fields, Barnabas. Go in to the auctioneer tomorrow and talk to him. There's no other way.

What are you on about, Eskra?

Maybe if you had done what you were told by the government. Not gone and bought that exemption for the compulsory tillage order. We might be growing wheat now for The Emergency and getting paid for it. But you had to be bull-headed. I don't see what else we can do.

He went to speak but she cut him off. How are we going to live? she said.

He watched her as she walked across the yard, her arms across her chest to make a barrier of her back to him, and he turned and walked behind the new shed. He stood very still and then he turned and kicked a dull sound out of a barrel half full with ashes, stood staring into the full sense of himself, kingdoms of the mind that are to a man what makes him, and he said to himself, what in the hell does she think, that I'm just going to lie here and take what's coming?

She stood in the sweet of peeled apples, placed around the plate the sliced fruit in grins. When she looked up she saw Barnabas marching down the yard from the new shed, his hands like stones that magicked into fingers. He stood by the back door and kicked out of his boots and came in red-faced and she sighed and turned away from him. He padded past her in his socks and went into the living room and poured himself a whiskey all scorch and satisfactory and he refilled the glass and went into the kitchen, sat down on the range chair. It was then that he spoke to her, steam issuing from a pot on the stove beside him. His face was bittered. You said to me how are we to live, as if I donny get out of bed every morning thinking about that, hoping for a way to make things better for this family. What kind of useless man do you take me for?

The ceiling rumbled above them as if Billy were dragging something huge across it. Eskra turned towards the stove. The dinner's near ready, she said. Call the boy down. She took a saucepan of potatoes and drained it and poured the skinned spuds into a white bowl patterned with amber and olive flowers. The potatoes piled like small steaming boulders and he sat there staring at her pop-eyed. He took a slug of his whiskey and felt it burn.

I will not be selling off them fields, Eskra, and with good reason.

She went to the door and called out in a high voice for the boy to come down to his dinner.

You find me a man around here with good reason and I'll listen to all he has to say, she said.

Barnabas stood up. Eskra turned to the turnips and buttered them.

What then, Eskra? We sell the fields and what? Rebuild the byre with the money? And farm out the cattle. Where? Grow grass in the yard? That new barn wouldn't house four of them.

We don't have to sell all of the fields.

She turned and took the meat out of the oven to rest and Barnabas stared hard at the joint and began to saw at the black bread. Leaned into the jam. Eskra put the potatoes on the table.

We don't have to sell any of them, he said. I'm going to go and get a meeting at the bank and get money off them so I am. I've already been talking to somebody about that at the bank. They said that reptile Creed would consider it.

Barnabas took the jam and smeared it on the bread and as he began to eat the jam blooded the sides of his mouth. She looked at him in disgust. The big red face on you, she said.

What?

We already owe the bank a debt for the new barn. And we can't even pay that. Why would they give any money to us, Barnabas, when we can't even pay them for what we already have?

What's that about my face you said?

Creed sent another letter, Barnabas.

Barnabas stood and looked at himself in the mirror and saw the jam on the side of his mouth and wiped himself, picked up his drink, took a long slug of it. She went to the dresser and took from the drawer knives and forks and asked Barnabas to call Billy again but he just sat down to the table. Eskra went to the kitchen door and leaned upon the jambs and called out. Billy came down the stairs like he was footing heavy weights.

Would you listen to who it is. It's Lord Clatterclogs, Barnabas said.

Billy looked at his father and smirked. There's jam all over yer face.

Shut up.

Barnabas got up off his chair and went out to the next room and fixed himself another whiskey, drained it where he stood, poured another and went back into the kitchen. He stared at the plated meat on the table, his face darkening.

What's that? he said.

What's what? Eskra said.

That.

What do you mean?

I meant what I asked.

If you are going to be like that, Barnabas, then it is what it is.

I suppose you think this a joke.

It's a side of beef, Barnabas. Pat Glacken came around the other day and gave it to us. Can you explain to me now what's wrong with it?

I won't eat it.

Excuse me?

I can't eat it.

Since when?

Any other animal but not that since after what's happened.

But you ate beef last week.

Billy leaned over the table and spooned potatoes onto his plate. Don't be stupid, Da, he said. Since when don't you eat meat?

Barnabas gave the boy a long look that held no expression at all, turned to look at the bowl of spuds and reached into it and began to spoon them onto his plate and then he put the spoon back into the bowl with a clink and leaned back, looked again at the boy as if he did not know him, and what was building inside him coalesced and was conjured quick into a fury that took the boy unawares, the hand that swung out flatly towards him and whipped across his cheek. Billy bucking backwards, stood up in shock holding his hand to his face. In that same movement he threw a look to his father of pure hate. Eskra stood up speechless and Billy fled from the room and Barnabas looked at her mouth gasping wordless like a fish. He stared at her dead-eyed. I'll break that boy's bake if he talks to me like that again.

Eskra stared at him like she saw a different man before her, looked at his face so long his features altered and fell away into an exaggeration of its parts, his lips ballooning into a fattened sneer that became all of his face and she watched him fork spuds into that same swollen mouth indifferent. He ate with the kind of patience of a man who is feigning thought about his food and it was then that Eskra banged the table with her fist. She went around to Billy's place and plated meat and potatoes and poured gravy over it and took it upstairs. When she came back down Barnabas was leaning back sucking on a cigarette holding in his hand his whiskey.

You've had enough of that, she said.

He gripped the glass and swirled it towards his lips. Eskra sat on the range chair defiant.

Barnabas.

He turned slowly towards her. I am the boy's father and he will not talk like that to me not ever.

He was asking you a question, Barnabas. Since when don't you eat beef?

A long sip of his whiskey for an answer.

Do you know what I think? he said.

I don't care what you think any more. I'm just sick of it.

I've been thinking about the day it happened. How people round here responded. Everybody came to help us that day. Everybody.

She did not look at him.

Only that's not true, he said.

He saw the damask of puzzlement on her face. What are you on about, Barnabas? she said. They all came.

He shook his head. They all came but one.

She could see when he stood that he wore a sly smile, like a man who had cracked the nut of a puzzle.

Everybody came who saw the fire and even Doctor Leonard who lives a good mile away, she said.

You're right. Everyone within reach. Everyone within reach but one. You know who was here. Fran Glacken and those eejit sons of his. The McLaughlin clan – even that imperious fucking father of theirs dragging his beard all the way over here. Peter came cycling his bike in his fucking wellies. And the others came after when they heard. But there was one fucking bastard who didn't show. And never came to offer his condolences neither.

She did not like what she saw in his eyes nor the way his hands fisted. The way he looked at her.

One fucking bastard, he said.

And who was that, Barnabas?

It was Pat the fucking Masher Doherty, he said.

Her face bunched up confused and Barnabas leaned back in the chair smiling to himself. He drained the glass of whiskey.

So what if he didn't, she said. Pat the Masher is a quiet man who keeps to himself. He has enough of his own troubles, what with that son of his.

I reckon it didn't suit him to help us.

That business before Christmas with his son. Sure he would have no reason to be upset with you about that. What happened with John the Masher wasn't our fault. It wasn't anybody's fault.

Don't be foolish, Eskra. Do you think that would not be remembered? From where that house is he could have done nothing but see that fucking fire, I'm sure of it. Watched us be burned out of the farm so he did. And I'll tell you what, Eskra. I'll tell you this. There might have been more to it than that. I can see the whole picture in my head so I can.

You need to stop this, Barnabas.

Stop what? he said. I'm not doing anything.

He stood and left the room without looking at her.

He awoke again from a malignant dream that spread its corruption within him. From what dark place in his mind it came he could not know. In his waking day these things lay hid and unimagined but at night they ripened like malign fruit and he awoke with relief into the dark certainty of the room, the assurance of Eskra's breathing, the quiet mesh of the house. His tongue slapped his mouth and his mouth was dust and he rose up before the morning, walked downstairs amidst the tangle of dream. What lingered there was like dawn shadow from a ragged tree snaking a suggestive and ghastly thing upon the ground unreal but shrinking now in the light of the sun. He reached into what was left of the dream and saw the face of a woman he met on a road. Nightfall, her skin moon's milk and her dark hair was curled and he asked her where he was going and she smiled and said nothing, walked alongside him, their hands touching and he asked her again and she turned around and said, all those who have died follow the same road, and when he looked at her again he could see she wasn't young at all but an old woman with her hair gone grey and her skin sored and then that face became the face of Matthew Peoples and he saw the awful things that insected out of his mouth.

He lit a lamp for comfort and fixed the fire awake. Sawed bread for breakfast and ate it dry watching the dawn, a blue skate wing that left a wake of blood on the horizon. When it was light he went out, a rawing cold speckled by spit-rain that promised greater rainfall and he looked towards a huddling of dark cloud shaped like an anvil. He went to the byre and began to clear out the remains, his hands reddening in the cold. He pulled at the charred wood, lifted fire-cracked stones, kicked cattle bones that lay concealed in the ashes. Caught amidst the byre the linger of the fire's stench. The metalwork shaped now like the letters of some occult alphabet signing for him sounds that led to a dark and final truth about the nature of man and beast. He removed pieces of the ruined remains to a site behind the new barn that he had begun to use as a dumping ground. He did not want to return yet to that taper field. Back and forth with the wheelbarrow all day to make with char a small dark hill. Nature had taken to the barrow as if it were a coat, gnawing the front of it until it was holed above the wheel. He could see the ground as he walked while the barrow leaked its load, left a trail of black dust upon the grass. The tangled ruins of the byre began to take shape with other ruined things behind the new barn, a cutting bar rusted to reddened bones as if it had laid down weary and died there. An old stove laughing at its predicament with hysteric grill teeth. Machine tools worked and put down by hands long gone.

He thought often about Matthew Peoples. Remembered the first time he saw him. Watched him lumbering up the yard, a white moustache on his face at the time that could have hoofed a horse. Jesus, if a whole tree could walk, he thought. Figured him for useless but Matthew soon learned him. That man could turn a hand to anything, could hedge and harrow, ditch and reap and sow. Could cure croup even. Told Eskra to sluice the young boy's chest and throat with a sponge in coldest water and sure it worked. Knew how to cure fistula on a horse too. Told Barnabas he needed a toad and Barnabas laughed at him but Matthew turned up the next day with a sack and produced a toad from it, a warted and bloated thing with eyes slow-blinking, a strange duplicate of Matthew Peoples himself. He held it in the air towards Barnabas. Hold it to the horse's hole, he said. Goan fuck yerself, said Barnabas. Matthew leaning back laughing. He began to rub the back of the toad off the sore. Keep yer head back, he said, for there's a wild smell off it. Barnabas half-turning his head in disgust. I'd say there is. You can stick your head up its hole for all I care, I won't be going anywhere near it. He called Matthew a juju man but Matthew stopped laughing and looked at him puzzled. There's no magic in it. It's the milk from the toad's warts will ease it so it will. He threw the dead toad into a ditch like a useless flap of skin. Said it would take about two weeks and sure as he said it, it did.

Eskra watching him at the window. Saw a shift inside him as if a mass of great weather were moving on to slub over distant hills not his own, took with it wind and pressure. Said to herself, finally, he's back to himself again. He's moving on from what's happened. She saw him bending to lift what was left of the purlin beam, oak a century old made light as pumice from the fire, and then he was bending down again, came up with a white rock in his hands shaped like a skull.

That same evening he stood in the light of the hall laid out in its shaded evening tapestries. He took his coat off the hook and sleeved it, stood a moment searching his pockets. He went into the kitchen and she watched him take the car keys from a hook on the dresser.

Don't tell me you are going to the pub, she said.

I'm not, he said.

We can't even afford the rationed petrol.

His finger tapped his nose. Don't worry about petrol. If we need any Peter McDaid can get his hands on some.

As he turned he stopped and stared out the window.

What is it?

He spoke as he was going out the door. Ah nothin. I thought somebody was coming in. Twas just somebody going past on the lane. A wee girl. Looked like one of Goat McLaughlin's granddaughters. The one that always looks cold.

An acid evening in which the world wanted some kind of blessing or warmth and he stood in it and took a gill of air and released it from his lungs. Light in his mind beginning to press into the darker reaches as if he awoke to find some huge impediment had been freely rolled. The light of a future looming before him for his eyes to see it. He parked the car outside the cemetery and found the plot in the darkening light. The earth still raw and the brown earth night-shifting into shades of purple. He saw the plot bore a temporary wooden cross. He did not know how old Matthew Peoples was. Never even thought about it. He could picture the man running towards the fire and the living thing that was his body in movement and the mind housed within, all that was that made the man, and he stared into the heaped earth trying to imagine that man as bones. The light within him gone as if in that moment he was taken down the smoke made him instanter into dust. He stared at the earth sat loose and in clods and the grass beginning to grow unevenly, began to smooth out a large ribbed footprint on the graveside. Saw the shape of his hand on Matthew Peoples' back, the flat of his hand that sent the man in. What rose inside him was great sorrow and he swallowed hard, felt wet on his cheek. To reach into the ground. To breathe life back into those bones. He wanted to speak, to say he was sorry, but the words sat dumb in his mouth. Finally he spoke under his breath. It was my own responsibility.

He turned and found the path towards the gate, took note as he went of the differing markers, headstones and crosses some of them standing as tall as a man, sized as if they were made to cast replacement shadows. The sky vast and darkening above. The gnawing ageless spit-rain. He saw how time made even stonework perish, the torque of the earth slowly twisting the stones so that eventually even the markers for the dead would be tossed out and the earth would make itself clean. What are these graves for anyhow, Matthew, but for the living and not for the dead, and when the living have left this life all remembering will pass with them, and you and me and everyone else will lie forgotten and stoneless and the sky goddamn the same over it. So what's the point of my saying sorry to you anyhow? Tell me what good will it do? Tell me who am I even saying sorry to?

The hinges on the cemetery gate squawked like a hungry gull and the sound soared sharp and was lost in the bruising sky. He turned around to latch the gate and his eye travelled to the sudden shape of Baba Peoples standing over the grave, as if she had taken form from the matter of evening itself, its darkening air and what it held concealed, or it seemed to him she could have ghosted from the thick stand of trees that huddled behind the cemetery wall in their perpetual sorrow, had sat there watching him as he stood over the grave, and he knew in that dim light her eyes were upon him.

Two days later. She hummed along to the melody on the radio, violins that had become sweeping and urgent and reached upstairs to the bathroom in spate. She poured hot water into the great tin tub and put onto the floor the cast iron pot and ran her finger through the water. She stripped and stood naked and eased in her toes and then lowered herself into the heat that stung her all over softly as if she had laid herself down amongst nettles. The shut door dulling the sound of the music. It reached her now melancholy and distant like the rumour heard of a stranger whose life was cut short. Behind the music she could hear the dull pings of Barnabas beating metal free with a hammer. She closed her eyes and tried to dream but what coursed from her thoughts was bitterness. This goddamned place. She cursed the obstinate notions that brought them here and she cursed the poverty of the place that had not changed in one hundred years it seemed to her, people living with next to nothing and happy to live as if the world had not changed, a few cars and lorries now about the place but that was all, and the poverty that remained was like an unwillingness that shined out of them, a temperament more obstinate than rock. And that look they wore she saw was ingrained, the hard stare of suspicion, a look in the eye like some biblical judgement that summed you up as foreign and told that unless you were born there you were considered none. She dropped her head under the water and saw her family. When they first came to Carnarvan and how they spent Barnabas's money easy and had within two years what it took others three generations to achieve. What was always in the air around here was something that would not be named by others but she would name it resentment. We do not deserve this after all that we have done. She hinged tighter her knees and slid deeper into the water until the echoes of the world began to lose their soundshape, the thud of her elbow on the tin, the staccato clattering of Barnabas, the start of rain. The noise it made on the roof amplified through the bath into something huge and susurrus, like the earth had found form to speak its secrets about the meaning of loss and other such things if only she could understand its revelations. And she thought then she heard the sound of knocking downstairs and she opened her eyes to the ceiling, through the water the ceiling plaster a white quavery thing she saw like a different plane of existence, and when she broke the surface of the water to listen, the world surged full-sounded and there was nothing at all to the day, no sound of knocking while the violins on the radio had ceased.

He rewrote some strange dark letter for the sky with the leaking wheelbarrow, through the yard and out onto the grass around the back of the new barn a twisting shape like the single arm of a swastika. Of its char and detritus the byre began to be cleared, and the floor stood open to the weather with its soot colour. Behind the hay barn was a dry-stone wall and he saw in passing a rock in the grass that had fallen over. The knit-stone was built by the hands of men that probably knew his forefathers, stood now like some demonstration against time. He bent to the loose rock and refitted it, and the stones kissed with a satisfactory smack as the wall took again its endurant appearance.

A turned tap of rain. Through shirt to flesh the rain-cold leeched and it took him a minute to notice. When he did he walked across the yard to the cover of the empty stable. He rolled a cigarette and watched the tobacco ash fall an aberrant spring snow, bellowed smoke into the rain that became one with the all-grey. The blackened heads of the mountains gauzy in the rain and watching down upon him like some convocation of elders huddling in judgement. Where he stood he could see Cyclop in the pasture field marching with an enormous bone in his mouth. His free hand clenched into a fist. Stupid fuckdog's as stupid as it fucking gets. He threw the fag to the flagstones and heeled it and became one with the rain, marched into the field where Cyclop was sitting. The grass had grown to an unruly green and bore in patches sprouting thistles like ornaments of fleur de lis. Cyclop watched him coming with his nose to the earth and his teeth clamped upon the bone, a long femur twice the length of his head and his orange eye lit with satisfaction. Barnabas called out to the dog from the edge of the field and began slowly towards him and Cyclop sat up as if he had taken a perfect read of the man's intentions, began to make a wary retreat towards the trees. The dog bit down twice on the bone to get a better purchase on it and Barnabas soon caught up and they stood under the canopy of a sycamore tree beside the old beech that sat the way it did in silent pleading. Barnabas saw the end of the bone was shaped as big as a man's heart. He grabbed hold of the bone and began to pull, his hand around the heart-piece, you stupid fuckdog you, and Cyclop dropped down and splayed his legs, held tight onto the bone, his lips drawing back to reveal a swell of sharp teeth and glistening pink gums. Tussling shadows on the hard-rooted ground they became, Cyclop wagging his tail and his eye shining humorous until he took a boot to his flank from Barnabas and he dropped the bone, walked off as if he had it within his nature to be insulted. The bone slimed with dog spit and Barnabas took it and carried it till he reached a ditch and threw it towards the brambles. Made a slug trail on his trousers when he wiped his hand on them.

He began through the pasture field towards the house and it was then that he saw the far shape of a woman leaving through the front gate. He marched upon the rain-speckled flagstones and went into the house, called out to Eskra, the room empty. He saw the teapot on the range and a single cup half full on the table and he poured the tea, stewed now into an approximation of bog water, drank it and wiped his lips. Why do I always get the cold tea? He called out for Eskra. The radio silent. Upstairs the floor creaked and there came the soft padding sound of his wife barefoot on the landing. He looked up the stairs and saw her looking down at him, her head and torso swaddled in towels, the blue and red of her agitated. What are you shouting for? she said.

Who was that woman? he said.

What woman?

Here, at the house. I just saw a woman leaving out the gate.

Barnabas, I was in the bath. What are you on about?

What are you bathing for at this time of day?

She tightened her towel. I didn't hear anybody, Barnabas, she said.

He watched her carefully as if he could sense something was being hid, thought he saw her mouth tighten, and then he saw her in another way, the bare white of her ankles and the long delicate way her arms held onto the towel as if she was hiding from him the best part of her and she saw what was held in his look, stepped back so he could just see her face.

I thought I saw a woman just now. Going out the gate, he said.

I would have heard something, she said. The radio just died. The house is gone quiet.

He gave her a long look. She unwrapped the towel from her head and let her long wet hair curtain loose and she turned for the bedroom, called down at him. Will you go and get the dry battery charged for the radio? The goddamn quiet of this farm fills me up with dread.

Billy came through the backdoor and slung his leather schoolbag onto the table, took off his father's old coat and threw it over the chair. Went outside again. Saw the horse a sack shape lying in the field and walked to her, bent down to take a look-see. What's wrong with ye, wee doll? He lay down sideways on the grass face to face with the animal and pulled a clown smile as if to cheer the horse and then he pulled his mouth wide with his fingers and stuck his tongue out at the animal. They eyed each other in as close a thing as there was to understanding between man and beast which was not that much at all. I know how ye feel, horsey. Things have gone to fuck around here. He sat up on his haunches and rolled a fag and looked over his shoulder, sucked it to life, reached out and put the cigarette to the horse's lips. Go on, take a wee drag. Ye know ye want te.

Eskra in the front room playing quietly at the piano, a passage worked over and over again so gently it was as if the music could bruise and break at her touch. Barnabas sitting in the range chair with his head leaning back against the stove tiles, his eyelids shut and strangely twitching as if he was eyeing some strange flight in the vast sky of his mind. Billy took a heel of black bread from the tin and sawed it into two thick slices and stabbed the curving point of the bread knife into the butter. He stood against the stove watching the fluttering of his father's eyelids and laughed at him. Yer eyes are going mental, he said. Barnabas opened a bellowing brown eye to him.

Billy spoke again. Something's wrong with the horse, he said.

She's lying in the field like a sack. Could be her leg or who knows what it is.

I'll look at her later.

Da.

What?

What's happening with the farm?

Barnabas sat up. Jesus, son. He saw Billy flinch. Your mother and I are trying to figure out what we should do.

Billy shrugged and went into the hall and saw his father's tobacco upon the lacquered console table, stole a wiry pinch and put it in his shirt pocket. His heart skipped when his father called out. Would you ever bring me out the tobacco from the hall.

Billy came in with it and Barnabas looked him up and down. I didn't mean to shout. Here, he said, threw him a boiled sweet.

The boy went outside to a sack of stored apples and took one and brought it to the horse, put it under her mouth. The skin of the apple had sagged under two seasons and the meat was soft and drying out and the horse wrinkled her nose at it. Billy lay the apple down in front of her and stroked a knuckle down the gullying dark of her nose, the horse watching him as if from a great distance.

Barnabas stepped into the bank manager's office and took a seat to wait. Murmured voices outside the room. A tonguing clock. When he turned in the chair he saw hung on the door the bank manager's hat and coat. The desk a polished oak and free of ornaments but for a heavy marble ashtray that shined empty. He pulled it towards him, rolled a cigarette, lit it and satisfied himself in soiling the marble. There hung upon the wall a watercolour of a pewter lake and he blew smoke towards the painting and clouded the lake with fog. He grew impatient, loosened his tie, turned around in his chair to watch the door goddamn it and looked again at the clock. When the bank manager came in Barnabas stood to greet him with a look of great solemnity and the man offered a hand that was cold and limp and he kept his eyes off Barnabas. He nodded for him to sit down. Said nothing about being late. Barnabas looked into the man's eyes and saw the man steal a look towards the clock, found he could not fasten them.

Now, Mr Kane, the bank manager said.

Call me Barnabas, Mr Creed.

Creed bore a small tight mouth and his short hair gleamed like wet snow. A young man opened the door and put down a cup of tea before him but offered none for Barnabas and he watched Creed bring the tea to his mouth and take small sups. Creed watched Barnabas dirty his ashtray.

Barnabas spoke his tale in the way he had intended to tell it and he told his story in full and spoke with all the feeling of what he had encountered and Creed listened and as Barnabas spoke he began to feel he was being pinned by Creed's eyes as if there was some part of him he would prefer to keep hid that was being examined. The man before him did not once smile and he did not speak until the end of his essay and the request that came afterwards and when he did Barnabas knew the fate of his case alone from the way the man's small mouth tightened.

You cancelled your insurance, Mr Kane?

Barnabas shifted in the chair and watched the man before him blink, waiting for an answer.

How was I to know the byre was for burning? I thought the insurance was needless.

But isn't that the nature of insurance, Mr Kane?

Creed loosened and retightened his small mouth and leaned back in his seat and seemed to pause in thought and then he hinged forward on his hips with his hands in pyramid fashion. Something in his tone when he spoke, of knowledge that could not be contested like some self-appointed oracle, or what Barnabas heard was the tone of a teacher. The way I see it, Mr Kane, is you have plenty of land. Sell it. Pay the bank back. Then you can come and talk to me. For now, regarding the new barn I will charge you just the interest. Sell the land, Barnabas. Then we can talk. It's a logical position.

Please, Mr Creed. Would you not listen to what I'm saying? I'm a good farmer.

I fear that is irrelevant, Mr Kane. Like I said. You know what you have to do.

Barnabas shifted like he was sitting on loose stones that had begun to roll out from under him. If I sell up the land I won't have a farm to rebuild. Where's the logic in that?

You don't have to sell all of it.

I don't have all of it to sell. If I did I wouldn't be able to buy none of it back. As if anybody anyhow in these times would buy it.

Creed looked again at the clock and began up out of his chair. Mr Kane, he said.

Barnabas stood slowly screwing up his eyes, leaned over the desk to the proffered hand, took the man's eyes and threw them some malice. You're some kind of fellow, aren't you? Tell me. What's your use? You with your papery hands.

Creed stood very still and held his eyes upon Barnabas, looked like some weirded reptile, old with grey eyelids holding so very still in great heat – not a muscle on his face was moving, and Barnabas felt the man's eyes enter past his own, bore deeper into him, begin to move about as if the man had the power to roam inside his head and find the place of his own agency and take that agency from him and do what will, and he wanted for the man to stop but could not speak for it, seemed the man had taken from him that power also, his voice, his warrant, his fate, and he bowed his head and turned.

Creed then gliding towards the door. Like I said, Mr Kane.

The sun flared bullion onto the street and burst starlight upon the door of the Austin. He did not see the world as it was but saw instead the darkening scrim of his thoughts. The fan of his fingers tightening into fists. He sat inside the car and looked blankly at the window. What was building inside him he could only hold at bay for a moment, as if a man alone could become sea wall, fend off the starless ocean that came relentless and all consuming, and when the sea rushed in it took him total. He beat and beat the wheel with his fists and the walnut dashboard shuddered from the shock of it and the knuckles on his right hand burst. He began to weep and he looked down at the mush of blood that was his hand. Knuckles then into his mouth and licked, blood's salt iron to the tongue. Worn myself to the bones so I have. People like me putting their back into this country. A place to live for our families. My wife and my boy goddamnit. He wiped his eyes with his sleeve, rolled a cigarette, sucked a long soothe, filled the car with smoke. He turned quick when he heard a timid knocking at the window. Smoke leaning thickly against the glass and a woman's hand that led to Pat Glacken. He rolled down the window.

Did you get the side of beef, Barnabas?

He dropped his burst hand onto his lap to hide it.

Oh I did, Pat. And wasn't it delicious.

I knew you'd like that now, Barnabas. You can't beat a good side of beef. A man like you. And where's Eskra today?

She's at home. The usual.

And how are things with you. The chest all better?

Aye. I'm grand, Pat. Nothin wrong with me now. Back to normal.

She held him in a look for a moment, saw the pallor of a man wanting sleep, under his eyes the silver dust of a moth's wing. Things pass, Barnabas, and then they're right again. You'll see. You just have to set your mind on getting past it. Mind what happened when Fran's wife, Ellen, died in childbirth, there was no talking to him. But look at him now. Reared them two boys near by himself and though I had a small hand in it, it was only a small hand for a sister canny be a replacement for a mother. And look at his farm now and them two boys turned to men.

He looked at her and nodded and let her talk and the words kept coming out of her mouth and he looked at the steering wheel and back at the glasses she wore, the thick lenses that insected her eyes and he wondered was she aware of herself, her glasses sliding off her nose as she spoke and the way she kept fixing them with a fat digit. The non-stop blathering. He put the cigarette into his other hand and sucked on it and leaned out the window and blew smoke away from her but it breezed back into her face. She waved at it with her hand. Anyhow, she said. Tell Eskra I was asking for her and tell her I'll be around in the next week or so with another good side of beef.

He looked at her and smiled. Anytime, Pat. That's wild nice of you.

He put his hand up to wave and realized he had presented his bloody knuckles and she saw the hand and the way he dropped it back down quick. She turned and he watched in the mirror the back of her as she waddled down the street. He sat staring out the window and blinked twice and he stood out of the car and began to walk, began towards the sweet dark of Tully's. Annie nodded to him and without a word pulled him a pint. Barnabas stood standing at the counter rubbing the hand. A wedge of skin flapped loose like a lid. The secret raw of his knuckle.

Sit yourself down, Barnabas.

Barnabas nodded. Aye.

The back door to the outhouse opened and a man came into the bar ushering before him the waft of stale piss. He closed the door behind him and with his other hand pulled at his fly buttons and as he did so he took in the sight of Barnabas pulling out from the counter a bar stool. He continued walking, waved a silent goodbye to Annie Tully and began to adjust the cap on his head. Barnabas reaching into his pocket for change saw the man in a mirror, froze, felt something move inside him, and when he turned around finally to say something, he saw go out the door the back of that bastard balding head of Pat the Masher.

Barnabas didn't look right to anybody who saw him when he left Tully's. Walking at a quarter lean with his hands jammed in his pockets and smiling to himself a smile that looked the far side of happiness. His mind warmed with drink. The sky had become murk and the murk cast the town in a grey absolute that sullied the earlier brightness. He got into the car and shifted in the seat and looked at his hand, a vibrant purple swelling, and he flexed it into a fist and grimaced and loosened it again. He started the

Austin and nosed it into the street but the engine cut out on him. Fuckdog, he said. He saw he was being watched for entertainment by some old boy in wellies across the street sitting on a chair outside the grocery and hardware shop. A pipe hanging from the old man's gummy mouth and some kind of smile upon his face like he was born fixed with it. The car gave a quick cough and a growl and lurched forward and he nursed the Austin up the street looking down at his hand, saw then too late what was coming towards him. The surge came thickly and consumed the car, snorts heaved into the air and the bellowing noise like low sirens, the chain-gang sound of hooves. They began to spill out from a narrow lane upon the street, their gait slack and their heavy hides of meat rocking slowly above their spindled legs. The head of Hugh Moss under a cap with an ash plant walking behind them. Barnabas had to stop the car, and the engine died out, his good hand whitening on the wheel as the surge began to encircle him, watched incredulous as if they were coming just for him, his vision narrowing down to the swell of different coloured hides, cows that trudged like they were damned to hell, a troupe of marching penitents ash-whipped and wailing dolefully as they misted the air with their breaths. Dead cow eyes staring at him.

She watched from the window the Austin beetle blackly up the road, the car lurching suddenly to meet the open gate. The way the car braked and then Barnabas getting out of it unsteady, saw her looking at him. He slammed the door. She could see from the way he stood that he was drunk and destroyed within himself, watched the way he came in through the front door leaving it open, marched past her by the living room door with his hands become fists. The way he just shook his head at her. And she saw then the state of his right hand and gasped so quiet he did not hear. Just a glance he stole of her as he went past. What he beheld in that glance he could picture the next day as clear as if he had studied a painting of her, the way she was upon that door, leaning half turned and lit in a failing grey light that put upon her face a pallor and dimmed the brilliance of her eyes, the blueness now that bore a look of such sadness it seemed to him later that what was held there was more than sadness, more than pain, was an approximation of all sadness and all pain and what it could look like in a woman.

She closed the bedroom door and drew the curtains and lay down on the bed with her hands by her sides, closed her eyes, lay listening. There was a quiet she had grown used to at this time of day that was different to what she heard now. Before, when the men had gone out to work and Billy was at school, the house revealed to her different kinds of silence like secrets. The comfortable silence of being on your own when you know others are close nearby. The immediate shock of silence that comes when you switch off the radio. That moment of silence when you come up out of your thoughts and you see the world as it is for a pure moment, the world as it always is, the fixed seat of the earth neither placid nor raging but resolute to indifference. What she heard now was different – a felt silence that spoke to her desolation, could feel her own earth shaking from tremors that shook free fear's darkest spirits.

The next evening he sat on the range chair with his legs crossed, watching her take down the blue china teacups. They never left the high shelf of the dresser but now she was putting them on the table to clean them. Between dresser and table the last cup slipped from her hand to the hard floor. My grandmother's china, she said. Softly she began to weep and she stood there slightly crooked as if she were suddenly grown old, a hand lidding her eyes and her other hand held aloft to where she had been holding the cup as if a phantom of it remained. Barnabas got up awkward out of the chair and went to her, stood there with his hand upon her shoulder as if he was fearful of pulling her towards him. He bent down to the broken cup and put the pieces on the table. I think I can fix it, he said.

I don't care about the bloody cup.

Outside Cyclop could be heard barking short sharp instructions to the birds or to the trees or perhaps he was just making himself known to the world, and what she said to him came soft and unexpected, like some animal dark and imperceptible had come towards him through great quiet and sinked him with its teeth.

Did you ever think, Barnabas, it is time to just give up?

He felt the drop-weight of a sickening in his belly as if something rotten inside him had fallen loose, found himself respond with quick anger. He pulled her by the chin towards him, bulled a look into her eyes. Whatever do you mean, Eskra?

He saw in her eyes a defiance that was hard lit and she did not flinch. He let go of her chin.

To put the house and the fields on the market, Barnabas, and go back to America. To see all this as something that was good for a while. To admit that we had a good run of it. That nothing lasts and that's the way of it. To accept in our case that it came sooner than expected. That fortune favours the brave only for a while. That maybe we weren't cut out for this place.

His mouth curled and there came to him an array of thoughts that had he acted upon them would have changed him to her for ever. He shook his head with violence, shook his head as if he could scatter from his thoughts the sounds of her words. The talk out of you, he said.

She stood with her lips rolled inwards so that it seemed to him she had no lips at all or that she was trying to keep something malignant within her. He kept staring at her, shook his head again. After all that I done.

You are not being realistic, Barnabas.

Tell me now what is realistic. Tell me.

All right I will. The costs of rebuilding the byre. The loan on the new barn. Having to pay for new animals. The cost of feed. Labour. How long we'd have to wait before there would be money again. Years and you know it. And how would we live in the meanwhile? Tell me. I always said not to keep putting all our money back into the farm but you would not listen to me one bit. You always did your own thing. You were foolish with your money in America, spending it like there was no tomorrow and you were foolish with it here, despite my saying it to you.

And what would I do now in America, me in the prime of my middle years, near enough to be growing old?

There's many a man who went to work older than you. My father did it.

Aye and the work kilt him. He died younger than me because of it.

As he spoke he saw he had wounded her, enjoyed the look it gave her. And the boy? he said. What about him? This is what he knows. This is what we wanted for him. That this be the place for him and no place else.

This place is nothing but damnation.

He stood there eyeing her with malice and she said nothing

more and he saw the fight was gone out of her. She turned away from him. Where is that Billy now? He didn't come home from school.

Wait, Eskra, he said. I have a trick up my sleeve. Just you wait and see.

Part III

H E AWOKE IN A rose dawn and saw a vision of what could be again. What came to him brought its own light of revelation and he lay there in the grasp of it, saw how the byre could be again. Eskra in the still of sleep and in that soft light made porcelain, her arm ragged-thrown as if it were wood washed upon the shore of some dream. He dressed quietly and went downstairs, rested his hands upon the sink and leaned towards the shaving mirror. Took a long look at himself. Who he saw was a man with eyes clawed by age and that man now rust-bearded, as if some transfiguration had taken place – another man emerging beneath his dark-haired older self, held brightly by a renewed and burning spirit. He reached for the razor and held it over his hand and it was then that he pressed the blade's edge into his palm, drew it. His blood opened to the world and he smiled at the pain and he made a blood handshake with himself. He reached to his beard and took between the fingers of both hands the rust-wire and pulled at his cheeks until it seemed the skin came elastic off his bones, could feel in his hands the beard's wiry resilience. Who he was now and that was it. He saw how he was after the fire and looked upon that yielding man with disgust. In his mind a vision of the byre stood again on the earth and he saw what would be done and he would call upon all that old strength to move the heavens and the earth, could feel spring's sap vital in his veins, that great power giving rise again to the trees and that which made green the trembling earth. He clasped his hands again into that bloody handshake. To be whole man again. A man who will not yield.

He stood staring out the kitchen window, saw the flagstones burning, how they seemed to hold within them their own light. When he stepped outside for water, to his bare feet the flagstones were cold. A supernal arc of reddening light expanding westwards over the mountains and he saw it as if it were warding off his own darker forces, that titanic of dark in his mind brought into veiling white light.

Later, he put on his boots, went to the stable and to a shelf that held a miscellany of old things and he nosed through them and put some items in an old and dusty satchel. The horse lying down watching him and he kept the silence between them till the horse nickered a soft hello and blinked. He reached out a smile towards her.

Embered fields held him as he walked. He heard his own breathing, the sound of the sea coned to his ear, watched a large bird wing and dive distantly, pump the air skywards again. The morning had reached its full brightness when he found the place and it was as he had remembered – a swathe of deadland dressed in rushes and stark trees that stood out of it lonely. The land here seemed more ancient, looked like swidden land that had been razed centuries ago and forgotten. It was held now in title by nature and sat upon the edge of the mountain bogland with a narrow fir forest at its westerly wing. That bogland came rolling down from the mountains all malign purpose, a creeping slower than time in its dun cloak that swept out all that was green. Travelling to claim the music box of the trees.

He walked bent through the rushes, looked till he found them, pellet-like between the sedge grass and the mud. Discovered their tracks. He followed the markings and figured out the run of a trail and he walked over to a lone ash tree and pulled a bowie knife from a scabbard in his satchel. He cut off a young branch and sheared it clean of its buds and he walked back to the beat and followed the path to a narrowing where the earth rose about a foot high on each side. He drove the rod perpendicular into the earth, took a wire noose from the satchel and rested it on his lap, removed some string, tied a slipknot twice around the rod to secure it. He tied the snare to the string and hung it over the track the distance of his fist beneath it. Took some twigs and stuck them through the hoop in the grass to hold the noose. His breathing came slow and concentrated and he thought about the smell of his hands on the wire, looked down at them red and thick-skinned with eclipses of dirt in his nails. Saw what little he had been doing with those hands all this time since the fire. He laid three other traps and it seemed to him the bright morning could not last and it did not. Through the haze came the distant sound of an airplane. He listened to it, a lone and angry insect buzzing against the sky's window, watched the sunless noon pass over him before he began tracking up the bog hills, shaping in his mind what it was he would have to get done to make real his vision.

He came into the house all storm energy, threw his coat on a chair and sought her out by the table. He stood over her with a smile on his face that reached up to his ears near lunatic, held a rabbit aloft like some kind of carnival prize. The gleam of a killer's eyes and the eyes of the rabbit glassed blind to her. She drew away from him in mock disgust. A drop of blood dripped in slow fashion towards the floor and she stood quickly, pointed.

Would you look at that, he said.

Get that thing into the sink.

He put the rabbit in the sink and began to rub his hands in satisfaction, looked at her again smiling fulsome, a long time since she'd seen him like that and she found herself returning the grin.

And do you know something else? he said.

You are going to tell me, I suppose, that you've cleaned the county of rabbits.

Naw, he said. I'll rebuild the fucker so I will.

Rebuild what?

The bloody byre. I don't know why I didn't think of it before. That it's possible. And I can do it without it costing hardly anything. I dreamed last night of a fellow who was about when I was a wee lad, a memory I'd long forgotten. They used say he'd pay for nothin not even the stone for his house from the quarry. I heard that he built his own house himself from the rocks out of his own field. One of them thran lunatics.

You are hardly going to do that, Barnabas.

No, will you listen to me. I'll get stone and wood. Ask about. There was once a time when people built what they could with what they could get. There's always ways and means. There's a heap of blocks lying unused at Fran Glacken's and maybe he'll give them to me. And we won't spend a penny. And we'll use the leftover savings to buy the cattle when I've done with it. We'll be as right as rain again.

As he spoke her face rose into a smile of appeasement and then it fell again. I don't know if this is a good idea, Barnabas. You'll get no help from those around here. You never did unless you were paying for it.

What did you think I thought would happen, Eskra? That they would all roll up here in their horses and carts in a big line of solidarity, with manpower and supplies and rebuild it for us? Give us animals to set us going again? Like something out of a film? The folk round here live with the fear of God in them but are Christian only in name. They can see only their blood's own shade.

Just think about what I'm saying, that's all. About our other options.

I woke this morning with a vision of it. I know in my heart if Matthew Peoples was here now he'd be saying this is the right thing to do.

The way she looked at him. It was as if he had prized open the rawest part of her, placed his finger into the quick.

She sat a long time in the range chair after he left the room, her thoughts adrift until a feeling came she had alighted upon something. She stood and went to the console table in the hall, pulled at the brass handle of the drawer, rummaged until she found it – a photo, the skin of it yellowing with a small cat's ear and she put it to her nose. Time smelled of dust and potpourri and other things she could not name and perhaps what she smelled too were things that came reaching for her from that day in the photo. What she saw was the yard ten years ago, men standing in their welly boots and waistcoats with their arms across their chests after stacking hay. She could see their shapes as they stood that evening in the kitchen, sniffing at the pot over the stove, heaving into each other for a seat. Ghost smells of sweat and hay and earth knit the air around her. She could see dirt from their hands ringing the sink.

She looked at the men as they were lined in the photo and saw the smiles they wore for the camera, smiles hitched up under hard eyes like trousers that would fall back down. What they could not hide was what was solid in their eyes, a knowledge of true difficulty, of lives lived in rare promise. Sun on their white shirts. Sun on the flagstones. Barnabas standing tense in the middle and staring into the void towards her with a wild man's gaze. The man was bright and burning and she saw then how it was and what could be again and she saw too what she did not know she was seeing. In the far side of the photo, one of the labourers holding onto another man's arm, trying to pull him back into the frame. Just the back of the man's head was visible, hair and shoulder matched in white and a hand hung loose. Her breath stalled. It was Matthew Peoples. Too shy to take part in it that day or so they thought for who knew the real answer to a man's shyness. That he did not want to be pictured perhaps, for to be pictured is to want to be remembered and who wants to think of their own death? Different strands of time began to fold on top of one another. Did an animal break free inside and knock him? Or was it the smoke that snaked around him and took him down? That same day of the photo he had given her a pot of cream he had made himself. For your hands, he'd said, and it had worked.

Billy came loping through the pasture field with the butt of a smoked-out rolly held backwards between finger and thumb.

Tongues of grass licking at his boots made sodden his ankles. He threw the butt into the grass and looked up to see the swift shape of Cyclop appear upwards out of a ditch, the grass bending as the animal roamed through the field. Billy shouting at the dog to come to him and the dog stopped in the grass and singled out Billy with the still of his orange eye-beam. Come here to me you. Billy at a run then moving towards the dog and he caught the animal by the collar, bent down to him. What are ye up to, eh? The undercarriage of the dog was cotted from the wet fields and the dog eyed the clouds as Billy talked to him as if something of more interest were to be found there. Billy roaming a hand through the dog's dark hide and he stopped when he saw fresh blood on the white fur of his mouth. His voice dropped. Are you hurt are ye, Cyclop? He took the dog by the muzzle and ran his hand through the fur and he searched over the dog and knew by the way the dog looked at him that Cyclop was not injured at all, that the dog wore the blood of another. He stood up and Cyclop went off at a run and he shouted after him. What kind of stupid dog are ye?

She watched him soap his hands in the sink, the water sluicing clean his soiled fingers. Saw how he stood up straight like he used to. A certain command he had, the broadness of his back flat against the weakening light, the way he pointed a thick finger towards the window. The sky, he said. See its colour. She came forward and saw the sky was an unnatural jaundice that laid a strange pallor over the world. He said it was unusual, perhaps to do with the lengthening of the days into spring, but what she saw produced a sensation she could not explain, produced in her a deep sadness. She stood by him and put her hand on his back and rubbed at his shoulder, said to him, I saw the bees today carrying pellets of pollen to the hive. The queen has begun to lay. And he turned and took her hand and said, see, I said everything would be right again. She saw then the slice in his palm. What happened your hand? she said. She took it and rubbed it gently, brought it to her mouth and kissed it. What did you do?

Nothing, he said. I came into contact with myself again.

She looked at him confused and smiled. They stood a moment in the quiet mesh of their breathing until Billy came trudging downstairs. She broke from Barnabas as the boy came into the room and Billy went straight to the stove and leaned over the bubbling rabbit stew, took a sniff at it. Jesus, I'm starving.

Eskra took from a drawer the good linen tablecloth and smoothed it over the table and Barnabas noticed the use of it. Billy spoke. We saw a German bomber today at school. The strange shape of it. It couldn't have been American.

Eskra looked at him and smiled. That's a long way for it to be from the war.

Maybe it was looking for ships to bomb, said Billy.

Maybe it was lost, said Eskra. Looking to get back home.

Barnabas came towards the table knuckling his cheek. Tis rare you'd see the Luftwaffe all the way out here. Twas likely the RAF. Them airfields in Derry are kept busy.

The stew was scalding and Barnabas watched Billy wolf at it like he had not a tongue to be burned in him and said so. Billy looked at his father and began to blow at his food and he ate with a dramatic slowness and when he had cleared the bowl he excused himself from the table. They sat together eating and listened to the boy clumping around upstairs. Barnabas leaned back and smiled.

Don't think I still don't believe this is a foolish idea, she said.

Will you remind me to get the battery charged for the radio?

Barnabas stood to make the tea and he leaned to look outside. How quick the night has come, he said. It was only minutes ago the sky was that funny colour and now look at it. The day has gone completely.

Eskra went into the living room to play the piano. Notes and chords sounded with slowness as if her fingers were learning new shapes, or it could have been she had to teach herself to forget her sore fingers. Billy sat to the table with his schoolbooks. Barnabas sat in the range chair reading the paper and then he got up and began to prod at the fire. He saw Billy writing in a notebook.

Is that homework you're doing?

Naw.

Well do your homework then.

Billy watched his father and closed over the notebook and Barnabas went back to his chair. He shut his eyes and after a while his eyelids began to flutter and his mouth hung loose as if he was agape to some inner vision. Suddenly he sat up, looked over at Billy's empty chair red-eyed, saw the boy had got up from the table and was cutting at the bread.

Did you hear a knocking at the front door, Billy?

Billy shook his head. Naw. You were dreaming.

Barnabas tilted his head. I wasn't. I was only resting. He stood up out of the chair and looked towards the clock. Who would be calling to our front door at this time?

He went into the hall and opened the door and was met by the sullen dark, the hall's lamplight uncertain on the steps against it. He called out hello, heard no answer. He stepped outside and

walked around the side of the house and called out hello again
and he stood and listened. Swabs of covert clouds dimmed the
moonlight and the night air met his lungs cold. Piano music
softly through the walls. He rubbed his hands and went to the
front door and stood. The webbing of night sounds hid to the eye.
The nattering breeze-shift of the hedgerows and trees. Two dogs
calling to each other in short sharp barks. Something else too. He
listened and heard a distant drone, like insects, looked towards
the North Star. Could guess what it was. He went back inside and
Billy was looking at him funny.

There was nothing, he said. Nobody at all.

That's what I said.

I heard just the sound of your airplanes. From the war. Far
off in the north. Americans I reckon. A huge formation heading
over to England probably. Couldna see nothing through the
clouds. If it wasn't for hearin them planes and the rationing
sometimes I often think what's going on in Europe is made up.
The Emergency some big yarn we're being spun to explain why
nothin gets done in this country. Bunch of useless bastards in
Dublin. The newspaper says the entire world is being reshaped
but here in this place you wouldn't know nothing of it.

He went towards the tea pot and poured it, put the cup to his
lips. Damn tea's gone cold again. What does a man have to do to
get a hot cup?

She went outside to see to the horse and found the day uncertain.
In the sky, dark and light like wary forces circled one another
and a conciliatory grey hung in between. She found the top half
of the stable door a quarter open and saw that wood and wall
were newly met by spider web. The gossamer shined at her with

its own light as if it could trap the uncertain sun, work it brightly within its own fibres and shine it. She saw no sign of the spider. She took a twig and twirled the web free of the door and in that moment a spider scurried sudden and as fat as her finger. She did not flinch, took the flossed stick and its occupant and tossed them.

The horse had not risen nor eaten. It seemed to her from the way the horse was sitting that the animal was not sick but protesting, as if the poor creature was angry about something. Animals make it hard to tell but listen hard enough and they speak it to you in their own way. She shovelled out the horse's manure and went to the pump for fresh water and pretended to the horse to change the feed. She bent down to the animal and spoke soft to her, produced a lump of sugar in her hand and held it flat under the horse's nose. From the rafters there came a large ticking sound and she imagined for a moment some kind of bat sharpening its teeth and she smiled at the notion, remembered when she first came here how wind and silence and that pure dark of a winter evening could let loose all sorts of nonsense into her head. The horse's eyes glossed and she wrinkled her nose at the sugar and Eskra drew her hand away from her. She put words soft into the horse's ear, knuckled gently the withers, skied her hand down the horse's nose. What's wrong with you, sweetness? Since when don't you like the sugar I could be putting in my tea? When she stepped outside she saw the previous sky was being torn up and a sheeting blue being hung in its place.

That clear sky took for a while, a rise in parts to a blue perfection that reached the eye to its limits. Trailing after it she saw rain. When the sky darkened with that coming rain she went outside with the washing basket and set it on the flagstones and rolled up her sleeves, saw a gull high above the trees winging whitely. The gull sounded at the world like a cart sent downhill with a squeaking axle, a rolling squawk that reached a high point of agitation. She walked the basket at her hip around the house and it was then her face began to knit. The orange washing line tied between two poles was empty. Twice her eye travelled the length of it, clothes pegs propped like rabbit ears and parts of the line fraying like old wool but there was no washing on it at all. She set the basket down and looked at it twice, searched her mind as to when she hung the washing the day before. She began to look about, looked to the junipers and to the hedgerow and she went over to the fence and looked upon the empty field as far as any wind could take her laundry, not that there was any wind for it. She saw in her mind the new white sheets she had hung out dripping. She marched into the house, saw Barnabas walking about the kitchen with a fag hung on his mouth and grey smoke wreathing the air above him and that far-flung scheming look in his eyes. She began looking about the kitchen as if somebody could have put the washing there and she went upstairs and looked in the press and in the bedroom and she came downstairs with her hands on her hips.

Did you take in the washing, Barnabas?

Why would I take in the washing?

Somebody took in the washing.

Why are you asking me about it?

Could Billy have done it?

Does anybody here know what that boy ever does?

Tell me then how the sheets are gone, Barnabas?

What sheets, Eskra?

Eskra sighed and shook her head, watched Barnabas walking

about as if he were resolving the parts of some inward puzzle and he stopped at the window and looked out at the darkening day. Fuck it's going to rain. I was just about to head out, he said. He turned and looked at her and saw her with her sleeves rolled, the sheer white of her arms and the way she was picking at the scabs on her fingers in anxiety.

Why won't you ever leave your hands alone?

She made quick stars of her hands like she was letting go quickly of something.

Barnabas. Somebody took down the sheets and put them somewhere. I hung them out yesterday and they're gone. They're not upstairs. They're not in the kitchen. Where else would they be?

He shook his head and began to chuckle. How could you lose the washing?

Do you think I'm being funny, Barnabas?

I'm not saying it is funny. I'm just saying. He began to knuckle his cheek. Are you sure you put them there? He saw how her eyes began to spark with agitation.

Now you're telling me I'm losing my mind?

I'm just saying that's all. You can't be blaming everybody else for you losing the washing. How can it be lost anyhow?

Where is it then?

He was silent a minute. Did you look in on the horse? he said.

What would the washing be doing there?

Naw. I meant did you look in on her? See is she getting any better?

Those are new sheets I bought after the old ones were ruined by the smoke. The new sheets. Are you playing games with me, Barnabas?

Why are you being so daft with me, woman?

The dapple and tap of rain against the window. They watched it persist against the glass as if asking softly to be let in, saw then in an instant how the rain in temper turned and began to slam and lacerate. The day took to an instant twilight and Barnabas shook his head. Arrah, I can't be going out in that.

That rain came with a venomous slant to cut a man wide open. The wind circled and outburst as it pleased, took the sloping rain and ran with it in bladed drifts that riled the trees and sliced at them. He watched the rain relentless for two days, scratched his growing beard, watched it until his eyes were full of it, each liquid bead unique and fated to the terminal of its journey. Billy left the house to walk to school and he was drenched no sooner than he was out in it. Barnabas only leaving the house under his coat to get water or muck out the horse. The goddamned house and his thoughts trapped in it, taking on the suffocating shape of each room with the walls pressing in, no space to think. He walked about the house, picked things up and put them down again, sat in the range chair and stood again, got the screwdriver and turned the chair over and began to tighten the seat. She could sense his energy coiled and seeking release.

It was the afternoon of the second day when he stood and began towards the back door, a day that began with morning upended by an evening pallor, the rain unceasing. He put on his boots over his wool socks and sleeved his grey gabardine tying the loose tongues of its belt around his waist and he put on his hat as if he could put a lid to his thoughts. Eskra behind him, sighing.

You're not going out in that, are you?

It's in my mind to get started, so it is.

It's going to rain itself out soon.

He went out into it, the rain slapping at his coat like they were old buddies born of the same fight, tyrants against their better natures. Flung from fists of wind came stinging ice-cold rain that blew northerly off the Atlantic. He visored his hat against it and he saw the yard overwhelmed, the flagstones slicked and by the side of the house how a drain held a piece of ruptured sky. He bent to the drain pool and put his hand into the water and fished out some grass and some twigs and saw it made no difference to the drain hole. Looked up and wondered about Cyclop, the dog somewhere hid like he knew better than the man not to be out in it.

The old hills stood dark and waste and over them passed cloud shadow that looked to him as if something huge and inborn to nature was winging overhead, an intimation of some great bearer of violence unseen. Just the need now to get the byre done and in a way that was as swift as possible and he did not want to stop the momentum he was building inside of him. Deeper down the road and the rain made mist in the fields. He looked up and saw the drained disc of the sun had been broken into flitches that strained through the churning canopy. The smudge of McDaid far off in his back field oblivious to the rain, the man hinged and hauling what looked like a lamb, and he wondered if the animal had drowned perhaps. He watched the man as he walked and it seemed McDaid was standing very still in that rain until he realized the man was walking slowly back towards his house, considered for a moment helping him but marched on.

The lane met another that veered left and he followed it up a gentle hill. These pasture fields belonging to Fran Glacken and he had his cattle already out after the winter. That man too hard on his animals and the ground couldn't be ready for it yet. The cattle stood huddling under trees, swung their tails and shunted at the air in front of them with their breaths. He came upon the drive of Glacken's farm, his hat soaked and the rain trickling cold over his ears and down his neck and to his wrists his sleeves were cold and sodden. He pulled his hand out of his pocket and blew on them and warmed his cheeks. He saw Pat Glacken at the window facing him, Glacken's house a white farm bungalow, and he waved to her but she did not see him through the rain. He saw then Glacken walking across the yard and the man saw him and stopped, squinted his pop-eyes at Barnabas as if he were an apparition, watched him approach up the hill, Barnabas moving through the teeming rain like a man passing through moments of his own life and whatever traces of him left were washed clean behind him.

Barnabas half shouted. Yes, Fran.

Yes, Barnabas.

Soft day.

Aye.

Glacken wore dungarees and a tan shirt with the sleeves rolled up to reveal freckled lobster arms. The rain rolled off his flesh and darkened his cap and he stood blinking against it. C'mon up, he said. Meself and Martin are skulling.

The yard mudded in the rain and a squat pig walked in front of them greaved with mud and Glacken booted it, sent the animal half scuttling as if it were used to such things. The swallowing dark of the barn and his eyes had to adjust to the light that pressed meekly from a small back window and he saw then the shape of Glacken's son Martin take form out of that shadow like a younger vision of his father, the same body and bald head, and he slunk forward shepherding a calf in the gulf between his legs.

Yes, Barney, he said. How's about ye?

Yes, Martin.

I see that new beard has shielded you from the rain.

Aye. And how's the new wife?

What new wife?

Barnabas nodded to the animal.

Martin let out a small laugh. Well, she don't talk back, he said.

His father motioned with his head. C'mon now.

Barnabas watched, knew well the procedure. Glacken leaning over the calf all sable and milk and Martin with a chain around its neck. The pink snout of the animal quivering between Martin's thighs as if it could take from the air a sense of what was coming. The man's strange odour and his huge hands around the animal's flanks. Glacken leaning dangerously as if he was intending for it violence though in his mind what he was about to do to the animal was good for it. He came at the calf with a yellow cup dehorner and he put it to the animal's head where the soft fur had been pared back to reveal the jut of first horns. Come here to me, sweetheart. Martin holding the animal with a look of concentration, his father going down upon the skull, cutting through the protuberance with the tool, the animal kicking up something fierce, the language of suffering translated simply into movement and then it let out a bawl. Jesus fuck, hold her steady. Martin roaring at the animal. Hold still, ye bold bitch. His father leaning over again, going at the second horn, the animal shaking now, the son trying to hold her still. Take a hold of her for fuck's sake. What in the hell are ye? The crunch sound as he worked the dehorner. He stood up when he was finished and pushed the bawling beast away from him.

Jesus, I hate the skulling of them, Martin said.

None of us likes it, said Barnabas.

Glacken nodded to him. How's everything up at your place?

Have you got a minute?

Glacken turned and motioned for the two of them to stand by the edge of the door and Barnabas stuck his boot out into the rain, watched it spatter. Glacken nodded. What's up with ye, Barney?

I'm setting out to rebuild the byre, Fran. Have to do it mainly from nothin.

Glacken frowned. Did you not have insurance, Barney?

No, Fran. I had it cancelled.

Glacken leaned his head out and took a look at the rain and he rolled his mouth into a spit. So yer all out.

I'm all out.

Knowing you, you have ideas.

Well, that's what I'm here about.

You want to sell me some of those fields then.

Barnabas gave him a strange look and he shook his head. Naw. I'm thinking bout something else you might be able to help me with.

Glacken looked at him surprised. And what's that?

That mountain of blocks under the tarpaulin behind the barn. I seen them there a long time unused. Was wondering if you'd let me have them. There's nearly enough of them for what I want to do. I can pay you back the full price of them when I'm back up and motoring.

As Barnabas talked Glacken began to knead the palm of his

left hand with his thumb. He spoke with his eyeballs full upon the yard.

Well, Barney. That's wild problematic so it is. Wild problematic.

Come on now, Fran. I'll pay you interest.

That doesn't stop it being wild problematic.

What is wild problematic?

That.

I'm just asking, Fran, is all.

The problem is I need em. I'm not done with em yet. I'm really sorry, Barney, but that's the way it is. Glacken turned around and nodded towards his son. Them boys are gonna help me put up a new shed for the new machinery. We've been waiting for the summer to build it. He pointed across the yard to where he would build it.

A long silence wedged between them and Barnabas began to look at an old shoe lying at the edge of the yard, its mouth stouped to the rain.

Just a wee bit of help, Fran, is all I ask.

Help has nothing to do with it, Barney. Would ye not sell up some of them fields to me? I've got two boys hungry now to put down their own roots.

Sure what would I farm if the fields are all gone to yous? Haven't you enough of them?

I'm wild sorry, Barney. Listen, when yer leaving would ye go in and tell Pat I said to give you a side of beef. It's there hanging.

I canny build a byre with raw meat.

I'll talk to ye man to man, Barney, about the fields if ye want to sell, but I canny help ye with the blocks. I'm wild sorry.

The men stood there plain and awkward and Barnabas saw himself standing like a fool. He searched for something to say that would save face, make it seem he had other things to talk about, that he was indifferent to the man's attitude, but what came out of him whipped unbidden from its own dark. Jesus, you're a tight cunt of a man, Fran Glacken. A right dog in the manger. Them blocks are lying there as long as. He shook his head furiously as he spoke and he saw then Martin stepping fast towards him and he took a hold of Barnabas's tie and roared at him, don't you talk to my father like that, and Barnabas gave him a shove backwards and Martin lowered his head and charged into him. The two men went to the ground and began rolling like the stars of some silent slapstick comedy till Fran Glacken roared at his son and kicked him in the ribs. Glacken staring pop-eyed at Martin who stood up red-cheeked, began fixing his shirt calmly, not once lifting his eyes off Barnabas who bent for his spilled cap. Barnabas began to brush dirt and straw off his arms and he stared at Fran Glacken, his breath heaving, a look in his eye of derision. In the silence that was held for that moment it became clear to all that the words Barnabas had said were said and would always be said and Glacken's silence stood itself between them in acknowledgement of that fact and Barnabas began to walk off down the yard, his fists out of his coat a pair of useless shining obols, could feel the hard orbs of Glacken's vision upon him. Down onto the road amidst the sharp sheets of rain that cut into him and he pulled his hat against it.

He stepped into the house with his clothes stained dark from the rain and in the shadows of his eyes lay storm pools. He stood there shaking his head at no one in particular.

Didn't I tell you not to go out in that? she said.

He began to mutter. I'll never ask nobody again for help, nobody at all.

She helped him out of his coat, turned a chair towards the stove and hung the coat off it. He stood over the heat with his hands flat out, water vapours beginning to rise off him like some spectre freeing itself of his body, water from his coat pooling upon the tiles, water in the hollows of his ears, and he put a finger into each earhole and shook them.

You've got dirt all down the back of your coat. What were you doing?

I tell you, when I was a youngster in America I remembered nothing of the rain.

Go upstairs and change out of them wet things or you'll get a cold.

He turned and she saw him briefly like a different person, the colour of his face changed by a rusting beard that was at odds with the darkness of his hair. How the beard had aged him quick. He stood a minute staring at the wall and then he turned for upstairs. He came back down in a change of clothes and poured himself tea and sat drinking it. He began to roll a cigarette and she ran her hand through the glisten of his damp hair and stopped. I'll get you a towel, she said.

You're all right. I'll get it myself.

He took to the stairs again with heavy steps, went to the press and stood looking at its contents, reached into the back and pulled out two balled sheets. His brow thickened. He stood looking at them, had just begun to open them out when Eskra came quickly up the stairs, swiped them out of his hands.

Are you mad, woman? Aren't those the sheets that went missing?

No, they're not, she said.

Well what are they then?

Those are the sheets that were ruined in the fire. Take a look at them. They're smoked dark.

Well, what in the hell are you holding onto them for if they're ruined?

Just.

He looked at her a moment as if she were the flesh and bone of confusion, grabbed at a hand towel and shook his head at her, began back down the stairs muttering. She stood with the sheets in her hands and looked towards the window, saw the rain had just stopped. The air held hushed and trembling and the world washed to a lustre that took the evening light and glittered it back in all its manifold colours. She heard then the back door close, pricked her ears for Billy's voice, but heard none. She put the sheets back in the press and went downstairs but what she saw was an empty room and the soaking coat gone from the chair against the stove.

The house of Goat McLaughlin rose to meet him in the spit-rain that lingered after the hard fall. He came to it from the back fields, saw the dirty white walls of the house alight in evening's amber. From behind a galvanized pig house came a black dog alertly forward. It woofed sharply and the other dogs came. One of them sidled forward on spindled legs with eyes shark-like and then another younger just like it. The three grouped watching Barnabas trudge the turnip field and begin to climb the barbed wire fence, saw him swing a leg over and stop, snapped loud woofs when they saw his trouser leg snagged on a barb. It clung tenacious as if it had its own animal nature and Barnabas roared out a curse at the dogs, at the fence, shook his leg but set free only beads of rain. Arrah fuck. He shook his leg again and took a look towards the house, had a feeling he was being watched, could see himself from a distance as if he had been stuffed to the gills with stupidity like some ridiculous scarecrow with its leg held aloft. He saw then Goat McLaughlin come spry towards him gathering the spit-rain in his beard. Pig shit smell off him. A pinch of his fingers and Barnabas was freed.

I wouldn't have recognized ye in that new beard ye have, Barnabas.

Barnabas nodded towards the dogs. Did you steal them wild cats from the circus?

Deep smell of dog and boiled meat in the man's house and he was watched as he entered by a pleading, sad-eyed Christ from the wall. He took a seat at the table while Goat stood on his short legs in the scullery with his back turned pouring tea. Barnabas sat poking a finger inside the new hole in his trousers. Goat sat light of bone on the chair, looked as if wind could lift him out of it. One of the black dogs appeared behind him and sat watching. The sound of pigs outside.

Tea all right for ye?

Tis a bit cold.

When I was a youngster, before your time now, the town and the countryside used to be swarming with pigs. Those mucs were called greyhounds, long-snouted and near as skinny as dogs so they were. Goat smiled and leaned into him. They had a wild habit of roaming. If you let one of them go wandering somebody else's cornfield the price of trespass would be sore.

Barnabas smiled back at him. Is that so?

Aye.

Goat took a drink of tea. I still canny make it the way my auld missus used to make it what with the rationing. She made tea so thick you could stand two men on it.

How long is it now since she's gone?

Five year.

As he spoke, the old man's eyes removed themselves from the room and just as quick they sharpened.

Barnabas spoke. You did a good turn coming out to help me that day of the fire, Goat. You and your boys. They came up to the place like lightning.

Goat McLaughlin nodded grimly. Aye. Ye were lucky they were working in the farthest field. Tell me, I hear now you're having further bother.

Who told you that?

Goat McLaughlin pulled his chair closer to Barnabas, leaned his pig smell into him. Barnabas saw how the old man's silver beard bore fading flashes of red and had to lean back from the smell.

The old man studied the man dripping before him. So what would make a man like you tramp all the way out here in this rain?

Barnabas cleared his throat, sat up straighter. I came to ask you for help, Goat. I canny get the money to get the byre rebuilt and I donny want to have to sell up my fields. So I'm asking for help. Scrap blocks. Any old timber. Anything your boys might have. Anything at all would do. Just so's I can get started and get to building again. Feed my family. You understand that, don't you?

The old man eyed him long without blinking and when he blinked he made a show of it. I understand that need fine rightly, Barnabas. Didn't I raise up three boys and a daughter of me own. But times are tough. I would imagine most around here would be likely to help if they could but most round here have nothing. Them boys of mine, each one of them is struggling with their own families to feed. The way I see it, it's not so bad. Your feet are put back on the earth now like the rest of us. Twill do ye no harm.

Barnabas winced. That's some position to take, Goat. I've a wife and boy to look after.

Aye. But you are alive, Barnabas, and not dead like Matthew Peoples and that is your great blessing.

Barnabas began to feel his head thicken and he looked into the old man's eyes and began to hate what he saw in there, the yellowing rheum and the righteous blue that shone out of them. He leaned in towards the pig smell. No one put a blessing on my house. And there's no need to bring him into it.

The old man watched the way Barnabas's face tightened. The great Lord is all the property we need, he said.

All I'm asking is if you'd put word about.

Goat eyed him and blinked another slow blink as if looking at an inner picture of the man and his eyes began to burn more fiercely. Aye, I will. But it is the way of the Lord that we must embrace suffering and adversity. Ye should have been prepared, Barnabas, for this sort of reckoning. It comes to all men, sooner or later. The great question in life is, are ye ready for it when it comes? That is the measure to my mind of a true man. Like I said, it will do ye no harm.

I'm not the kind, Goat, to go through life lying down.

A second dog entered the room making a high clip on the floor tiles with its nails. The dog's black fur shined near blue and it stood with red eyes watching Barnabas. The third dog appeared and the first dog yawned and Goat McLaughlin watched Barnabas stand up. He stared at the old man in disbelief and shook his head at him, saw the chorded folds of his throat, found himself wishing for a moment the old man's death. By a knife, probably. Something blunt to make the pain endure.

Would you ever go and tell those hounds of hell to fuck off.

The spit-rain stopped in solemn sympathy with the man and in the sheen of the road he saw the world corrupted, the sky, the trees, the mountains, the fields, remade now into a shadow world in which one could not perceive their true forms. What he saw in those shadows was a lesser truth of what the world was and what he saw around him was what the world is and nothing else goddamnit. He walked and could feel the breeze enter cold through the hole in his trousers, saw in his mind the leering face of Goat McLaughlin, the scrawny old man with bird-like talons for hands. That puckered face sucking it all in. Deliberating on my ruin like some un-anointed priest.

He followed the road home and rubbed the scab the razor left on his hand, searched his mind for ideas, felt all the while as if he were on the brink of some revelation. He passed one of McDaid's small fields and saw the corner of it flooded with rain. A rust-gnawed gate stood sentry to it and he unlatched the loop of old blue rope and entered the field. Sheep black-faced staring at him. He walked towards the corner where the land sloped and held a huge rain pool and he went over to it and surveyed the field's drainage. The liquid silver of the rain pool mirrored the world so intently it was like a rag of sky torn free. In it he could see the sky satin white and the limbs of trees, a barren beauty like some kind of sprawl-boning clamour of the dead. When he returned to Donegal he was first struck by such trees. Could watch their different shapes all day. Not one the perfect image of a tree but each one oddly unique. Some of them huge and thickened with snaking ivy so that it seemed life was being constricted out of them, the trees breaking free near the top to gasp for air. There were trees cleaving like married old couples. Long-necked superior larches and firs aloof and furred a thick green. Old sycamores that were strangers to time. An oak he saw daily at the back of a field naked and dead like a stunned invert octopus.

McDaid was sitting in front of the fire eating when Barnabas came through the door. The house held in an almost religious silence. He looked up at Barnabas and laughed. Jesus, ye look like a dying bastard.

That field of yours down the lane is taking the full run of the rain. You need to get that drainage sorted or it will be ruined. I'll give you a hand digging it.

I lost a wee lamb this morning.

Drown, did she?

McDaid shook his head sadly. Naw. It were got by a dog.

Barnabas snorted. Did you get the gun to it?

McDaid nodded to a shotgun on the table. Maybe if I'd seen something of it.

He sat spooning broth from a bowl and then pincered his fingers into the soup, produced a small bone and sucked it. He reached towards a bottle and poured a dram into the same bowl and drained the bowl with his teeth. Wee sup? he said.

What is it?

Poitín.

That stuff will burn a hole through your head.

A wee slice of the black bread then?

Go on.

He watched McDaid saw the bread and then the farmer

turned conspiratorially and his voice dropped to a hush. Fancy a wee taste of something different, Barney, now that the butter is rationed to fuck?

As he looked at Barnabas his lazy eye was upon the door.

Like what?

A wee taste on the bread.

You've not been at Eskra's honey have you?

McDaid went to the other side of the room where he had a simple kitchen laid out and he reached towards a shelf and took down a brown pot. He hunched his shoulders over it and began to smear something upon the bread, brought it over on the flat of his hand. A wicked smile lit his face and the bread he held out for Barnabas had a fatty smear on it.

Jesus fuck, Peter. What's that?

Try it. It's quare unique.

McDaid sat into a tattered, mud-coloured armchair and looked as if he was squeezing in a laugh. He held himself still and leaned forward eyeing Barnabas intently. His eyes flashed and he licked his lips. Go on taste it.

Barnabas put it into his mouth and ran his tongue over it. What he tasted was old and oily, came with a heavy tang of turf. Something else unknown, deep and rancid, and his face curdled and he stood up and began to spit the food into the fire. McDaid slapped his thigh and his face creased up with laughter.

That's the funniest fucking sight so it is.

Jesus fuck, Peter. That's sick as a dead dog.

It's something different all right.

What is it?

You won't tell no one?

I canny wait to tell the world about your great culinary discovery. What is it?

McDaid sat for a moment and then winked. It's bog butter.

Barnabas looked at the man stunned. Jesus fuck, he said.

I was up with the cousin Willie Lafferty cutting turf last summer and we found this thing in the moss and dug it out and we figured it for one of them bog-butter finds they always be talking about in the paper. The damn thing old as the hills probably. I took it home and forgot about it till the other day and then I had a wee taste of it. Doesn't taste so bad to me considering.

Barnabas stood and shook his head in disbelief. He took the jar and looked at it in amazement. Damn it. Peter. You must be gone in the head. Who knows how old this is? Most of them finds are about two and a half to three thousand years old according to what I read. Hold now. That must be a hundred generations.

I had it last night on me spuds.

There's people in Dublin who'll want to be hearing about that.

Arrah, fuck Dublin. Fuck the lot of them and the restrictions they put on us. All they'll do is send some inspectors up who'll not let us cut turf for a while. Who needs that? I'm doing everyone a favour.

McDaid leaned back into the armchair and swung his wellies up lordly onto a stool. Barnabas sat there ruminating. When he spoke he was staring at the butter in amazement. When you think about it, somebody churned that with their hands and put it in a place in the moss for safekeeping. Sat there all this time them thousands of years and them people long gone and everything with them. Not a trace of them but what's in that jar. We're an ancient race. What are you going to do with it?

McDaid slapped his thigh and began to laugh out loud. Sell it about as lard, he said.

When he was done laughing the men sat a while in silence. Then McDaid spoke. Ye look troubled, Barnabas.

Barnabas groaned quietly. Problems with the bank.

Aye.

Well. I'm rebuilding the byre anyway.

Good on ye.

There is a way it can be done.

Spit and sawdust?

The load-bearing wall is gone and a lot of them stones are ruined. So what I need are blocks. I've asked about but nobody wants to help.

Who'd you ask?

Fran Glacken. That Goat McLaughlin.

Sure you'll get nothin off that Fran Glacken. That man's been fighting with his own two brothers this last twenty year and none of them talking to one another. And all over some access to a field. For a while there his own two sons weren't talking to each other and both of them under the one roof. And that Goat. McDaid shook his head. He's too much of a thran cunt to deal with.

I've a few quid hid someplace to buy some animals again. But other than that it's either rebuild or sell up. Eskra thinks we should leave. I'm not going to be selling nothing, so I am.

McDaid shook his head. Jesus Christ, sir. We canny be having that.

He stood and took the bog butter and sealed it and put it back on the shelf and he turned around and stood where he was, began to scratch at his blue jaw. His eyes lit with an idea. I know a place where you can get a heap of good quality stone. As much as you like of it. And it won't cost you nothing nor bother nobody at all too. It belongs to nobody at this point in time. All you got to do is keep quiet about it.

It were the Saturday morning before Christmas when John the Masher came up to our house with an iron bar in his hand. I seen him coming through the bedroom window frosted cold and before I'd even got a good look at him and the trouble he was carrying, some part of me knew not to go outside to him. I hid at the side of the window and watched him come into the yard and I could see he was funny, his cheeks all red like his face were flaming and his head were thrown back. Roaring out my name. Billygoat. Billygoat ya bastard. The sound of his roaring sent the ordinary day veering into someplace bad. My heart going off like a gunshot. I thought he was mad because maybe he had been found out about the car in the field and maybe he thought I told on him. And then there was that other thing too what it was we done to that wee girl Mary the Moss under the trees after we went to see her that I will not speak about. I was avoiding him since then and now he was outside, his voice full of violence, shouting all the while for me. Downstairs the auld doll was labouring through one of them piano pieces, 'O Twine Me a Bower' or some shite like that, and I heard the piano stop mid-tune. I walked slowly down the stairs afraid the creaking sound of the wood would give me away and then the auld doll comes out of the living room with her face all white and the look she gives me. She says that young Masher boy came up to the window while she was playing the piano and tapped the glass with an iron bar, looked into the room with a wild leer on his face.

Something god-awful in his look that frightened her. She says his eyes are rolling in his head like he was not right. She stood in the hall looking at me with her hand on her belly as if to hold it there would keep both of us from alarm and then she called out quietly for the old boy. I whispered to her that I'd seen him go outside. I followed her into the kitchen and what did she do but she went up and locked the back door and a good thing she did. The Masher comes round the back and peers in the window, the iron bar fat in his hand tap tap tap off the glass. And then he is at the back door trying to get in and he starts banging the door something terrible and the door shook and a strange noise came out of the auld doll's throat. I went over to the stove and took a hold of the poker just in case, the door juddering from the wild kicking his boots were giving it. The Masher calling out the whole time Billygoat, ye cunt ye. I were wild embarrassed and worried he might say something that would ruin me and you could see the shape of his head a dark stain in the ribbed glass of the back door. And then I saw through the main window the old man coming quickly down from the byre, not quite at a run as if he were all calm and Cyclop beside him, and all we could hear then was the sound of a thump and the sight of The Masher been dragged by his hair up the yard. The old boy put him down on the ground and bent to him with his fist, put a right dent into him the best dinger of a punch I seen in a long while and The Masher just curled up into himself a useless heap, the iron bar rolling away by his side. He looked like a scarecrow with the stuffing pulled out of him and the auld doll she was white when we went outside and the old boy was looking up at us and not a bother on him. It's all right he said. He looks over at me. This here's Pat the Masher's son isn't it? He began to shake his head like he was sad for him. That boy's lost his mind again, mad as a bag of crows. The auld doll tells me to go find Big Matty and the old boy tells her he sent him home early. He sends me then up the yard for rope and I go into the byre and take some off the wall where it's hung on a big nail and I'm thinking of the enjoyment I took seeing The Masher beat up like that, the cows looking stupid at me and snorting. The old boy, he ties The Masher's hands behind his back in case he were going to offer up any more trouble and when I see him like that I began to feel sorry for him. Then he stands him up and leans him against the wall, the crazy look in his eyes was gone and he looked like a wee child uncertain and weak. The auld doll whispers, asks what he is going to do with him and the old man looks at her and says to her I'll take him up to Sergeant Porter. She looks at him and shakes her head and says to take him to his father instead, you take him to the guards now and he'll be sent away for Christmas and for who knows how long and those places are criminal. But the old man shakes his head at her. This is serious business Eskra he says. Somebody could have got hurt. The auld doll tells me she is still shaking from the shock but then I look at her and she looks fine to me. I stand there stupid in the yard not wanting her to ask me anything but she does anyways and I says to her I messed around with him for a bit but that was a while ago now and that he was acting wild strange so I stopped spending time with him and she stands there shaking her head at me. Stay away from him now you hear? All the time in my mind I seen terrible things, not the silly things we got up to before but that other thing we did with Molly the Moss. What we did with that wee girl I did not want to think about and it was all I could do because I was terrified now it had got out in some way. The white skin of the girl laid out, never seen such a thing so exciting nor exquisite and that look then in her eye. What it was we done.

H E STOOD OUTSIDE TRYING to guess the coming weather, saw a fault over the earth that rived the morning sky. Over the sea and the western reaches of the world sat a ridge of low cloud like dirt snow sided on a road. What it met shined from over the hills, an eternal blue that spoke the world could be perfect if it wanted to. He mucked out the horse's stable and fed her and when she had eaten he walked her into the yard. Watched the sclerotic way she walked, screwed his eyes at her, could see nothing strange nor obvious upon examination. Just the way the horse held her head as she wambled, spoke again that reluctance. Is it that you're getting old on me? he said. As he spoke he heard the words of Matthew Peoples telling him about the horse that day of the fire, could hear the ring of the man's voice, heard the man's words in snatches, that strange and sleepy tone, and he stared at the man before him in his mind but he could not get a fix on his face. He began to harness the horse and when he drew over the noseband the horse threw her head into the air and snorted, an instruction perhaps in horse-talk to leave her be. Now, now, he said. He whispered further encouragement to her and led her slowly up the yard to the new shed, parked her beside the cart that leaned its long shafts upon the flagstones. He turned the horse around and had begun to fasten her when he saw Eskra step outside. She held in her hand a meat-stripped bone for the dog. She saw Barnabas and the horse and began up the yard all rush through the skitter of chickens.

Can't you see she's unwell? she said.

Barnabas sighed at her. I've a heap of stone to get for the byre.

And what about the horse?

Do you want me to get this done or not?

Of course, Barnabas. But the horse is sick. Could you not borrow one?

McDaid only has that auld half-donkey.

Cyclop ambled over curious to the conversation, lay down between them. He behaved before them like some kind of lion-heart returning from war, his dark and thick coat vined with thorns that hung from his neck like a garland displaced, the whites of his ankles mudded. He sat watching the entertainment with his front paws stretched lordly out while thumping his tail and waggling the dark triangles of his ears. He watched with one eye the slinging voices in the yard, looked at the woman when she hitched up her voice and he looked at the man when his voice rose to meet hers, unrolled a wobbling half yard of tongue that told of his appreciation. And then he shared a look with the horse as if they were above such things.

Eskra sighed and turned with the bone and waved it at the dog. Don't you want this or not? The dog appraised the woman and the bone with a cursory glance and he turned his one eye towards Barnabas and the horse. Sometimes I wonder about that dog, she said. The horse and the dog looked at each other again. Eskra lobbed the bone up the yard and the bone rolled to a stop on the flagstones beside a cylinder of chopped wood. Cyclop stood and stretched out his back a mute and keyless accordion and brought himself back into shape with a yawn. He walked towards the bone and took a sniff and left it where it was, returned to his flagstone seat. Barnabas watched Cyclop make that saurian yawn that could make it seem the dog housed within him an entire other nature, some berserk violence waiting to be unleashed, and then he quit looking at the dog and spoke to the horse, you're a good girl, now come on would you. Saw the withdrawal of Eskra and her plum shadow from the flagstones.

He took a turn off the main road that led up long and slow into bog and dark hills, no more than a grass-humped track. The better nature of that sky before him. From far off he heard schoolchildren's voices skirl on the wind like sirens, screams like some fragment of a dream. He watched the horse take to the hill with no sign of trouble. The way she had loosened up out past the house made him think she was being temperamental, and she walked now at an easy gait, her head nodding as she walked to the cart's softly squealing axle. The days of rain had given some life to the land and he saw the wild grasses reach up eager out of the earth like teeth tearing at the sky for the sun's fleeting rays. He saw everywhere the ferocity of spring, the upswing against death that held within it an unfurling bass power that brought bud into leaf, bulb into flower, felt within himself a measure of that same ferociousness, could hear against the sky the sound of his soul singing.

As the road rose deeper into the hills, nature in its appearance seemed fouled to him. The fields losing their green to become wan and toothless. This bog a tattered place ruled by an aberrant nature that denuded itself of any markings of man, shook off his sheuchs and stone-wall perimeters, set sawtooth briars

to grow where they pleased. The distant white smears of lone
sheep occasional as if they had been scattered by wind. The road
bending gently up the steepening hill and when they reached
halfway and the road levelled briefly he allowed the horse to rest.
He rolled a thin cigarette and turned to the land below him and
lorded chugs of blue smoke over it. The townland of Carnarvan
with its scattering of houses, and further to the east the town
on the hill like some dull shrine to the living. He thought about
when he first returned to Donegal with Eskra and the boy. How
he saw this land with marvel. The sea and the sky and the hills
pressing themselves newly upon him. The play of light in its
ceaseless shape-shifting. He saw the way light could sway in
the rain like a dancer, shimmer like a swished skirt, foot itself
elsewhere. And he saw the place for how old it was and watched
the countenance of the hills in their ever-changing solidity,
as if the place could re-imagine itself at any moment, these
mountains ancient creatures shifting in their sleep, dreaming
their own myths.

He turned and flicked the cigarette into the ditch and began
to lead the horse upwards. What flickered then into his mind
was an old memory, to the tongue the fresh-picked taste of raw
jam from the bramble. The hills rising up as if they were another
realm of time he was walking into.

He didn't see the old man on the road until he was almost upon
him. An ancient face tongued by wind and rain. He saw what lay
beneath the man's papery skin was not bone at all but bog wood
as if he had risen ageless out of the moss, contoured and shaped
by the land's slow heavings. The old man's eyes were half lidded
pinkly and his head was held back as if to see out the peeps of

them but Charlie Cannon was blind. He'd often given Charlie a lift into town in the days before the petrol rationing, and even then his was one of the few cars on the road amongst the horse and traps. Now the man did the long walks on his own, could be seen eyeing the long hill up to church in the town with his cane. He saw how Charlie walked now with the cane slung under his arm, his body an all seeing thing, the land become a part of his nature. The blind man stopped when he came close to the ensemble and he held his head up curious. Barnabas waited till he came close and said, how are you getting on, Charlie Cannon? saw with amusement the man's puzzled face trying to get a latch onto his voice. Owling wild eyebrows shaped sensory to the wind like palps and then the old man's brows fell and his voice was heard softly. That you, Barnabas Kane?

Charlie Cannon, you've got eyes in your ears or is it ears in your eyes, who knows. And you don't even need your cane. Look at you. There was me thinking you were blind all this time. How you've been fooling us.

Charlie Cannon let out a soft laugh and his left hand fluttered.

I don't need no eyes to see what's on this road. Aren't I on it all this time?

Would you not live someplace easier?

They say an ancestor of mine called Ranty lived up here with his eyes gouged out. That some mean bastard took them out with a knife. Kept living up here anyhow as blind as the eternal night. Once you know a place you know it.

As the blind man spoke he gestured with his left hand to give shape to his words, as if he did not trust what he said because he could not see how it registered on the face of another. When he spoke his left hand shook and when he listened it lay restless by his side. The men talked more, about the farm and the fire, and when Charlie Cannon asked what caused it, Barnabas spat on the road. Well, Charlie, I've lost long nights of sleep trying to figure it. I haven't ruled out in my mind it were started deliberate. Time will tell, won't it?

The blind man was silent a while and then he pointed to the deadland around them. What brings you up to Blackmountain, Barnabas? Yer too early I fear for the cutting of turf. Unless you want to get soaked out of it. He laughed softly.

Barnabas found himself pointing up beyond the hill to show where he was going and then he lowered his hand and let it waver as if he was suddenly uncertain the man was blind at all. I'm bringing the horse for a walk. She's been unwell. I need to build her strength up, he said.

He heard the lie as bare as the land around him and it had a worse taint. The old man nodded slow and said, aye, but when he spoke again Barnabas saw the jittery hand had stopped moving. Sounds to me that horse is spavined so she is. You'll make her lame taking her all the way up to this place.

She doesn't seem that way to me.

Maybe so. But when they're sore like that they get spooked wild easy. You should beware taking her up this hill. Listen to that wind. It carries nothing but the ghosts of the dead long gone from out of here. You'll get the horse spooked so you will.

You're a wild man for the superstitious talk, Charlie Cannon. And what are you doing so happy in their company?

Sure I'm nearly an auld ghost myself.

Goan, would you.

The old man laughed quietly and he nodded to Barnabas goodbye. Barnabas found himself waving back, watched the blind man continue down the road without need for the stick. He slapped the haunch of the horse and began to laugh and shake his head. Ghosts, he said.

The steepening road tired out the horse but soon they reached the pass. A different world then amidst the tops of the hills and the view of the land fell away behind them. A place called Drumtahalla and he knew not much about it and to his right the lonely green of the Meeshivin forest. Used to be that forest sprawled everywhere. The breeze came emboldened, whistled and hissed, took on a knife edge. Deadskin scree upon the slopes of the mountains and just beyond the pass he could see the white of Charlie Cannon's cottage nestled into the hills and an old ruin beside it.

Horse and man came through that pass and then the road dipped and he saw it lean long and lonely stretching it seemed into the forever of dark and distant shapes, other mountains unknown to him, the bog's expanse of endless browns within brown. They were following that lonely road when the horse stopped suddenly in protest. He pulled at the animal but the horse did not budge and she rested her dark eyes upon the land sullenly. What the fuck's wrong with you? In the breeze, the horse's mane fluttered but the animal held still and he went to the cart and took a bucket. He stepped into the bog and bent to a nearby stream and filled the bucket with bronze water. As he bent, his eyes fell upon the roots of an ancient tree left exposed agonizingly close to the stream, the trunk long gone and the roots hung out useless over the shifting land neither met by earth nor water. That tree probably as old as five thousand years. He saw how this place was once forested and full of men and women no doubt who walked about an ancient race with similar concerns, the need to eat, the need for shelter, the need to keep warm their children. And he watched a bird wing blackly over the barren turf, let from its mouth a forlorn call.

He put the bucket under the horse's mouth but the horse showed no interest. He produced an ash-plant from the back of the cart and began to whip the animal but the horse did not budge and he lost his temper, began to beat her with his fist. He punched her in the shoulder and slapped her on the withers and then he turned in frustration. Stood thinking. Behind him the animal began to move slowly forward into the bladed wind.

He came upon the place as he had been told it, saw two stone cottages alongside a stream. They stood forsaken beside three dead and twisted trees that once stood sentry over them while beside one lay a lamb's skull grinning up at him. All that stood of these houses now were their walls like old teeth bared to the wind in some sardonic grimace, and he saw how one of the walls had fallen in as if time were something huge that fell against it. Who had lived here he could not know but Peter McDaid told him it was the famine some hundred years ago that drove them out and that people were long past caring.

Each house open to the sky and he stepped inside one, the ground sprung with a carpet of heather and he looked at it and tried to imagine that somebody once lived in this place, once pressed bare feet to its floor, maybe weans were born here, who knows, grew up here, were loved here, died here, or were driven out from hunger to who knows where else, and he tried to imagine the sounds of their living but instead he heard the silence of the years passing over it. He looked at the walls two foot thick and packed with earth and he began to loosen a stone.

Later, he unhitched the horse and turned the cart around and fastened the animal again. Upon the cart he began to make a grey mountain of stones. He reduced one of the old houses to a low wall, heaped upon the cart as many stones in weight as he guessed the horse could carry, the cart fit to take more but for that damned beast of a horse. When it was time to leave the animal was reluctant and he looked at her, saw a skitter in her eye, the flip of an insect on the surface of still water. What's wrong with you? he said. Is it that you're angry? He whispered to her encouragement and apologized for hitting her earlier and then he shouted at her until she strained forward, pulled the cart into a squeal of protest under the dead weight of those stones. She took to the road slow and he walked alongside her while the wind rose to their backs and harried them. The day dragging what light there was to the west in heavy chains and it cast upon the land its monolith shadows. They made their way amidst the groans of the cart that sounded in unison with the wind and they travelled slowly through the pass till they met the land and the road twisting downwards, lumps of rock like jut bones and far off grassy fields. He turned an eye to the load to make sure no stones were coming loose and he walked alongside the horse holding onto the harness. The road steepened and the cart made another groan and the horse made a strange squeal to accompany it. He looked at the animal and didn't like what he saw and he told the horse to steady, took a tighter hold of the harness. The horse squealed again and the sound of it bore clean through the wind like a blade. He pulled the horse to a stop. They stood a minute like that facing downhill and what winged then in front of them was a butterfly, a crimson Peacock with peering blue eyes on its wings, and it shook itself up into the air before them and dived again, came to rest upon the horse's nose. In that instant the horse took fright, reared up her head and screamed, began suddenly to move. Barnabas roaring out at the horse but the animal moving regardless, picking up speed now until he was running alongside her shouting, what's wrong with you, would you hold on, and he pulled at the bridle but could feel the animal pull easily beyond his strength. As he ran he saw the road lean dangerously downwards and he pulled at the horse but the animal paid him no heed, and he began then to shout out words, words that in another place or circumstance could have raised the dead, but here they could not put a stop to a horse that came under the influence of gravity. The spiral of the road and the speed of the animal and the sun dimming quickly as if it could not dare to watch, and he found he had to let the horse go, watched what happened with horror. The rear left wheel of the cart wobbling and then disintegrating as the wood buckled and broke, shot spokes into splinters. The cart took a quick lope dangerously to one side as if it were some kind of stone mastodon being brought down by hunters, toppled towards the earth in what seemed to him a miraculous slow arc of movement and it took sideways with it the harnessed horse a shrieking brown blur.

A caress of lamplight held Eskra's sleeping face and faded into dark up the wall. Her features weightless as a child, her skin made buttermilk. She sat on a chair resting her elbow against the deal table while she held against her head an enclosed hand. Her other hand open and so gentle upon the wax tablecloth it would seem she came through this life without pressure or weight or any bearing against the world at all. The east outside came pitch against the glass and the night sat hushed so that when she slipped into dreaming the drifting images that came took her back to Vinegar Hill, and she heard the tones of her dead father's voice, heard it bright in a way she could not while awake – his voice that came strong even in sickness, and she a little girl hugging him bone-tight and she saw in the shape of his eyes their true colour, saw pitted in his soul the sadness that shone an awareness of his coming death. And as she dreamed she saw the horse stood over them watching her with the eyes of a woman. Billy then stomping into the room in his boots and she fell away from her father, fell into the room with quickly opened eyes and a feeling that lingered of sadness. Yellow lamplight forming to make the shape of her son who stood pointing by the window. He's back now so he is. Billy turned and was gone outside in noise and rush.

She stood by the side of the house with the west lit in its last embers. Watched the slow approach of a swinging lamp. Billy a fragment of the dark running down the road and she saw then what was coming towards him was not Barnabas on his own but Barnabas and another. Up the lane like slow-herded animals, the hulk shape of a cart behind them mountained with stones and she recognized then the particular walk of McDaid, the man's forward lean with his elbows pointing out like he was walking into wind always. The wellying waddle. How Barnabas coalesced into the man she knew, his eyes yoked to the ground. She saw then it was not the horse and cart they were leading but McDaid's cart and mule and they brought it to a groaning stop in the middle of the yard.

Where's the horse, Barnabas? she said.

In the lamplight they began to unload the stones.

Barnabas turned. Billy, get up here and give us a hand.

The boy came forward and stood narrow against the thickness of his father.

Barnabas, she said. What's going on? Where's the horse and cart?

She watched him grunt and grab a stone off the cart, place it upon the flagstones. The billowing stone dust caught in the lamplight looked like ten thousand distant suns, born into glitter and dying there.

Barnabas, she said.

He turned to her dirt-faced and she saw in his eyes a great weariness and he did not speak but sighed at her. McDaid turned to her and spoke, his voice awkward and soft. Barnabas had a wee accident up on Moyle Hill, Eskra. The wheel came off the cart. Turned the whole thing upside-down so it did. Lucky no one got kilt.

Eskra's hand went to her mouth and she stepped forward and put her hand on Barnabas. Are you all right, love?

Aye. I'm all right. It was the goddamn horse's fault. Got spooked so she did.

He turned back to unloading the stones and she stood a minute watching till her voice became high with concern. What happened? she said. What happened to the horse? Where is she?

Barnabas did not answer and she pulled him by the back of his shirt and he turned to her dead-eyed holding against his chest a long flat stone.

Take it easy now, Eskra, said McDaid. The horse is up at my place. I put her in the barn to recover.

Eskra's eyes widened in the dark and she bunched her skirt and abruptly made off, set off up the road calling for Billy to follow behind her.

The boy a fleet form running past her half-seen in the darkness. He merged with the moonless sky and the trees and the fields so that all became single dark matter. When she got to the shape of McDaid's house Billy was almost whole again, stood with the horse in the middle of the road, the pair of them faintly visible against the sky's obsidian.

She was in the barn, he said. I took her out.

In all the commotion I didn't think to bring a lamp, she said.

Haul on. I'll go into Peter's and get one.

He came back out with a faltering lamp that would not burn any brighter. He held it close to the horse. She went towards the animal and began to feel all over, smoothed her flanks with long and slow and kneading gestures and the horse quaked when a hand came upon her hind leg. Eskra held still, the sound of the horse snuffling and breathing against her own breath nasal in concentration. She could see nothing else wrong with her, just pain flagged in a limp when they began to walk her forward.

She's limping so she is, Billy said.

She's bruised and spooked but she's whole and that's good.

She began to walk the horse slowly towards their house, whispered into the animal's ear voice kisses.

Barnabas returned two days later to the old houses in the mountains with Peter McDaid and his mule. The animal squat and still under a sparkling diamond sun that strung out shadows of the men in hinging shapes. Stone by stone they revoked the claim of those two famine houses to the land, land that had let the hand of nature go to work in its wearing relentlessness. What was left of the walls came down and they loaded the cart, the pair working in unison, their hands and faces whitening from the dust. They stopped to drink water and chew on old apples and Barnabas threw into the bog an apple core, watched with amusement as McDaid chewed the core and ate its pits and stalk. In the afternoon he saw McDaid leap into an odd shape and then the man lying down on the moss.

What's wrong with you, Peter? Barnabas said.

Me back is having spasms. Tis a hoor of a thing.

That's the cyanide in them apples. That's what it is.

McDaid lay tense with his hands by his side, lay staring at the cloud shapes, read into their natural forms things that he knew, dogs and cats and men's faces and even items of furniture, saw the shape of his mother's old dresser in the tall stretch of a cloud.

The last time my back spasmed like this I was at the far end of my fields. Raining like a total bastard. I had to lie down on me back and pull the coat over me head from the rain. Lie there like a dying animal.

He began to laugh at himself and stopped from the hurt. Ah fuck, he said.

When Barnabas had removed the last stone that would be needed he took a long slug of water from a bottle. He stood still for a moment staring at the ruined houses as if he could not believe what he saw. He proffered a hand to lift McDaid and the man rose like a corpse. McDaid slowly began to arch his back. Do you reckon you have enough? he said.

I've been keeping rough count.

McDaid walked slowly over to the cart holding onto the small of his back and he began to push at some stones to test they were piled firm. He stood again on a mound of moss looking down at the loss of the two houses. Do you reckon we took from this place its history? he said.

Barnabas held in his mouth two unlit cigarettes and he sucked them to life with a match. Blue smoke ghosting about his face and he handed one to McDaid, knuckled at his cheek. I'll bet there isn't a single person in Carnarvan who could tell you a thing about the people who left this place. Just look at it. The people here are so long gone none of them at all are remembered. What's left is just an idea of people. A folk memory. It is nothing real.

His eyes travelled the silent land around them, the barren slopes of the mountains that leaned up to the sky. They no longer have stories whoever these particular people were, he said. They might as well have never existed. All signs and sins erased.

If you could sit down and talk with stones. The stories you'd hear out of them.

I'd say there was nothing here but suffering. I'd say there was hunger and they died or left and went someplace else. That was the way of it.

C'mon, let's get to fuck away from here. I think I'm starting to mistake the sound of the breeze for ghosts.

The mule held himself sure-footed and stoical down that hill and in reward the afternoon sun went to work on his shape. It took the animal's long grey ears and made on the moss a rabbit's head for him and it took the mule's stout body and stretched him out upon the bog until he walked grand and noble, a horse pulling behind him a mountain.

*

The first days of April brought showers teasing and temperamental that made it too wet to start building. Each time the rain fell he would escape to the stable, stand in the doorway, his eyes adrip with loathing. The stones in their tidy piles graded into different sizes and in the new barn sat a mound of sand and bags of cement piled like loaves that McDaid had brought to him. That cousin of mine has fuck all use for them, he said, has them sitting there for years so I told him I needed em. Owed me a favour.

Dreams almost every night of his own agency and power and the byre rising up under a white sky and then those dreams turning to frustration where nothing got built at all, days running out in those dreams holding in his hands the useless stones, dreams that could have tired out even the interminable night's patience.

The horse was still sickly and kept in the stable most days and he stood beneath the stone lintel with his back to her watching the rain, watching the sunken shape of the byre taking the full of another shower, watching the byre with a gluttony to get it built. An entire week of this kind of weather would drive a man mad so it would. He began then to stay indoors blowing smoke against the kitchen window, leaning his face against the glass, imagined it an invisible force holding him in.

My hands are itching to work, he said. I feel like I'm twenty-one again.

Eskra behind him in the room folding clothes. It's an unfortunate time to start, Barnabas. It's the same every year. Why don't you wait another month?

I want to take Billy for a week out of school.

What for?

She paused in the middle of the room and saw the way he

leaned his fists upon the counter as if his entire will were directed into those fists and he could at one push remove from the house the kitchen.

Just for one week, Eskra, to help me get started. Mixing that mortar and lifting them stones on me own will be slow and heavy work.

She shook her head to the unseeing back of him.

Listen to you. Always complaining about your lack of schooling and having to learn everything you know out of books. Always saying you could have done more with your intelligence. Is that what you want for your son? I'm not going to have him like those other children round here that treat school like it's not important.

Just one week. It won't hurt him.

No.

Look, the bastarding rain has stopped again.

He stepped out into a dry and matinal dark that concealed all signs of coming weather. A lamp placed on the flagstones that lit around him a pale corona and put everything else to dark. No rain during the night and he sensed the morning might hold, churned at the mortar with impatience. Laid the byre's first stones down. As the morning swung over him he turned and watched the bluish light push over the mountains and it seemed to him like the final movement of some old and weary creature that had travelled overnight the full circumference of the earth, while the daylight that came hesitant behind it could not hold all the creatures within its kingdom radiant.

Hours later he looked up over the low rise of a new wall, saw sunshine sparkle upon the pump. He washed his hands and went to the house for breakfast. Caught sight of Eskra through the window. She stood by the stove half lit in that bright morning light, motes of dust adrift and lit in their strange and softly orbits, and the light that held her as she rubbed at the webbing of her fingers made her look pained and beautiful. To kiss her with the reach of his eyes. He tapped at the glass and she came towards him and he pointed towards the byre. Would you look at that. She smiled.

When he went inside she poured him porridge and she rubbed at his shoulder and they ate their food together.

Later, after Barnabas went back out, Eskra stood to the stove and stirred again Billy's porridge, poured it bubbling into a nut-brown bowl. The bang of the boy on the ceiling and she called out to him again. By the kitchen window she heard a rogue bee's drone as it smacked itself off the glass and she walked over to let it out, saw the shape of Barnabas walking across the yard, his sleeves rolled and the skin to his wrists already caulked grey. What rose then to meet her was a wasp, came straight towards her face, and she took a step backwards and batted at it. The wasp dipped low towards the sill and turned and swung up towards her fast, all black-bunched thorax, its abdomen long and sickle curved, and she saw the sleek poise of its stinger. Her stomach tightened. She did not like to harm any creature under the light of the sun but in the countenance of the wasp she saw a sightless and dangerous aggression. She reached for a tea towel and swiped the insect towards the window, heard behind her the trudge of Billy down the stairs. She reached for a glass and cupped the insect against the window, watched it launch itself angry against the container as Billy came into the room. Get me the newspaper, she said. He went to the table and picked it up and came towards her rubbing his eyes with sleep and she took the paper and sealed the glass and told him to open the door. She let free the wasp, watched it take high into the air like a speck of soot, disappear over the stable roof. The head of Barnabas popping up from behind the low wall. If that boy is up send him out, he said.

She came towards him. I was going to ask him to come with me to the beach, she said.

Arrah, Eskra.

It's Saturday, Barnabas. We've been cooped up here all week like animals.

Barnabas looked up at the sky and muttered a long curse.

Billy sitting at the table stirring honey into his porridge. She saw her own blue eyes in him as she spoke. Let's go to the beach for a walk, she said. When they went outside to fetch the bicycles, Barnabas hunched up red-faced from the byre. That boy's staying here, he said. Billy stood awkward with his hands in his shorts and looked towards his mother with an intense look of pleading until she nodded to him. Go and call the dog, she said. She turned to Barnabas. Can I not have some company on the beach? He can help you after lunch.

Before they left Billy had called for the dog and did a circle of the yard but the dog did not come. A busying breeze behind them on the road as they pedalled and Billy kept searching the road, expecting to see the dog as if he would appear at any moment from one of the fields, wet and wild and that eagerness brightly from his single eye. They came to the beach two miles up the road and it lay festooned with dark ribbons of seaweed. A slate sea that made it seem the world did not bend to meet itself but continued straight and true into the eternal.

They left their bicycles by the machair dunes and Billy ran towards the water. He stood in the caul of a previous tide that lay spectral on the sand, leapt back from the advance of the water. He turned and took hold of a long cylinder of seaweed and began to flay the beach. Eskra walking slowly towards the water in bare feet, the lullaby sound of the sea and the salted air lush, and she bunched her skirt to her knees. The cold bit her toes as she entered the water to her ankles. Part of her dress fell from her hand and she watched it soak and darken, let the rest of it drop. She reached her hands into the water, a numbing cold and the sea's salt stung the rawest part of her fingers, and then she felt the pain ease. She began to squeeze her hands into fists and released them, opened her palms in the water skywards as if making an expression of grace.

Behind her on the beach Billy began shouting to himself and threw a wrack of seaweed into the air, watched it flutter birdly and glisten. He turned and frowned when he saw his mother squatting strangely in the sea with her dress floating around her, the slow way she washed her hands.

The sea lay itself upon the beach without anger or rush, sighed as it made its retreat. They walked the length of the strand to a place of basalt rocks and they watched the tide recede and saw wobbled shapes of themselves on the sand's shining surface and shrinking marks of their feet. Billy walking awkward behind his mother. Ma, he said.

She turned around to look at him.

Why is Da rebuilding the byre? The cattle are all dead.

She studied him where he stood, the boy all bony elbows and long and awkward feet, saw the way his gaze was both daring and avoidant.

It is in your father's nature, Billy. To keep trying. What else do you want him to do?

The boy shrugged.

Your father is going to get us out of this mess. The bank did not want to help so what is he supposed to do? The alternative is to give up and move away. When I first met your father he was smarter than any of those men he worked with. He was filthy and greased all the time from the work and he drank a little too much but inside him he had intelligence. I saw it straight away. I saw that if your father had been born with better chances he could have been somebody great. That man had to build up a life from nothing in America and what he built for himself he built with no help. You know, when we came back here, I had it in my mind we were returning him to what should have been. That he had a right to be here in his own country. And that you could grow up in your home like I never did. And then what happened, Billy, with that fire.

She stopped and began to shake her head and stood staring at the sea. Billy walked past her.

In the back of his mind your father has never forgotten where he came from and what that was like and what that kind of life did to him. You know, he would rather die than go back to all of that again and lose everything he has. Do you see what I mean?

As she spoke she saw Billy frowning again. But why don't you just sell up some of the fields? he said.

Eskra did not answer him.

The distant shape of a person on the beach walking in their direction and a small shape breaking away towards the water, a dog chasing a stick.

*

Goat McLaughlin marched breathless towards the Kane farm making sharp and short whistles at his dogs, the animals fanning out into an advance party of three that scuttled and sloped as if alert to some danger. They slid quick through the gate's ribs, one of the dogs trailing blue rope from its neck and it made towards Cyclop's water bowl and began to lap from it. Barnabas heard the old man's whistles and looked up, saw the invasion of dogs, Goat moving quick-footed up the yard, his talon hands loose and jiggling. Barnabas muttered. Bring forth the prophet. Barnabas stretched his back and looked down at his hands and slapped the dust off them and he stepped out of the byre and stood in front of the pile of rocks in the yard, met the man's advancing gaze. Yes, Goat, he said.

Yes, Barnabas.

The men did not shake hands but stood there eyeing each other, the old man clad in purple knee-patched dungarees and his eyes kept flitting to the stones behind Barnabas. A shine in his eyes that told he would speak and would be listened to. I didna want to disturb ye, Barney. Donny like to see a man taken from his work.

Well, here you are.

I see yer rebuilding the byre.

That is so.

The old man paused a moment and looked at the staggered wall beside him and dropped down his chin. When it rose again his words came out lit by some internal fire of indignation and his hands began to jiggle intensely. Them stones, Barnabas. Those stones that ye took. Don't ye know, Barnabas, there's a desecration involved? Ye took from the land what is not yers to take. Ye cannot expect nobody to say nothing about it.

One of the dogs came towards Barnabas and began to nose at his feet, a tight and curling tail it sported and Barnabas gave the dog a menacing look, lifted his boot and pushed the dog away with the flat of his foot. The animal retreated sullenly and Barnabas eyed the old man, stood silent for a moment. What are you on about, Goat?

Beard to beard they stood and beneath the brushwire of the other's chin Barnabas saw the old man bite down on his teeth. His eyes never leaving the stones. His mouth made a strange shape as he spoke and he began to wag a weazened finger. Ye know fine rightly what I'm on about. Ye took them stones from the famine houses up at Blackmountain. Yes, ye did. I heard fine rightly. Everybody round here knows. That accident ye had on the hill. Them stones do not belong to ye, Barnabas, and they must be put back even though the desecration is done. We will figure out a way.

Barnabas said nothing for a moment and then he let loose in the man's face a great laugh, stood there with his mouth open and the black of his back teeth visible and then he snapped his mouth shut, leaned in towards Goat. The old man's eyes had scorch in them enough to light tinder.

As Barnabas spoke his mouth tightened. I got them stones from me own land, Goat. And while you're here let me tell you that you've some neck coming in here telling me what to do. When you wouldn't help me out with nothin. He shook his head at him. You are a pious, superstitious old bastard who for all your Christian talk could not see fit to help another man when he was down. Now I've got to be getting back to my work.

He turned and began to walk towards the byre and the old

man stood a moment quaking. When he spoke his voice had found a higher register of anger.

Them houses belong to our tradition, Barnabas. Yer making a mockery of the Lord. They were not yer stones to take. They belong to our people, people round here who were starved by the famine. The bounties of this land are not here to be used indiscriminately by local strangers like you.

As he spoke he was wagging his finger and then he stopped himself, seemed to find control and his voice dropped down. I know ye are a reasonable man, Barnabas. I know ye are doing what ye think is right by your family. Look. I hear you've no longer a cart of yer own. I'll help ye take the stones back so I will.

Barnabas's eyes began to widen and he curled his mouth and walked back from the byre to the old man, stood right up to him. Nobody owns them rocks, Goat, but the dead and the dead have forfeited all rights to them. There's a life to be lived here first. Nobody takes nothing to the grave. Not even you.

The old man met his glare. The earth bears all things freely when no one demands it, he said.

Barnabas leaned in to the heat of the man's breath. Tell me, he said. Who the fuck consecrated you priest?

The old man stepped back. He shook his head with fury and his eyes began to bubble and burst. Ye are sowing division, Barnabas Kane. Ye are turning yer back upon our fellowship. Cutting yerself off from this community. Ye should listen to what people are saying about ye. Ye have no animals, Barnabas, yet ye are building this byre. What kind of foolish thing is that? Ye should sell up and support your family. I'll help ye take back the stones. Those stones are our bones, Barnabas. Ye don't want to isolate yerself from this entire community now do ye?

As he spoke Barnabas saw Billy and Eskra come through the gate, saw Eskra stop when she heard the old man's raised voice. She directed Billy to go in through the front door of the house. Barnabas felt his fist begin to boulder and he held it in a way that would have been fit to fell the man had it not been that Eskra appeared then from the back door. She stood with her arms folded but said nothing to alert the old man and he leaned in towards Goat.

You ever tell me again how to look after my family and I'll rip that great beard of yours right out of your head. This byre will be rebuilt with your help or not and when I asked you for it you wouldn't give it to me. Now give me head peace and clear the fuck off.

The old man thumped a foot, turned and saw Eskra, and his voice dropped low.

Ye think me a hard man but I just want for ye to do what's right.

Get off my land, Goat.

It's a good thing for ye none of my boys are witness to this.

You can send any of your boys over to see me any time they like, Goat. They'll get a great welcome. I've got a twelve-gauge Browning behind the backdoor for trespassers and I'd just love so I would to take off a foot.

Goat eyed Barnabas with a look that would break an ordinary man apart. Barnabas stared the old man back, stared so hard that the old man's features began to dissolve into a mush of skin and hair and bones. The spell was broken by one of the black dogs that began to giddy about the old man's feet. He turned and made two sharp whistles to the other two dogs and they snapped their heads to their master, followed the old man out the gate.

Barnabas pulled a chair out from the table and let out a long sigh as he sat down. He began to cut the black bread on the board in front of him, leaned towards the butter and knifed at it. Do you remember that one time years ago, Eskra, when we came here, what Fran Glacken said to me? He said to me I was a local stranger. The cheek of him. The big smiling face on him and I nearly hit him. Do you know what he meant by that? Did I ever explain it to you? It meant that I was not the same because I was gone out of here. Because I had emigrated. As if I had a choice in it. This fucking place. I never treated anyone any different when I came back and I never lorded it over nobody. I'm the same as them but I'm different because I went away and that's the way they see it.

He chewed on the bread and sent his tongue to lick at butter on his beard.

Maybe them cunts are right calling me a local stranger. I can still see this land in a way that they aren't able. And for all the time spent here I still canny get a handle on the place names – every nook and cranny with a bloody name on it. You know something – Matthew Peoples knew it fine rightly too. The old bastard was always taking a hand of me because of it.

She saw as Barnabas spoke he began to make a face, pulled a mocking impression of Matthew Peoples. One time I was asking him about the best place for trout and he starts putting on this expression and I knew he was pulling my leg. Oh, that would be down by the whin pool, he says, now you know where that is, don't you? You'd have to cross the seven bloody magic stones near Cloontagh but not go as far as it, naw. Go past the bloody potato field of James Duffy. Not the big one but the wee one. And you'll find it then by Altashane. He says all this to me with barely a straight face. Just a yonder beyond the fairy circle that's near the fir trees.

When he stopped talking he leaned slow over the table towards the teapot and poured himself tea that dribbled from the spout onto the tablecloth. He slapped it down, took a drink. Damn it, he said. This tea would freeze a man's balls off.

It's made only a while ago, Barnabas.

He turned and began looking out the window and all that was turning to dusk.

Being of the land, but not of it, he said. That's why we can expect nothing but difficulty from them. Nothing at all.

When he turned in his chair he saw Eskra trying to smile at him but what lit her eyes was sadness.

Anyhow, he said. We'll fucking show them. I showed them once before. I'll fucking show them again. It won't be a bother.

He rose under a great dark each day to work upon the byre and as he worked he would look at the sky and wonder. Dawns that came like the aftermath of slaughter, a battleground of the gods during the night. Or some mornings it seemed there was no dawn at all, just a pale light that sent forth a day stunted, slung down upon him its cold. He would work regardless, work with his sleeves rolled soon to make a sweat while the weather tensed and threatened but kept favour. He began to work up a cadence, an old rhythm that his hands knew, his feet in lockstep, a meeting of mind and stone that spoke to him of fundamental things. His hands upon the stones as if he had delivered each one from the earth. The stones loosening memories as if they had within them shamanic powers, memories that came like drifts of clouds from over some blind horizon of mind. Saw himself aged twenty, a strange and fearless creature who would not know the man he was now. Hanging off a corner without a harness nearly sixty floors up. The sally and slap of the wind and Manhattan beneath him like some epic ruin. The fearlessness of that kid. It scared him now to think about it because he had learned the taste of fear. He saw in snatches the faces of men he had worked with, could remember most of their names – Patch Barry and Matty O'Brien and Sonny Bracken – and one by one they left the work and fell forgotten into America. Sonny the best friend of Patch and both of them Mayo men and everywhere you saw one you saw the other and the high talk out of them. He recalled, too, the times he spent with the Mohawks up in the Gowanus. Jim Deer inviting him up to the streets of Brooklyn they had turned native. That dim, smoke-thickened room called the Spar Bar and Grill where he would drink and listen to their speech like strange music. The Mohawks did not look like Indians at all, wore their hair short. Jim Deer with his hair greased and the way he laid out his long hands and big moon fingernails upon the table or wrapped them both around his beer, his silent way of looking into the deepest parts of you. Deer's sweet baritone voice explaining how his father died from a fall off the skeleton of a railroad bridge over the St Lawrence, and the man's eyes like stones in the telling. They all had such stories yet worked the skyscrapers anyway, drank till they could stand no more and when the time was right retreated to their home at Caughnawaga, a reservation on the St Lawrence River. Deer said, in the river's silence you are in the company of your dead. Barnabas had learned to forget the dead, had put Donegal out of his mind, but the way the Mohawks returned home so easily awakened in him something dormant. That aching place of his childhood. The death of his parents stirring sorrow in him as if from the grave they would not let him forget. The last time he drank with Deer he asked him why they were so fearless. Deer answered, death is an invisible presence all around us. We just pass through. None of us know how close we stand to it.

He saw himself standing outside the byre beside Matthew Peoples.

So long ago now the life lived like a dream and yet he never forgot the Mohawk saying it.

He smoked as he worked, stood up when the fags were all smoked and he would straighten his back and roll himself five more, stow them in his shirt pocket. He worked with each fag hanging from his mouth, smoked in near-circular breathing. When the horse woke from sleep she would stick her head out the stable half-door and watch. A strange creature she saw back-bent and heaving over rocks, a monster with the body of a man and the mind of a bull and smoke blasting from its head in the half light like a dragon, if the horse knew of such things. As each day rose the shape of Eskra would appear made spectral by the kitchen window and she would come outside to Barnabas in her dressing gown and place beside him a cup of tea, ask him how he was getting on. He would smile at her and work on. The tea going cold until he would remember about it and he would slosh it down with a wince in one drink. Nothing worse than cold tea. Soon enough the byre rose up all four walls to meet its maker and it began to lend some of its appearance, dusting his hair and face and thickening like stone the skin on his fingers. What he felt in his mind as he worked was the deep humming flow of a river. Working each day until his shadowed self became lost in the bluing dark and then he would stand back and look at it, the byre turning silhouette to the merging of night sky and hills.

That same day Billy and Eskra went to the beach the dog did not return and by evening Billy had grown desperate. In the yard he saw one of Cyclop's bones freshly dug out of the earth and he stood over the bone and kicked it, called out at the top of his voice for the dog. The bone skittered hollow on the flagstones and the dog did not come and an awareness then came over him. He chased after the bone and kicked it towards the new barn shouting the dog's name. He met the back gate that dipped rickety when opened as if it had grown tired of holding itself, and he walked out towards the edge of the back field. The grass came to his ankles and he shouted again for the dog. In the sky a fresh-hung moon like a pill to stay the night's pain and his voice reached out into the grand silence but did not hold there. He looked towards the darkening scrim of the fields and he thought of The Masher and his strange bird-like whistle and he stopped shouting, turned back for the house. When he stood in the yard he called out again but the sound of his voice fell lonely.

He saw his father in the range chair with his shoes kicked off and his legs stretched out towards the table. Toe-white poking through a hole in his sock. Some kind of grandness to him now with his belt undone and a hand upon his belly as if he were pregnant with satisfaction, while Eskra sat quiet and focused, bent over herself stitching a button to a shirt. When Billy spoke his father pointed to the radio with a jabbing quick finger. Billy stood awkward for a moment and then he stamped his foot. Jesus, will ye listen to me? he said.

Barnabas stared at him. Would you ever shut up. I'm trying to hear. The Russians are nearing Berlin. Could there be anything more important?

Eskra turned around. Let the boy speak, she said. You've heard the news today already, Barnabas. Nothing's changed in the last hour. She turned to Billy. What's wrong with you, love?

Cyclop's still gone, he said. He never came back after yesterday. I've been out looking for him so I have, but there's no sign of him.

Barnabas groaned and Eskra dropped her voice into a whisper. He'll come back tonight wait till you see, Billy. Cyclop lives his own life.

Barnabas rolled his legs in towards him with dramatic fashion and he stood up. For fuck sake, he said. A heavy blink as he walked across the room and dialled up the volume, sat down again with a humph and stretched out his legs. That damn dog does only as it pleases, he said. Now would the pair of yez shush. That boy Hitler is on his way out.

He saw Billy running up the road from school, his bag bouncing eager on his back, watched him reach the yard and stand staring over the dog's food and water bowls. The boy turned around with a tight look on his face and he dropped his head when Barnabas called him over, walked towards the byre slapping his hands by his sides. Barnabas stood up off his haunches. Go in and change into your work clothes. I need help out here. As Barnabas bent back down, Billy's face hardened into a look of hate that went unseen by his father. He walked wordless towards the house and soon after Eskra came out. She went towards Barnabas with her arms folded and when he saw her he stood up agitated. What is it now with that boy of ours? he said. He saw she had tied her hair up different that made lonely the full shell of her ears. Whitely they stood out and a new tightness to her mouth he did not like the look of.

Can you not see he's worried sick about that dog.

I didn't think of it.

I'm worried about Cyclop as well, Barnabas. I was going to say when you came in that we should go and search for him.

Barnabas leaned back and began to light a cigarette. Why doesn't he go out looking for him then?

He says he wants you to go with him.

Arrah, Jesus.

Barnabas took off his workboots and put on his wellies and he shouted for Billy to come downstairs, that they were going now in a minute. He put on his coat and stood by the door and waited. Billy came running down the stairs. Put on your welly boots, Eskra said. The boy kicked off his shoes and stepped his bare legs into puddling boots while his father's old coat hung on him like a pair of huge wings. They were walking up the yard when Eskra called behind them. Take this, she said. Barnabas turned and saw she held an unlit lamp.

No need, he said.

It's going to get dark in an hour. Just in case. He might be injured or something. She waved it at him as if he did not have a choice in the matter.

They set out through northerly fields calling out for Cyclop. The dog a wary beast at the best of times and in his mind Barnabas saw the animal sitting somewhere covert between trees, his tongue lolling in amusement. They trudged towards the perimeter of Fran Glacken's fields and began to veer west down the slope of tapering pasture until they met impenetrable whin that held its yellow to itself like stilled flames. They swung around and came by a stream and crossed it and in the trees birds began to make their last calls and blend into the deeper darkness. Billy stood in the middle of the stream until his father summoned him onwards. Through trees and the sloping fields and they came upon a view of Pat the Masher's house distant and dark with no light in the windows. Billy looked at the house and in his coat his hand began to tighten around the haft of a knife.

They walked a wide circle, all the while calling out to the dog as the dark crept slowly around them. Barnabas turned to the boy. C'mon, he said. It's growing dark. We can finish this tomorrow.

Just a wee while more.

Barnabas sighed but kept walking.

Their shadows began to fuse into one and passed into that wider dark that claimed them man and boy the same, the stars too dimmed by cloud and a moon that lay hid so the night became but one dimension. Barnabas stopped and lit a low moon from the lamp and held it up before them, saw a moth wing itself at the lamp's glass.

I mind when that dog was a pup he went about the place like a dog with two dicks, peeing all over the place. You'd be carrying him in your hands and next thing he'd let go on you. On your trousers and everything. He'd piss in your eye, so he would. The great piddler of his age. Cyclop was the wrong name for him. Should have called him Piddlin' Pete.

Who was it gave him to you?

Oh, some auld fella from up Glebe. He wasn't fit for looking after him. Had a heap of them. The dog seemed glad of the change. If only we knew what we were getting ourselves in for.

They came upon a narrow lane guarded over by trees that stood feather to the night, followed it, Barnabas's voice bellowing into that dark as if he had some kind of authority over its province. He listened to the way sound travelled, the whump of wing-beat, a small animal's rustle and scuttle, walked wide-eyed to pick out like bruising fruit the colours of the dark. At the end of the lane they began to close a wide circle, came upon the main road. Smell of moss and muck and damp and then through trees they heard a dog's barking. They stopped and held their breaths and Billy called out and ran. Barnabas calling after him. Walked quickly. Heard a creature on the road and ran towards it with the lamp, the shape of a dog, and what was held before them when they saw it was another. A skinny mongrel standing slantways and suspicious before it skittered off. Billy's head dropped low.

McDaid's house loomed and Barnabas went to the door and knocked. The door opened and lamplight made a sight of McDaid in yellowing long-johns with his fly wide open and his cock on show. His feet planted in wellies. Barnabas nodded towards the man's crotch. Jesus Christ, Peter. The electric eel is making a run for the river.

McDaid looked down and laughed and he fixed at his long-johns. Jeez, boys, you caught me nappin.

They stepped in and Barnabas told him about the dog and he eyed them back with the odd alignment of his gaze. How old is he now? McDaid said. Maybe he's sick and gone off to die in one of the fields the way that dogs do.

Billy shot the man a look of hurt and Barnabas saw it, reached out to his son and rubbed his head. Naw, he said. He's too young for that carry on.

Queenie peering curious between McDaid's legs. He looked down at her. Don't mind me, Billy, I'm just thinking out loud. How old did ye say he was?

He's eight so he is, Billy said.

Well what's that in dog years? McDaid reached down as if asking the dog. Let's see now. That makes him about fifty-six. My own good age. He'll be all right then so he will, for I'm fit as a fiddle.

When they entered their own house, Eskra went to embrace the boy but he went sullenly upstairs. Barnabas stood pulling at his sock. That dog, he said. When I lay my eyes on him I'm going to give him such a mighty kick up the hole.

The brass bell above the grocery and hardware shop door pinged its hopeful ring, reached for the sky and died there. Eskra standing beneath it on the street staring across the road. What she saw was a chimney smoking so thick it seemed to her to have caught fire. The smoke chugged like blood arterial, as if some dark heart were pumping it relentless, and she stood under the shop's sign and found her feet had become lead. A small bird fluttering panic in her chest. Oh no, she said. She cast her eye at the people on the street and pointed but nobody seemed to notice, saw a young farmer with his hands hooked in his pants coming close by. He saw her pointing towards the roof and he stopped and unpursed his lips and squinted, and then he turned to her and shrugged. Tis nothin, he said. He left her standing there staring at the smoke and she watched it until she saw it thin out and whiten. What is wrong with you, Eskra? A bit of smoke and you think the place is burning down.

She wheeled her bicycle down the street and turned the corner, came straight in front of Pat the Masher. He stood at the top of the hill in quiet colloquy with the priest who lay a soft white hand upon his shoulder. The cleric's eyes met the eyes of Eskra and he dropped his hand to wave to her. She stopped before them flushed. I feel like such a fool, she said. I thought that one of the houses there on the street was having a chimney fire.

The priest looked at her a long moment and smiled. Better to be safe than sorry, he said.

She looked at Pat the Masher. And how are you, Pat? she said. I haven't seen you in a long while.

The Masher stood close to her own height, thick-boned, always fidgeting with his hands, but he had a way of standing gentle. His head was bald but he had hedgerows over his eyes that could house birds. He smiled at her a little and when he spoke he sounded nervous. Kept clearing his throat. She knew in that moment she had intruded upon something. She took the weak grip of his hand. Good to see you, Eskra, he said. Tis getting warmer so it is.

He spoke as if he were sighing and she saw how he looked exhausted, the skin under his eyes pooled with the dark of sleeplessness while his eyes looked loaded with burden. He was not looking after himself, his clothes stained and he wore a blue rope-belt that reminded her of Matthew Peoples. The way he stood awkward, began to look down the street, began to futher with his hands, and she wanted then to get away. Well, she said. I must be going.

The priest smiled at her. And how are you and yours, Mrs Kane? Are yous doing well?

We're doing all right, she said. Barnabas is out rebuilding the byre and it is going up quick. It was either that or sell up the fields. He says it will be restored in the next month or so and then we'll be right again. Between you and me I can't wait to hear again the sound of new animals.

Pat the Masher spoke quietly. That's good to hear.

And how is your boy doing? she said.

In the instant that she spoke she saw a change come over the man's face, as if what she said had caused him some harm, the hedgerow of his eyebrows coming down in distress and he made then the smallest of grimaces, turned his head away. As he turned she saw his gaze uncouple from the world around them and become a strange unseeing. The priest taking quick steps forward and he began anxiously to rub his hands. Well, Eskra, we must all be going about our business. And he held out his hand for her to shake it.

The town a twenty-minute cycle behind her when she saw them amongst dusty nettles, head-bowed in a ditch as if ashamed at their own grandeur. She stopped the bicycle and wheeled it back and laid it on the road. A thunder of pure blue to pound the day and she reached her hand in to seize them. Nettles bit at her hand like the bee stings she was indifferent to and she removed each blue flower by the stem, stood on the roadside and stared at them. What the bluebells evoked in her was unspoken, nature's mastery over a part of her being she could not account for. Perhaps it was an awareness of time's passing, another late spring and her fleet life through it or maybe it was just the shock of their beauty, that a light so piercing to her heart could be as simple as this.

She picked up the bicycle and began to walk, thought again of Pat the Masher. That man did not look right at all. I hope there's no new bother with that son. The day-bright of fields and the bluebells in the basket. The bicycle back wheel clicking in satisfaction. The day felt loose to her and she swung in answer to its easy rhythms, looked up left at the lane that rose for the hills as she passed it and thought of Barnabas coming down with the horse. Light and peace now upon the mountains. The air a pure crystal. She followed along the road and a lorry passed by her. The driver signalled hello and she waved back though she did not know the face. When she reached the turn for their road she saw Billy coming from school along the main road. She stopped and waited, watched him shape into view, his short auburn hair standing skywards and his fists balled by his sides and she saw more clearly in his march the cut of a young Barnabas. Billy saw a pleased smile on his mother's face and watched it fall away when he spoke. Has Cyclop come back yet?

She shook her head slowly. He wasn't there when I left after lunch. He'll come back, Billy, I promise. He'll come back when it suits him.

She pulled the schoolbag off his shoulders and wore it on her back, wheeled the bicycle beside him. He marched ahead up the road. She called out to him how was school and he answered her with some vague mutterings and she did not follow up on it. As they walked past McDaid's house she saw Queenie sitting lordly on the step, a beast both sad and proud and she made them all look her minions. Billy did not stop as was his usual, but marched past the dog. He disappeared around the corner.

When she reached the turning she heard Billy's voice call out. He's back. He's here.

She heard him shout the dog's name a long eager call.

Her eyes passed beyond the trees and followed through the gate and she saw by the front porch the dog curled up and Billy running towards him. From her heart fell a load she had not realized she was carrying. Billy began to call the dog, but the dog lay there indifferent to him, exhausted perhaps after some epic journey through the fields, and she watched as Billy approached Cyclop and bent down to him. The boy put his arms around the animal and in that moment he leapt back, stood and stepped away with a jerk as if the dog had snapped at him, and Billy began to stagger backwards looking down at his shirt. He held out his hands and as he turned towards his mother she saw the horror that was held mute in his face, the boy's eyes opened wild and his hands steeped in blood. She was not aware of herself dropping the bicycle to the ground as she ran towards Billy, nor of the school bag that bounced on her back, and she grabbed a hold of Billy's arms looking to see where he was bitten and she saw that he wasn't, and in that small moment of time a vision of something else took form and expanded, held itself clear before her, and she ran towards the dog and saw how Billy took a step backwards, as if he held her accountable for what was, and she bent down to the animal and lifted up his head and what she saw was the glassed eye of death and a wide smiling gleam in his throat that had been cut into it with a knife.

Behind her, the boy howling.

Billy stood by the horse in the stable and leaned his head against the animal, held himself still in the must and silence and then he reached his arms around the neck of the beast. Heat-flesh brought to his ear the animal's storm workings, what stirred internal sounding like weather surges and governing all else the boom and ghost echo of her thundering heart. What he kept seeing in his mind was an awful vision of the dog and his mother's drawn face and he could not stop seeing them until his mother came into the stable. She went to him and she saw in the gloom his cheeks shining from his tears and how his lower lip was trembling. She reached out for him, sensed the tensed fibres of his arms, held him until they softened. The boy stood between woman and horse and the horse stood staring out of the barn with her eyes upon the yard and then the animal reared her head backwards and sneezed, broke the spell of silence. Billy pulled back and groaned. Oh, Ma. She's gone and sneezed all over me. Eskra could not help herself, tried to stifle a laugh and couldn't, and her laughter caught the boy by surprise and he looked at her upset, and then he started laughing too, and the horse shook its head at the two of them. They held each other as they laughed and Eskra's long laugh petered out and met sorrow waiting at the end of it and the two of them leaned in towards each other and sobbed. When their tears ran dry he let go of the horse and she wiped his face with her sleeve. She held his face in her hands and saw in his eyes a look of fear that left her shook, as if what the boy had witnessed was everything that was solid of this earth and its forms deliquesced, and she went to speak to him but did not know what to say and she was glad then for the sounds of Barnabas outside until she figured what it was he was doing. The dead-weight dragging sound of the dog being brought up the yard, and then Barnabas appeared backwards, walking past the door, hauling the body of Cyclop in a gunny sack. The boy tensed and made to move from her but she stopped him from going outside. From his cried-out eyes he gave her a pleading look. I don't want Da to bury him without me.

He's just moving him someplace else for now.

The hauling ceased and they heard Barnabas cursing, the agitated click of his heels on the flagstones, his face then appearing at the door. What are yous doing in here? He leaned against the jambs and squinted his eyes at the two of them. Do you know any reason, Billy, why somebody might do this?

He saw Billy shaking his head quickly, furiously, and then the boy made a low sound as if he had not the strength to talk. Naw, he said.

Barnabas stepped outside and stood looking at the byre and then he turned around to them and spat on the ground. I'm going over to Peter's to see if he's got a can of petrol. Gonna take the car up the town to talk to that sergeant. See what in the hell is going on around here.

She stood by the front door watching the road for Barnabas. In her mind she began to see a reason for what befell the dog. It loomed and pushed against her reason and she tried to hold firm against it, but what pushed powerful was an intuition – that it was that tiny Peoples woman who could do a thing like this. She could not tell it to Barnabas. She looked at the bloodied step and saw it catch the light like porphyry. By the gate lay the bicycle and beside it on the ground lay the bluebells that had fallen out of the basket. She picked the bicycle up and laid it against the wall, lifted the flowers and walked through the gate and hurled them into the ditch. She turned and saw Billy watching from the bedroom window, his face a whisper to the glass.

She was saddened and angry and she went into the kitchen

and took a bowl and cold water and added hot water. She kneeled to the step and washed it with both hands and her hair fell loose in her face. She rinsed the blood from the flagstones where Barnabas had dragged the dog to the sack, tried to imagine what kind of person would have the sickness to kill a dog like that, cut its neck on the step and leave it out for the boy to see. No thing for any child to see at all. Blood spilled at the back of our house and now blood spilled at the front of it and this place nothing but wretched. She turned and for a moment saw the trees and watched the way with grace they moved and she said aloud to herself, the wind sways not the leaves evenly.

Dog blood mixed in the water filmed her hands a translucent red. Dog blood a shadow of itself on the step after it was washed out, as if the life-force of the animal there remained. Dog blood a pool beside the step for two wasps that swung down from behind her. She watched them test and taste the blood and saw some vile conspiracy in their movements, that evil could find work out of evil, and she felt a sudden and deep sickening. She swung at the wasps with the cloth and flattened one of the wasps into a pulp while the other swung up agitated. It made a loop in the air and swung by her face and then shot for the roof and disappeared. She stood and removed with her shoe the mess of dead wasp, saw the disarmed point of its stinger, heard then behind her another drone. Two cars coming up the road.

Barnabas swung the Austin in front of the house and a black Garda car parked alongside him. Eskra watching the sergeant climb slowly out of his car. The way he stood. His shoulders slack as if he was weary of such trouble and the look of him barely forty. His face was slack too, his cheeks blue-shadowed and a soft end for a chin, and he wore a belly that pushed out at the buckle. Too many days with his feet up and she saw now he left his cap on the front seat if he ever wore it at all. But she saw something different in his eyes, the bright steel of composure that gave the lie to his demeanour and he caught her watching, looked at her grimly and nodded. Take me up to see this dog, Barnabas, he said.

They stood by the new barn with Cyclop lumped in a gunny sack. The jute had darkened with blood and when Barnabas rolled back the sack's opening his hand brushed off the dog's cold nose. He drew his hand back quick and wiped it off his trousers. The head of the dog held loose in the policeman's hands and his eyes met with the vitreous unseeing of the dog's eyes and then Barnabas spoke. This dog's dead only a short while. There was heat still off him when I lifted him. The blood was warm on the step.

Aye. Aye. That may be so.

Barnabas watched the man examine the stiffening animal, the slow-breathing like this was nothing new to him, the way he ran his fingers like a vet through the dog's fur, felt about the legs and up to the neck where he held gently the dog's snout without fear of it snapping open, trained a thumb through the fur around the mouth. He stood then looking at dried particles of blood on his hands, rolled them between finger and thumb, smelled it. He stood and turned and walked down the yard to the pump and worked a quick heave and sluiced his hands clean. He stood there looking at the byre with long interest and he leaned back and began to walk towards Barnabas.

I'm glad to see, Barney, you got yourself up and going again. There was talk there for a while this farm was done for. Aye. Aye. He turned towards the byre and nodded. An antique look you're going for. As he spoke he smiled as if he could not help it.

Barnabas frowned and he looked down at the dog in the gunny sack and began to swivel his foot, looked back up at the Garda with a squint eye. Tell me, Pat. What are we going to do about the dog dead here? The one with the throat cut out of it.

The Garda looked at him and he looked at the sack and he made a funny shape with the side of his mouth and then he sighed quietly, gestured with his eyes as if he wanted to say something. Barnabas looked at him. Do you think it was them Travellers that did it? I scared some of them off here a few weeks ago. Came right into the yard so they did and began rummaging as if there was no one living here at all.

The Garda shook his head. I doubt that very much.

Vicious cunts whoever they are doing that to a dog. It's the kind of them to do it.

The air shook with the sound of the back door closing harder than she had wanted it to and they turned and saw Eskra coming towards them. She walked with her arms folded to her chest as if she was guarding against peril itself and she did not give a damn that her hair had fallen loose. She stood to the Garda and did not meet him with the respect he was used to. What are you going to do about this? she said. She nodded towards the dog. Whoever did this to an animal should be well met by the law.

The Garda pursed his lips and agreed with her and Barnabas looked towards his wife. Eskra, would you go in and fix the Garda a wee sup. Something for his travels all the way out here.

Eskra threw him a look. Would you not go get it for him yourself? Have I nothing to say to him?

Barnabas looked at the Garda and he looked again at his wife. Please, Eskra.

A slow smile came upon the Garda's face and his eyes lit up. He raised a hand and brought finger and thumb into a near circle. Just a wee dollop, Eskra.

She looked at him and wiped the hair out of her face. I don't see anything around here to be smiling at, she said.

She turned and walked down the yard, her arms still folded, and the Garda turned to Barnabas. Is that what you'd call the American temperament?

Barnabas shrugged. That woman is usually soft as butter, as you well know.

Well, said the Garda. I respect what yous have gone through here. And it must be terribly bad for the boy to see it. It's extreme all right. To see that done to a dog. Aye. Aye. Though I'm not sure realistically what I can do about it.

Barnabas squinted at the Garda again. I don't understand, Sergeant.

Surely you do, Barnabas.

Barnabas gave the Garda a long look, saw the man standing expressionless with his hands by his sides as if there was truth in plain sight between them and he was waiting for Barnabas to seize upon it. The Garda began to look out upon the fields and nodded in their general direction where a low sun lay flat upon them. There's blood on that dog's fur that is a day or two old. Flakes of old blood, Barnabas. That's not his own blood whatever way you look at it. You're a farmer, Barnabas. You can take a guess. You must surely be able to picture in your mind what that dog was up to.

Barnabas looked at him, blinked slowly, spoke with a tightening throat. Sergeant. That dog was just an animal. I want you to go and find the person who did this. It was my boy Billy who found him. That's no sight at all for a boy to see so it is. Just a youngster.

The Garda nodded slowly. Aye. Aye. I agree with you about that. But you see, I can go around and make specific enquiries about who might have done this to your dog. But then I'll end up finding out about who has lost newborn lambs from this area, likely within two or three miles about here, and then I'll have to be coming back to you with costs for the damage or a summons. And I don't want to do that. And I don't think you could afford it. It's blood for blood. And I'm figuring, Barnabas, you don't need any more trouble so you don't. You've surely had enough of it. And I can tell you are climbing your way out now with this byre getting built. Good for ye. You'll have new cattle out on the fields for the summer. That's what I'm saying to people when they're complaining to me about where you took them stones from. That's what I'd rather see. So perhaps it would be best if we just let this one be, Barnabas. Let the sleeping dog lie, so to speak.

Barnabas swallowed, began to speak and found himself speechless, saw Eskra coming up the yard towards them with a glass of whiskey. Words began to misshape in his head and he could not seize upon a form that made sense to him, and he looked upon the Garda, the smile that rose on his face for Eskra, the hand that swirled the whiskey and took the drink to his lips, the bluing pink tongue that flickered briefly into the glass, the hand that returned the tumbler, the shine off it of the sun. Saw the way the Garda's eyes half closed briefly as if he was considering the travel of the whiskey's warmth inside him, down into the place of comfort. Eskra leaned into the policeman and stared. Her voice softly heated. So, Garda. What are you going to do about this?

The Garda turned to Barnabas and smiled and nodded towards his car. I've just had a talk with your husband. He can fill you in.

He began towards the car and Barnabas in his mind stood mired, could not figure upon a single clear thing.

The dog buried in the sack in the back field and the night spent quiet. The next day, under the beady eyes of blackbirds, Barnabas went back to the byre. That evening he stood drying his hands on a tea-towel and straightened it out on the stove's hot rail. Looked over towards Eskra. Are you noticing any wasps about? I'm working on the byre today and I must have seen four or five of them. One of them a persistent little bugger so it was.

I've seen a few about. Two on the step yesterday but they came for the blood. Normal enough to see them now with the days warming up.

I wonder if there is a nest about. Fucking pests.

The back door opened and Billy came in and dropped his school bag, made for the stairs. Barnabas sat in the range chair and called to him. Come here would you. Billy stood in front of him, his head hung and his blue eyes hopelessly dark.

Will we get you a new dog?

What would I want with a new dog?

Did you hear what I asked?

The boy was silent.

What's that I hear you say? Is that a yes?

Billy silent, still looking at his father, his eyes seeming to grow darker.

Barnabas took a hold of the boy's wrist and pulled him towards him slowly, and then as if it were a trick, he yanked the boy in close and began to tickle his ribs. Billy protesting with flailing arms, let out an angry squeal.

What's that I heard you say? Did I hear you say you wanted a new dog? Did you hear him say that, Eskra?

Barnabas took in one hand the boy's flailing arms while Billy squirmed to break free like an animal. Leave off. Leave off. Barnabas with thick fingers tickling him until Eskra came over and pulled the boy free of him. Billy standing there spent and crying.

Can you not see, Barnabas, the boy is upset?

Christ, I was only trying to cheer him. Since when can a father not tickle his son?

Billy went for the stairs and slammed the kitchen door behind him.

Eskra shook her head. There's no need to be so rough with him.

He's not a child any more, Eskra.

Well you were treating him like one.

Arrah.

Later, a burst of orange from the sun lit up the kitchen, stood golden a while before it fell out of the sky. Eskra got up from the table. She made tea, turned around to him. I might have an idea about who did that to our dog, she said.

Believe me, Eskra. You have no idea. No idea at all.

What do you mean?

Just. You wouldn't know.

What do you mean by that? What was it the Garda said?

Said?

He said he had talked to you when I asked him what he was going to do. What was it he said?

Well. He said—

He said what?

Barnabas stood there, saw himself mouthing useless air to the Garda. He said— Look, Eskra, he said would look into it.

That was what he said?

That was all.

Did he not have an opinion about who did it?

Naw. Now would you leave it at that?

Low cloud darkened the town and put rain brisk upon it, the streets like the plucked hide of some great bird and the wail of a lorry's horn from the far side of the town its dying call. She tied her blue headscarf and ran for shelter, stood in the grasp of shadows beneath the draper's awning. An old man cycling past with a pipe unlit in his mouth and his eyes squinting to the rain and she leaned back against the window's dull reflection of herself. The grey lean of the sky and she saw that the rain fell just for the town, that distant clouds were clear and bright. Goat McLaughlin then coming towards her. He crossed the street oblivious to the weather with his head held high, was followed by one of his black dogs that came towards her shark-faced. She saw in how Goat McLaughlin walked that he had grown indifferent to nature, could picture him bent in a coat amidst great heat or out in the snow in his shirtsleeves. He brought with him a stench of pigs that reached into her strong and the mongrel took to sniffing her legs and then it mounted itself up on her leg. Goat McLaughlin kicked the dog down. Sorry about that, Mrs Kane.

She began to retie her scarf and the old man leaned his smell into her. A wee word, if ye will?

She watched the way he leaned back on his heels as if to take in the full sight of her, saw a vigorous light in his rheumy blue eyes. His white shovel beard reaching to his chest. She could not put an age on him. What can I do for you, Mr McLaughlin?

Sure ye know to call me Goat.

That's no name to be calling a respectable man.

He shook his head and smiled as he did so. After all this time, Eskra Kane, and ye still don't know our ways.

She caught the smile that rose up from his beard and mirrored it back. As if anyone could learn them.

He stood silent a minute and she was grateful for the quiet and then the old man cleared his throat. I was wild sorry to hear about yer dog, Eskra. Ye know I'm mad for dogs myself. Hate the sound of harm being done to them. I'd cringe if I ever met a Chinese fella, what with the way they eat them and all.

His words put a cloud on her face and her eyes watered. He raised his hand towards her arm and rested it on her. I didna mean to upset ye.

Eskra swallowed and lifted her head and regained her composure. She looked down at the dog with its taut curling tail nosing about the street. The old man sucked on his cheeks. It hurts me to hear about such cruel treatment, for what's in a dog is its nature and no more won't ye agree? Born with the nose of a wolf. Ye will call around to me this evening, Eskra Kane, and I might have something for ye that would put a smile on the face of yer youngfella.

He leaned back on his heels again with a look that took her fully in, nodded his head to her, turned and was gone, a figure that seemed to fade to the last in that rain.

She waited two days and then she went to his house. He brought her through the meat smell of his house out back to a chicken-wire pen beside the pig house. She winced at the din of snorting swine. Do you not get tired of the noise? she said. The pen was fashioned around a dog hut that looked like it had been built by drunkards, a ragged assembly of plaited wood planks while it wore for its roof a rusted sheet of tin. The roof was slid back and she saw a litter of coal-coloured pups nestling against their mother. A smile lit her face and he saw it, came beside her and reached down and pinched a pup by the scruff, lifted it up to her. She took the pup in her arms a tiny bundle all fluff and sleepy eyes and an anxious pink tongue flickered at her fingers. She brought the pup to her cheek and let it taste the flesh of her. Goat McLaughlin stood with a smile rising like the dawn out of his beard, hocked his thumbs into his mucked trousers.

Is it a he or a she? she said.

Can ye not see the big dong on him?

Eskra looked at him strangely.

Take him home with ye and give him to the youngfella. He held her in his pincer eyes for a moment before he spoke again. And while I have ye here, there's a wee thing I want to ask ye about.

Eskra stood eyeing the pup's face, the crusted eyes, and then against her skin came the nose's cool quiver.

That Barnabas of yours. Rebuilding that byre. Ye know where he took them stones from, don't ye?

She turned to him and bundled the pup in her arms like a child. The way she looked at him then, a look he could not measure, could not tell if she was playing stupid with him.

What is it you are saying to me, Mr McLaughlin? That byre has been nothing but frustration to us. Are you not happy we've got to sorting out the problem?

What I'm saying to ye is this – he stole that stone, Eskra Kane, from old famine houses. Stole them from houses that are other people's graves. Ye might not understand this, ye being a foreigner and all, but them old houses are a part of us. Them stones are our bones so they are.

What famine houses are you talking about?

Blackmountain, he said.

Eskra went silent for a moment and she looked in her arms at the pup. She wanted to laugh, the thought of Barnabas going up there. The warped ingenuity. That blaze she saw in his eyes as a young man and here was the measure of it.

Goat McLaughlin began to pull at his beard and he did not blink looking at her.

Are you talking about those old ruined houses way out in the middle of the bog? she said. Tell me, Mr McLaughlin. Those houses weren't even fit for use by animals. I remember seeing them myself some years ago on a long summer's walk. They were lying in ruins in the middle of nowhere. Nobody's given a damn about those houses in a hundred years. So tell me now, why it is you are taking offence. Has he hurt anybody?

What he has done is an offence to every man, woman and child of this country.

You did not answer my question. Has he hurt anybody in a material or physical way? I doubt very much that he has, Mr McLaughlin.

The old man began to knead his boney hands. Call me Goat, would ye.

Whatever, Mr McLaughlin. I'm surprised at you. If those old ruins meant so much to you, you might have done something to fix them. You need to quit that kind of talk. You should know better than to be at a man like that when he's down at his lowest. There is one thing Barnabas is not, and that is a thief. Barnabas is doing right by us. He's doing his best. He's rebuilding that byre and I say good for him. So long as he's hurt no one I stand by him every bit of the way.

Taking them stones, Eskra, is as good as stealing.

Tell me, Mr McLaughlin. How is it stealing when that land is not owned by anyone?

The old man stood agitated and he looked at the ground and brought his head back up to stare at her. I fear for ye, Eskra Kane. Taking them stones is a curse. It makes a mockery of the Lord. They come from other people's misfortunes. They're part of the land, relics that must be remembered. I'm not going to do a thing to stop him and neither will anybody around here but everybody knows. If he were an honest man and a local man he would have stopped what he is doing when I asked him.

Eskra's eyes pointed with anger. If he were a local man? Barnabas is from here as much as you are. And I'll tell you another thing while I'm at it. I might be American but my blood is as Irish as your own. Your problem is you do too much remembering. You spend your time living in the past. That's the way it is around here. You live with ghosts, feeling sorry for yourselves. Always looking backwards. You don't know how to live facing forward, how to get things done in this country. She stopped for a moment to take her breath. And let me tell you another thing. There has been no more an honest man all his life than Barnabas Kane and look where that got him. That damn fire took away all our stock. It nearly took him away from me. I will say this, Mr McLaughlin, the last thing we need from you now is this sanctimonious horseshit.

As her voice rose the old man's voice failed him and only a bare whisper remained. By the light of the Lord, he said, and it was then that she interrupted him. Would you ever put a stop to that blather? She saw in that moment Goat McLaughlin for what he was, saw past the iron filings of his beard to the ashy of his skin, skin thin as grease paper and apt soon to dust away, saw behind the burning blue eyes that what burned there was fear, and where others heard a hard and righteous gale, she heard an old man's bluster. It was then in her mind the strong wind of the man died out.

She threw him a look of pity and he caught that look and saw it for what it was and felt useless before her, and she reached out towards him and placed the pup squirming into his hands.

I'll be off home now, Mr McLaughlin.

He held in his hands the last rock that would make a vertex of the gable wall, put his face in close to the stone. Quartz particles sparkled for him and in that way what he had built held a gleam to his eye despite the day's cloud that dulled it. When he stepped down off the ladder he saw the byre's structure was stood strong on the earth. He had built it lower than what had been there before, now a simple single storey, and it awaited timber for a roof. He walked to the pump and washed his hands in the cold water and went into the house, stood watching Eskra remove from a vase daffodils brittle like dry paper. She turned and saw the roof of his teeth.

What has you grinning?

Tis done.

What is?

The stonework.

A smile lit her face he had not seen for a while. He stood and nodded towards the back yard. Come out and look.

She saw the building stood solid and strong a ragged likeness of what stood before and she leaned her head against his shoulder. She said, do you remember those first nights when we got here? When the house was in pieces and was frozen and there was nothing down on the floors at all but rotting boards. And the amount of work we had before us to build up the farm? We were young and we were foolish but we did it. And look at us now. She giggled. It is like we're doing it all over again.

Only now think of all that we know, he said. It's different.

She took a look around her at the day's perfect peacefulness. The stilly waters of the sky and the breeze soft to the trees and the settle of their breathing together. Inside her the swell of good feeling that felt certain in her bones. You were right not to sell any of the fields, she said. I didn't believe this could be done but you did it.

He told her he might have difficulty getting timber for the roof straight away, that he might be a while in getting it, that this was the nature of these things. And if all else fails we'll take down a few trees of our own. Anyhow, I've the slates for the roof all sorted out. Peter says they'll need to be cleaned up a bit but they're as good as.

She said they would figure it out somehow, that they had figured it out as far as this, and she gave him then a squeeze of her hand.

He turned around. Is Billy about? he said.

I haven't seen him.

He winked. Come on then. The lion in me needs to have a wee lie down.

Two days before the fire coming home from school I heard him in the trees, was nearly certain of it, that funny bird call of his whistling at me. I knew it rightly, so I did, knew it was him and I knew then he must have escaped from the mental home. Me too afraid to stop and look into those trees and I could feel the blood sent ready to me legs, was hearing his call in my mind coming for me like a noose toward my neck. I had a wild bad feeling then, saw how he would hide himself in the forest, so many places to go hiding. Waiting for his chance. Me walking home with my ears sharp as a blade and my hand on my knife in my pocket. Kept listening out for that bird call wondering how it is they could have let him escape.

Then that day of Big Matty's funeral and me pimpled to fuck in me shorts and I coulda ate a horse too cause I'd slept in and the auld doll made me miss breakfast, sobbing over her tea she was. The saddest day ever and all I could think about during it was I wanted to get away and go down the back of Doherty's Hotel and have a fag. We were stood amongst the gravestones and I tried to imagine for a while what dying was like and I could only imagine it with me still being there to witness it and I took to wondering what it was like for Big Matty to die like that and then I had to stop thinking of it. When I was a wee boy Big Matty used to be always messin with me. The wee finger was gone on his left hand and he used to have this trick that made it seem like he had all the fingers on it and then he'd shake it and the wee finger would disappear. I used to ask him how he lost it but he'd tell me a different story every time and I would believe him. One time he said the fairies stole it off him cause he cursed them one night when he was younger and on the drink. Said he slept in a sheuch and when he woke it were gone and the rest of the day he spent lookin for it to no avail. Another time he said he got it blown off him in the civil war, said it were them gorilla fighters shot it off him and every time I thought of that later on I always pictured him fightin against monkeys, I never did know what he meant. The auld doll said there was no way Matty fought in the civil war and that he got no further out of town than that lump of a horse out there in the stable. She said he must have lost it in an accident. Maybe a threshing machine or the slip of an axe she said but it isn't our business to ask him.

She were talking to some old dear in the cemetery and the old man was chatting to that scary auld bastard Goat McLaughlin and then that crazy wee bitch of a granddaughter of his Molly the Moss is standing beside him. The thing that I done to her with The Masher I cannot speak of it and the way she was watching me now I began to get stressed. She stood there smiling at me with that devil look in her eye and then she comes over, the silly bitch leaning in with her face and arms chaffed blue from the cold she wasn't even wearing hardly nothing. She begins whispering to me all conspiratorial and I knew she could see I'd been crying and I reached out and grabbed her tit real quick and she pushed me back and stood there looking at me with those huge eyes. Her voice dropped low beneath the din of the auld ones and she leaned in to speak as if she had within her the answer to all mysteries like the teacher would be saying. And as she spoke I saw a fellow walking towards us, it was her older brother Jeb and I was sure he was coming for me, that he saw me make a grab at her and my throat went tight as fuck. I did not hear what it was she was sayin other than she was on about The Masher and she made mention of the fire but I was lookin at the brother wondering what he was going to do with me and then he's standing over us and he just smiles at me like I'm some eejit and drags her away. Off she goes tottering like a wee lamb back for its milky mother and she tilts her head backwards to send me a big smile. I heard her voice in my mind ringing with its mystery and I got a sick feeling in my stomach because I wondered then if she knew what I knew, that she might well do from the tone she took with me, that it was obvious to her, the thing I had been thinking all this while, that it was The Masher started that fire to get back at me. I know he did but how can I tell anyone? I know it was him that burned the byre for what I done to humiliate him with that girl and to get back at the old man too.

Part IV

THE END OF APRIL passed dryly into May and he saw the horse was happy on its feet. An eagerness from the animal when he went in to see her, the way she nosed her head towards him with affection and took the apple with appreciation from his hand. When he led her out of the stable to roam the side field there was no resistance and the horse began to stroll alongside the sun's contour of herself on the grass as if paired again with her better nature. The byre once again a presence in the yard they were happy about. It stood with a cement floor awaiting a roof, cast over the yard and fields new and large shadows of itself.

He went into the stable and took the bicycle and cycled the mile to the roofer John-Joe up at Glebe. The man stood in his sixties with wrinkled skin and hair the full earthen colour of his youth. For years he had worked as a blacksmith and his hands were still red and rough because of it, stood always as if his arms were wielding heavy tools. He held a hand out for Barnabas and Barnabas took it, the man's skin like pumice, and John-Joe listened carefully as Barnabas explained what it was he was doing, that he had no money for the job and what little he had was to pay for new animals but they could chop down trees and he would fix him up later no doubt about that at all when he was back at full swing. But John-Joe shook his head for he owed Barnabas no favours. I can get you some old fir lumber for nothing from up the yard, Barnabas, and you might even get a purlin beam out of some of it though probably you won't. I wouldn't say it's first grade and that might explain why it's lying there but that I can do for you. Things are just too tight right now to work for nothin or on credit Barnabas. I've had just two jobs to do this three-month and one of them fell through on me yesterday and I have an unexpected wedding to pay for goddamnit, Mary my youngest, he said, and as he spoke he swelled out his belly and began slowly to shake his head.

Barnabas went and took a look at the wood and began to knuckle his cheek. Arrah, John-Joe, you know I canny build a fucking roof with that.

She watched the days pass under every kind of weather, a neutral grey sky, bursts of sunshine, rain gentle upon the roofless byre. Barnabas going off on the bicycle and coming back at the end of each day empty-handed but for some lengths of wood he picked up some place. She watched him grow more frustrated, slip back at times into his earlier troubling behaviour, the kind where he would snap at the very walls as if the shadows were leering at him. She saw to the chores of the house and would check on her bees and heard in their tone the mild sound of agitation. Could not figure what was wrong with them. In the evening she would play a little piano. Leaning into the music. The notes on the page arrayed before her a perfect abstraction and she would reach into them and try to make them real. The music came in snatches of beauty, stumbled and sped and fell apart again as if the music could not be set free from their ideal by the stiffness in her hands. She stopped and felt the raw webbing between her fingers, looked to the pictures arranged on top of the piano. Saw her mother and father as they were newly married, her mother straight-backed in a chair, hands placed awkward before her. Her father clean-shaven in a way she never knew him. A boy's face with lug ears and small uncertain eyes. Another photo of her father taken years later with those same eyes deepened with knowing. A newspaper on his lap and a white pipe in his mouth beneath a black lunette moustache. She saw in each photo how her parents were staring into a future void unknowable to them, and she met their gaze over that passage of time, looked back over a bridge of knowledge of all that came. Their struggles and their pain and their small successes. The jaundice that turned her father yellow, became for him a slow death from cancer. How his demise left her mother poor and ruined – the man fading to ragged bones in the bedroom, a whittled emblem of the family's fortunes. And she thought then of the byre, the way it was stood and how great it was but how in a certain light its rooflessness made it seem already like a ruin, as if the building had amounted to failure before it was finished. As if she could see it from some strange future, see in it the ruin of themselves. It was then an idea resolved inside her and she stood from the piano and went out into the hall, put on her coat. Went to visit Peter McDaid.

He left the deadland holding two taupe-brown rabbits in his hand, the necks of the mammals twisted as if each of them had turned to see what it was had brought them their moment of death. The day swung to a pendulum point of dusk and as he walked the hind legs of the rabbits brushed the grass. The deadland began to merge with the brighter hues of fertile fields and he came towards a large gate, swung the rabbits over the peeling iron bars and climbed the top of it, began up a hill. As he neared the top he saw the land level out and realized he was in a cattle field, by the far trees dumb-staring silhouettes that stopped him where he was. I will not walk amongst them. He turned back and swung the rabbits over the gate and followed his body over it, took off in a wider circle. None of this land his own and he thought of the stupid bovine stares and he began to think of Matthew Peoples, the lean of him on a spade, a big-boned shifty weight of pure strength. A waddle up the yard with Cyclop at his heels. The melody of his laugh on a joke, the rising tune of it. He thought of the man and the dog standing in the yard and it did not seem real to him that both of them could be dead. He recalled a time when he brought over to the man's house a flank steak, Matthew Peoples opening the front door while tightening his rope-belt. Watching how the man dropped three mucked spuds without cleaning them into a pot over the fire and the way then he dropped the steak into the water after them to boil it. The brown froth on top from the mucked spuds. Barnabas standing up out of the chair in outrage. Jesus Christ, sir. You canny boil that fucking steak. He could still see the way Matthew Peoples was shaped over the fire, tried again to picture him clearly but could not.

The day fell upon its blue hour and everything in that light seemed to him intensified, as if the evening had thickened the trees and nature's canvas had become enriched with mystery. A storytelling of rooks made raucous the air and he came upon a path that cut through whin and bramble and passed through a stand of trees. It was then he met upon a plain view of Pat the Masher's house. He had not thought of it and stopped, the house in that bluing light softened to an indigo and everything in it held still to a whisper, no smoke drawing from the chimney and no people about. Something in his mind began to loosen and move forward and he could feel it as an idea taking shape, began towards the house before he had an answer for it. He walked down those sloping fields until he stood before the house, saw with disgust the disarray of the back yard, the tin cans strewn amidst broken boxes and pieces of timber, farm machinery lying whole or in pieces as if somebody had once attempted their repair before letting them to rust.

He walked into the yard and caught its smells, paraffin and tar and something else he could not decide on, like faint gone-off food, and he went slowly towards the window, looked in, the house dark and the outlines of a chair and a kitchen table. He turned and stood facing the direction of his own house and he knew then what it was he was looking for. Saw the window afforded a clear view – a distant darkening roof that was his own. You could see us fine rightly, he said to himself. You could see the whole of that fire. And you sat here doing fuck all. He turned for the door and put his hand upon the latch and it was then he looked out across the smallholding, saw the shape of Pat the Masher walking across the field, froze with his hand upon the latch, let it go and turned quick, across the yard then towards the fence unsure if the man had seen him.

He hung the rabbits in the stable and called out for Eskra, heard just the silence of the place. Washed his hands and poured luke-warm tea, fucking Christ, and held the cup by the throat. Leaning down to hitch up a loose sock when he saw in the tail of his eye a person pass the kitchen window. A man standing to the back door and then a quiet knocking. The door handle turned to open. Who in the—? He stood up in expectation, was near to his full height when he saw who it was come into the kitchen. Ah, it's you, Peter, he said. I didn't know who to be expecting.

Tis me all right.

Peter McDaid stood in his wellies with one eye on Barnabas and the other cast towards the window and he stood scratching his blue chin.

Eskra not about is she?

Naw. She must be late coming back from the town.

McDaid walked towards the deal table by the window and took a seat, moved a book out of the way to make space for his big hands, began to lean over them.

Do you want me to make up a fresh pot, Peter? The tea as usual around here has gone cold.

Naw, I'm all right.

Barnabas took his cup and sat down opposite. Did you take a look at the byre?

Aye, I saw it last week. It's a fine shape, Barnabas. A fine shape.

Wait till you hear the most ridiculous thing. I'm up in Tully's having a pint the other night and there's this fella there, a lorry driver who goes up and down to Derry, big thick head on him, never talks, and then he tells us this story. He says he was out by the Point and all of a sudden something makes a wallop on his windscreen and when he gets out to look he sees it is this huge owl. Imagine. This creature all brown and broken he says and curled into itself and its heart still beating cause he says he could feel it in his hand. And he doesn't know what to do with it so he picks it up and rests it on his coat on the floor of the lorry, drives around looking for a vet but he canny find one, so he says then to himself, I need to get rid of it for what I can do with a battered bird like this anyway? So he puts it in an auld bag and throws it into a ditch. This is after trying to rescue it, you see. So then I says to him, was it still alive? And he says to me, aye, I think so. So then Olly Mooney pipes up and says, would you not have killed it first? And the man turns around and tells him, I didn't want to have to kill it again.

Barnabas let off a gunshot laugh and then he stopped and blinked. McDaid was trying to force a smile but gave off instead the smell of trouble. Barnabas watching him in silence. What's wrong with you, Peter?

McDaid sighed. I got to talking with Eskra, he said. The other day. She called over and had a wee talk. Asked for me to have a word with ye.

As he spoke he reached his hand into his pocket and his eyes cast about as if he did not know where to rest them. He produced a white envelope, placed it on the table.

Barnabas looked at it. What's this, Peter? he said.

McDaid slowly swung his eyes to meet Barnabas, saw something change in the man's face, a sleety dark that fell quick to his eyes and when McDaid went to speak his mouth was chalk. It was Barnabas who spoke first, talked real slow, began to shake his head. Arrah, Peter. Tell me this is not what I think it is.

Cold weather passed between them and then McDaid's tongue warmed loose. Eskra came to see me, Barnabas. Suggested it. It's everything I ever saved this past few years. You know how I could do with the extra space. It's just the one field and it will pay for the byre roof. I'll be happy to see it back to you in a few year. You can buy it back from me when yer good again.

Barnabas held both hands before him on the table and

he stretched out his fingers and looked at them in a slow and strange fashion as if he had just awoke to the use of them as appendages, and then he made his hands into fists. He looked out the window. The cowling evening upon them and that same abandoning of the light pressing down on his eyes. He stood and spoke real slow, continued shaking his head. Why would you go interfering, Peter? Getting in the way? Why would you do this? I'm nearly out of this, Peter. Nearly out of it. Can't you see the byre is near built? After all that trouble I went to. Why would you go and insult me like that?

The more he spoke the more his face took on an incredulousness that deepened the sleet in his eyes, made his cheeks burn. McDaid looking at him speechless.

Barnabas continued. Naw, he said. I'll tell you what it is, Peter. You are taking advantage of me now. That's what's going on. You are taking advantage of my situation. You've been sitting there waiting for this moment.

Barnabas pushed back the chair further and fixed a stare towards the door. McDaid stood slow as if he had become his own mule after taking a beating, his eyes low, and then he looked at Barnabas sadly and shook his head, took back the envelope, fumbled it into his coat. Ye have it all wrong, Barnabas, he said. Ye have it all wrong.

Naw, I don't think so, Peter.

McDaid shrugged awkwardly and began for the door, stopped before it and turned to look at Barnabas. Well, he said.

Barnabas spoke. Aye. That will be the last of it so.

That same night after the house finally went quiet Billy could still hear his parents in his dreams. All night they came to him in shouting, his father's roar accusatory and titan against his mother's defensive squalls, their voices like some kind of weather that rode in furious over the sea, met the house and quaked it, shook and smashed crockery off the dresser. He was beset by such dreams all night that came in swells and abated, and who he saw at times were hardly his parents at all, for he had dreamed them out of shape, twisted and freakish apparitions composed of parts of themselves and other people, faces he grasped to love but faces that could not hear him or see him, and sometimes he saw in them John the Masher's face and he would shout and shout to silence. His father merging into his mother into some malevolent deity of one. It seemed to him all night he was beset by these visions, and in the dawn light when he awoke he felt tired and tormented, and for a while he sat on the side of his bed rubbing at his eyes with his fists, the dark silt of those dreams ashed upon the morning in confusion until finally he stood and heard the house was still.

The way she walked to the yard pump gentled the morning air, a gown soft-swung and bare feet soft upon the flagstones, her toes curling against the cold. The height of the sky a blue vertigo – the kind of day to leave the doors open for a while to let in the keen air. The porcelain jug in her hand bore an empty white belly layered with fine cracks, could have been a secret map of lost rivers long dried up, and those cracks were licked wet by pump water that was sent silver into it. She went inside and reached for a tin and saw they were near out of tealeaves. The kettle on the boil. She made a weak brew and left it to draw longer.

The storm with Barnabas was days behind. Each of them bruised to the other and she saw how hurt the boy was, the way he wore that hurt in his eyes as if an inside part of him had been darkened by them. After a day she and Barnabas made their peace and she had resolved with him to try better, admitted to him that she had made a mistake. That she had lost her nerve and did not trust him.

Things will improve, he said.

They have to, she answered.

Too late she saw the gap that opened permanently between Barnabas and Peter, the man no longer calling around, a sweeter man there never was but there is only so much sourness sweetness can take without becoming bitter. She told herself Barnabas would come around and see it how Peter saw it. That they would make their peace.

She took oats from the jar and soused them in the pan with hot water and set the pan on the stove. Pinched at the salt and sprinkled some on top of the water. Another wasp at the window. It flitted at the glass and she stepped away from it and saw it swing for the open door. Out and away with you. Upstairs the floor timbers groaned and she heard the sonorous noises of great suffering, Barnabas shifting out of bed and complaining to the walls. She leaned on the jambs and called up to Billy and waited till she heard him shout he was up and a few minutes later he came downstairs dressed for school. He sat at the table and played with his porridge. Grumbled at her. This tea's thin as piss water.

Don't you talk like that. That's the last of our rations.

He pushed the cup away from him.

Give it here.

He sat there fumbling with his thumbs and stole quick looks at her, something fraying about her general nature, the way her hair was shot with more silver. She watched him sit hunched as if protective, saw on his left hand ink marks that wandered spiralling to his fingers, a schoolboy's tapestry of violence in weaves and scrawls and an ornate skull and cross bones.

Why do you draw on your hands? she said.

Dunno.

Barnabas came plodfoot down the stairs bit down on a fag, the man fully dressed but for his bare feet. He sat down on the range chair and produced a pair of socks. Saw Eskra watching him. The way she spoke barely under her breath. Why don't you cut your toenails? He looked at her and said nothing, turned to the boy. When you get home from school quit whatever you are doing. I have a job for you.

Billy stood up and shrugged and bent for his schoolbag. Aye, whatever.

Don't you whatever me. Barnabas grabbed him and began to ruffle his hair with affection and the boy resisted against him, broke free with a staring red face. Leave off, would ye. He went out the door.

The air between Barnabas and Eskra a delicate thing that could bear little pressure upon it. He went out to the yard and closed the back door behind him. She began to clean about the house, went to the back door and opened it again, drafts of cool air bellowing into the room that fluttered the pages of a recipe book on the table. She went to the radio and turned the dial and stood a moment to listen. Could not recall what it was she heard, but the music brought suddenly a dim memory from childhood. A brass band in a park. Musicians in black. Sitting beside her father. Her mind grasping for details that were lost to her, faint smells found of roasting peanuts. The music on the radio swelled and subsided and left her holding the ghost hand of her father, and she stood there, saw herself as a child, felt herself as a child, felt for a moment grief for the loss of her old self.

She took the sweeping brush and went to the front door and opened it. Heard on the breeze a distant dog's woofing, a high octave of birdsong. Caught the music of the bees and heard it off-tune, an odd discordance. She swept up the hall and went into the kitchen for the brush and pan. She found the brush in the turf bucket and shook her head at Barnabas leaving it there like that, the man was unbelievable, began to nose about for the pan, found it behind the back door nestled against the shotgun. She took the brush and pan to the hall and bent to the small hill of dust and dog hair and she went outside with it to the hedge and bent and lowered the dirt into the thicket. She walked back to the house and it was then the strange music of the bees reached into her. She began towards the side of the house, her head cocked to listen better, wondered what it was that made so strange their droning. She came closer and what she heard was shrill and worrisome and what she saw was not seen until she was upon it, until she lifted the hive roof. What she had heard and believed to be the bees were not bees at all and that few of her bees were living. In that small moment of time she saw the carcasses of her hive strewn about, the mesh floor some mediaeval orgy of body parts like the leavings of a battlefield blooded. Bee wings torn off and strewn about to catch the light in their tiny way and shine it silver, pieces of black bee legs like loose strands of tobacco, thoraces disembodied and heads rolled as if they had been beheaded, and in a way they were, and she saw most of the bees' abdomens were missing. What bees were left complete were lying on their backs as if astonished at such butchery, and the insects that had invaded murderous for her bees filled her ears with violence – a plague of wasps that swung dangerous, made fizzy the air. In that moment she lost her mind to them, batted her hand at the wasps, a movement that was reflex and helpless, and the draft of her hand brought the insects upon her. A pail of wasps rose up narrow-waisted, swung at her with their stingers. They broke the white seal of her arms, the skin that lay thin on her hand bones, the delicate arch of her neck, pierced the promenade of her forehead, the plash of perfect skin between the eye and eye-bone. She felt the pain pulse white lightning in her eye and then thicken until it was felt in the whole of her head. She batted blindly, uselessly, staggered backwards the hot pain like pokers scalding the insides of her and her mind fell away from her. Jagging breaths and backwards then and she lost her balance and hit the ground, wasp venom ferrying itself within her, her-lips-her-skin-her-limbs thickening with it, and the strength gone out of her arms and she lay there on the green grass involuting and useless.

The spring sun shone and from the sky came chill drafts that made the leaves tremble. Out of the sky came a cabbage butterfly, a dark blind eye on each of its white wings and it beat the air briskly, fluttered high a soft kiss to reach the branch of an ash. And when it had rested a while upon a greening new leaf, it dived itself back down, its wings held over its head in the poise of a fallen angel. In the moment he came for her he saw the butterfly upon her, resting serene on the curve of her waist, a white orchid. Bent and took her in his arms.

He watched her open one eye, the other lidded swollen, a marbling of red and blue and she murmured to him my bees are lost. What he heard was a mesh of words unintelligible, her bottom lip fattened and her hands and arms and throat puffed up. Upon her forehead was a swell like she had been felled by a stone. He heard in her breathing a wheezing and he put his fingers onto the ashy of her skin, took her inside and sat with her by the bed until Billy came home from school. Sent the boy off for the doctor.

He went outside and walked slowly towards the hives, saw the place was devastated, heard a quiet that was total. Later, he told her they were all gone, the larvae and the eggs all taken and the honey was eaten also. She did not speak, lay there inert with one eye open towards the ceiling and then she turned away from him. He went into the kitchen and took from the press a number of blue glass bottles and he filled them with sugar water, hung them around the hive, put them inside the house, upon the deal table and on the sills of the windows, put two each side of her in the bedroom, hung them outside around the house. Later when he went to check on them he saw those placed by the front of the house held dead or drowning wasps in their dozens. He stared into a trap and felt pure disgust. Something else unsettled him. What he sensed perhaps was in the air itself or in his tasting of it, an odd and faint pungency, and when he looked up from the trap he knew that the world was askew to them, that somehow they had fallen out of kilter with what was, some invisible order, and he could not understand what for or how so. A whirling universe of chaos and dark and the light bending sharply away from it, could sense as if a door just opened to him the nature of the trap greater than he had ever imagined.

Two days later she rose to a yellow afternoon that lit the room. The house so quiet with all its windows closed she could hear above all else her heartbeat. She stood in front of the mirror and saw her face had lost its shape. She dressed with care and went downstairs and bent to tie her shoelaces and found her fingers hurt. What had to be done now was resolute inside her, had formed into a solid visual shape as she had lain there. Through the mesh of pain in her body she saw it. Now I know what's going on. My family. She sleeved her coat and stole out the front door and did not look towards the ruined apiary, could hear Barnabas banging something in the back yard as she ghosted out the gate. What kind of evening it was she paid no heed and as she walked past Peter McDaid's house he saw her from the field and waved meekly and saw the wave unmet, watched her pass down the lane. She met the main road and began to walk in the direction of the town, began moving her fingers through the hurt, sucked on her swollen lip as she walked, ran her tongue over the place where the venom had been entered.

Fir trees banking up a hill to her right netted the last of the daylight and thickened the air with resin. When the road met a stone culvert she took the left past it, a rutted lane that leaned down a hill and bent around a corner. Halfway down she met the white of a house. Did not knock to enter, opened the latch of the door without stopping and walked in. When she stood in the room she saw in it few furnishings and that nobody was home. A rocker with worn arms sat beside a fire that looked a good while dead. On the air the stench of the unwashed, while hung from a rafter above the fireplace was a black fowl. She looked in the second room. A brass double bed with a single blanket. A thickening of that stale smell. She began to look about the house for her missing white sheets, found nothing.

As she came towards the town she walked past people who

knew her – an old woman called Mrs Doherty who slowed to talk and looked at her aghast when she saw the state of Eskra's face, the fattened lip, the lowering swell of her forehead, her left eye askew. Eskra marching past her, walking with her hands fisted and burning, felt a swelling and heaviness in her legs. How she must have looked to others she knew too well from the way their eyes fell upon her, two men staring hard from the back of a passing cart. Across the town centre she marched towards the double-door of a pub. One door shut and the other open to a cramped foyer and she stepped into that dark and opened a frosted-glass lounge door. A grey and greasy window lit the bar and she stood in its watery shadows, the counter to her right without a bar keep and a turf fire burning. A table of three men stirred by the door to gawk at her, one of them leaning over his drink with his finger in his nose. The mouth of the man closest to her fell open when he saw her face, lifted his foot off a stool. Eskra saw what she came for at the far end of the room.

Baba Peoples sat with her back to the door beside an old man and woman. There was meekness in the way they were, hunched and no talk out of them and their hands were cradling their drinks. Eskra came behind Baba Peoples and closed a fist around a length of her thinning hair, yanked her backwards off the stool, began to drag the woman across the room like a sack. An odd sound left the lips of the old woman, a muted shriek that sounded more animal than human while she kicked her measly legs uselessly beneath her. Eskra dragging the old woman towards the door and one of the men stood quick and came behind Eskra and took a hold of her shoulders, tried to swing her away, forced her to let go of Baba Peoples. The old woman scrambling to her feet and as she moved Eskra shook free of the man and hit Baba Peoples a slap hard on the cheek, could feel in that slap how brittle were the woman's bones. The old woman flew from the slap and when she got up from the ground she took in the grotesque swells of her attacker. Her eyes shook with startle. Eskra's voice reaching up into a yell. You little tormentor. You're no better than a witch.

The man who stood behind Eskra took her firmly by the arm and she tried to pull free but couldn't. The barman appeared squat and bald and began shouting. Hold on there now, he said, his face reddening, but he did not come between them. Eskra shook herself free and stared at her restrainer as if daring him again to touch her, and she turned around and faced Baba Peoples. A voice rose up from behind her. She's only an old woman. What in the hell did she do to ye?

Eskra turned to the table and pointed to Baba Peoples. She's been tormenting my family. This last two months now. Doing things to us. She's been holding us to blame for the accident that killed her husband. This woman is bitter and twisted, no better than a little witch.

Faces turned to watch the words register on the face of Baba Peoples and she stood in that glare smaller than she ever stood, her failing grey hair unkempt over her face. She stared up at Eskra, took a step towards her, spoke then with unexpected defiance. I did no such thing, Eskra Kane. To ye or yer family. Yer making it all up.

Eskra's voice became cat spit. Listen to you and all your lies. You little fucking child hag. You did to my bees and you did to my family. And I know you did to our dog.

The old woman took another step towards Eskra and reached her hand into her dress pocket, produced a small seamstress scissors. She held it in the air before Eskra and stood defiant. The

barman shouted firmly at her. You put them scissors away, Baba
Peoples. The old woman leaned towards Eskra. I resent what yer
sayin, Eskra Kane. I never done nothing to yer family other than
ask ye for money. And got none. Now say it to me again, woman.
Call me a liar.

Eskra grew more vexed. The lies out of your mouth. Admit the
things you have done. You're trying to drive us out.

All eyes in that room were upon the two women, the eyes of the
men watching each other, watching the women, eyes that spoke
of a wariness of interfering, while some of those eyes took from
what they saw a strange enjoyment. As they stood there in that
room the hand of Baba Peoples rose up quick with the scissors
and it came then towards her own head and they watched in
mute horror as the other hand followed, took in her fingers a
sheaf of her own thin hair, how she defiantly cut that lump of
hair to the skull. She dropped her hand and the cut hair slid
off her head and fell with a flutter to the ground. The barman
gasped and a stool behind Eskra screeched and a voice shouted
out to stop her. Baba Peoples spoke again. Let her say it to me
again. Go on, say it, Eskra Kane. Call me a liar.

She held the scissors ready and the barman red-faced moved
towards her but Baba Peoples turned and warned with her free
hand for the man to stop. Eskra eyed her venomously and her
voice when it came out was belling. What a display, Baba Peoples.
You should be ashamed of yourself. You can do all you like to
your hair but you and I know the truth.

As she spoke the old woman struck the scissors to her hair
and with each strike made a ruin of her head, savaged the hair
off herself until she stood in the middle of that room balded.
She stood pointing her yellow eyes at Eskra while Eskra eyed her

back, the old woman's scalp faintly shining in the greased light and tufted. Then the old woman spoke.

I hope ye are happy now, Eskra Kane. I hope ye sleep well tonight. And I'll tell ye another thing that ye do not know. That dog of yers was got by a farmer, I won't say who it was, because his lambs were being slaughtered by your dog.

She watched as her words entered through Eskra's eyes, saw the woman's eyes flutter in confusion. Turned then and put the scissors in her pocket and righted her stool and sat down to her drink, the back of her head appearing to every one watching as some strange and shining defilement. Eskra standing in the room, everybody else in that room watching her, and they saw the way then she hesitated before them, that what began to alight her eyes was doubt, that the other woman's actions had spoken a greater truth, and as Eskra turned to leave the bar she felt a pure and bottomless dread, that from the way the people were now looking at her, she was the person being judged.

That crazy Masher bastard kilt my dog I know it, and he won't rest till
he gets me, who knows what he'll do next. I carried this truth in me for
weeks after the fire like a curse and then one day I says it to the auld doll,
it just falls out of me so it did. I tried to tell her it was The Masher that
done in Cyclop and that he started the fire to get back at the old man for
having him sent away to the mental home but she just shakes her head at
me. That boy she says is locked up in the asylum forty miles away and he
won't be getting out probably never, that is the sad way of these things.
Why couldn't she listen? What went on with Molly the Moss in the forest
were all his fault, he was just leading me on. He was behaving all natural
like it was something he normally done and I suppose I was pretending
that it was all normal to me too. We went looking for her to tell her to
keep her mouth shut after she seen us when we left the car in the field and
it was like she was waiting for us. We walked past her house real slow
and she came outside and followed us and we nodded for her to come
for a walk. Her hair like twirly auld straw and them big blue ringy eyes
on her and something brazen in her bearing. In the blue of her skin she
always looked frozen. The Masher kept on giggling and whispering to me
saying she's wild stupid and we gave her a fag and the three of us smoked
with her walking behind us. We're looking at her and she looks at us and
says what did you think I was going to tell? I would never say nothin. We
traipsed about the place, out around the edges of her grandfather's fields

and then we went up the hill into the planting. The Masher was hooting laughing when we got into the trees and his voice was ringin the tops of them and he was as giddy as a dog with two dicks showing off. It began to darken a wee bit the further in we got and we got to where it was a good bit darker than daylight the trees so thick, and it was as good a place as any and then we just stood there all awkward. The Masher bends to the ground and picks up the branch of an old tree and he starts banging it off a trunk and it makes cracking sounds that echo in little shocks. I'm standing there with my hands all stupid and start looking up at the trees looking for birds or whatever making awkward conversation and then she just says I'm wild tired so I am, and she lies down on the forest floor on top of all them needles. When we go to her them needles are stuck to her hair and they are stuck to the undersides of her arms and when she lifts up her dress up to her neck you could see them stuck to the back of her whole body and the two of us we start kissing her tits laid bare they were to the world. Her breasts small doughy rises and we're just lying there licking at her and she's lying there not saying a word with her arms by her side like she doesn't want to touch us. And then I don't know why or what came over me but I just reached and pulled her dress all the way off, I didn't even think about it none. And I can see her now all whitely laid out and the bluey rings around her nipples and the tuft of hair between her legs like the wee head of a baby. Her knickers had come off and the way she stretched her arms back to allow the dress to come off made me think she liked what we were doin to her. It felt like heaven and hell right then the way we just stayed there licking at her a pair of scrawny cats to the buttermilk and I was too nervous to do anything else, the closest I'd got to a girl before was feeling Mary Laffin's tit through a jumper. That time was only a grab and as I lay there over her with my two hands flat on the ground feeling a soreness in me wrists from the leaning and me knees getting wet from the moss I could hear the silence of the place over us, the thick quiet of the trees listening and then the hoot of a bird overhead watching us no doubt too and wondering at the weird sight of us. And I didna care if anybody saw us and a hunger came over me like fire something strange. I sucked away on her tit and did not notice that he was away up off her and when I looked up it was too late and my heart leapt out of my chest when I saw him standing between her legs with his cock freed out of his trousers. He veered it towards her and stuck it at her and there was something wrong with him and then he began to shudder and he was done before he even got it in. The Masher on his knees lookin like a fool and she let out a high-sounding laugh at him and then she took a hold of me in that same moment and unbuttoned me and guided it into her my mind going into a pure whiteness and I heard her make a small pig squeal as it went in. A voice trying to scream inside of me it were wrong and I knew through and through it were and I couldna stop even though I hated the pure sight of her, the silly wee bitch, and when we were done the place's quiet like the wind that's died after a storm. And I saw then that The Masher while I was up on her had run away in shame and that was the last time I seen him till he came up to my house with the iron bar. The all-white of her laid out like snow and the way then she looked at me after we were done with it, a long soft look she gave me, and I pure as hating her.

S HE TOLD HIM SHE was still sick and would not tell him what was wrong, sat in the range chair where she walled herself in and did not rise from it. Sat there mute to him. He puzzled at her behaviour and told Billy his mother was still ill from the wasps. The next day the boy came home from school red and agitated, skulked in the shadows of the kitchen scowling at his mother, watched his father as he fixed the fire, followed him outside until Bernabas turned and cocked his head towards him, would you go get the oil for the lamps, some of them need refilling. Billy just standing there and when he spoke his words poured out. He told his father he was being taunted at school, that they were saying his mother had beaten up the old woman Baba Peoples, that she had cut off the woman's hair to mark her. Barnabas looked at the boy in confusion and he began to shake his head, started cursing at him, told him to go away and fuck with such nonsense, but Billy shook his head and said it was true, that he had seen the old crone himself at a distance that day on the road and her hair was all gone off her. Looked like a fuckin bird so she did.

Barnabas stood before Eskra with a lamp. Asked her about what happened. Met the shut door of her face. He stood there looking at her speechless. Finally he said, what is it have you done, Eskra?

What is it? What did you do to her? She did not speak and turned from him and blind then he became to his temper. He dropped the lamp, shook her near to standing out of the chair, pincered her cheek with his fingers. Met an eyeball that bore blue chill to him. He spat when he spoke. What in the hell is going on, Eskra? Did she do something to you? What?

The face before him then of a different woman altogether. The swelling had gone down and her face took its old form but in the eyes now he saw a total change. Leave me alone, she whispered.

In the aftermath of what was they scarcely spoke and he watched her continuing retreat from him, a shadow in the range chair passing hours listless, seemingly listening to the radio, or he saw her ghosting wordless through the rooms. The way she began to go out on long walks in all weather, as if to get away from him, and he would watch her, walking their fields but never those of another as if she were trapped on the farm, hemmed in by something other than boundary. It seemed to him she eyed the world now from someplace remote, a place where she could control what it was of the world she let into her and he saw too a difference in her bearing. It was as if she had lost her love for him but would say nothing of it. Barnabas watching on with a dread feeling. He tried to get her to eat and every day made some kind of dinner, usually of eggs and potatoes and meat, and he would make her breakfast in the morning but she would sit before her plate or bowl and pick at it. Will I get you the doctor? he said. She did not pass beyond the gates of the house and she spoke only a few words to Billy when he spoke to her and the boy began to look at her askew as if she were some malevolent twin of his mother, began to come late from school.

Barnabas did not know what to do with her so he began to spend more time on the byre, worked himself each day into a total exhaustion. He went with the axe to the stand of trees between the pasture and taper field and felled first the ancient oak. Palms burning from the swing and bite of the axe. The oak yielded to him and in that moment it seemed to him all of nature adjourned to watch, the weather holding itself mute, for in the few seconds of its falling the great tree let out a sorrowful groan. It smacked the earth and it seemed not just the leaves on the tree but the very air was trembling. He felled a mature evergreen and he chopped both trees free of their branches and used the horse to drag the harvest into the yard and he piled up the useless branches into firewood. He went again to see John-Joe, dug into their savings which was to pay for the new cattle. John-Joe the next day appearing with a horse and cart and strapped on the back was a large motor-powered band saw. They ripped the air with the noise of its cutting and over the course of a day cut the trees into slices of timber. Carried the lumber to the new shed and stacked it in piles and sheeted it up and Barnabas asked him how long he would need to leave it dry for. John-Joe began scratching his dark head. That depends, he said. The least, I imagine, is a month.

The early days of May brought a cold and mean sort of weather. He drove into town for supplies in the spit-rain and he saw how people had changed to him. People whom he might have expected to stop and say hello no longer paid him heed. He went into the hardware shop and was made to wait until last to be served, and when he was, it was by the store-owner's son, for the store-owner, John Doherty, looked through him as if he were a ghost and went out back into his house. He drove home that day clamped down on his teeth with his hands white on the steering wheel. That same afternoon he saw the priest appear in the drizzle on his bicycle, cycle through their gate under a wide black hat and leave his bicycle gently against the wall. Barnabas hid behind the new shed, watched with disdain the way the priest walked so light on his feet, went around to knock on the back door and put his hand to the glass to look in. Calling out Eskra's name. Barnabas staying where he was until he saw the cleric cycle back out onto the road. Knew she had gone out on another long walk again.

He stood before the roofless byre and listened to the emptiness of the farm, this time of spring and all that should come with it, the song of the animals as they would have been taking to the fields in their chorale. The way the cattle knew his voice. Their aliveness. Their stubborn cowness. He stepped up the ladder and climbed the front wall and looked to where he would fit the rafters and then he looked down into the waiting byre, saw how he would place into it a beating heart. The bellow of cattle and their goading, the old knit smells of feed and shit. He thought of the way Eskra was behaving before him, that goddamn woman, and he could not understand her any more and did not know what to do. No longer even a mammy to the boy. Seemed as if she no longer had the ability to hear them. A few more weeks to wait for the timber and then he would roof it and slate it and the byre would be done and when it was, surely she would right herself again. Everything could start all over. The way he was treated now in the town. He leaned over the stonework and banged it with the base of his fist. A taste of salt air faintly from the bay and from his height on the wall he saw the land as it was encircled around him, McDaid's back fields, the lands of Fran Glacken, that white house of Pat the Masher's with its mess and stink. He leaned over the wall and spat onto the flagstones.

He saw her at the table when he came into the room staring at a plate of picked-at food. The stove near gone out. He stirred the fire and fed it and poured himself cold tea. Turned the radio on. A song filled the room and stopped him on his feet. An old jazz song, a Duke Ellington number, and it brought him instantly to her arms in Vinegar Hill, dancing in her mother's apartment. He leaned into the radio and turned up the volume and called across the room. Come here to me you. Her head slowly half-turning and then he was upon her, took her by the hand and pulled her out of the chair, began to lead her in a softly dance slow-circling as if dragging a scarecrow with stick feet. He whispered to her, you remember this, don't you? Steered her into the swing of the music and then her feet found form on the ground and she began to relax into him, allowed him to hold her a little better, took a hold then of his hand more firmly. Her head fell to his cheek. The byre smell off him. The man become byre, become wood and nails and brick and timber and the dust of it all in his hair and the wire of his bearded cheek and she could smell off him too the grass and the trees, could smell off him all of Donegal.

He said to her, come back to me, Eskra, will you? Come back to me. Please. What's done is done. I don't care about it.

Her voice rose to him like the ghost of a voice from long ago. You will look after the boy, Barnabas? Won't you? I don't know who I am any more.

What are you on about, Eskra? You are his mammy.

She felt his arms tense as they moved slower now to the music.

Don't you see, Barnabas. Everything is different now. Everything has changed. We cannot live here any more.

He stopped on his feet, let go her hand, bulled his eyes into her. What are you talking about, woman? he said. The fucking byre is nearly all built. I've gone and rebuilt it for you. For us. For our family. I've gone and paid to cut the wood while you were lying in your bed. I built the thing with my own bare hands. You must be gone in the head. His eyes blinded and he turned and stamped out the door, left her standing in the room on her own.

Dreams of disquiet held him like a vice and then his mind was loosed into the room. He opened his eyes and lay there grasping at a dream, like hands trying to hold water. The bedroom clotted with semi-dark and he shifted and listened to the quiet of the room. Turned and saw Eskra had got up. When he went downstairs the kitchen was dark and bore no sign of her, the bucket unfilled with water and when he opened the stove door he saw the fire was not lit. He cursed and went out into the morning and found the sky was low and luminously white as if something sacred was held just beyond its beckon. The pump let out a long, languorous screech like some strange bird calling and he filled the jug with water. A scruff grey cat appeared as if in answer to the pump's call and it loped across the yard watching Barnabas. The cat stopped and braced itself to run, sphinx ears and streaks of rib bones beneath black-and-white tiger marks, and then the cat leapt quick into a field. He walked towards the gate with the jug in his hand and he leaned out to take a look at the road, looked as far as he could see towards the corner but saw no sign of Eskra.

He started the fire and laid it with turf and waited for the stove to heat, put on the radio and sat down. News of the war and football results and he stood up and turned it off again. The fire was warming when he saw the time and he called for Billy to come downstairs. A short while later Billy appeared in a rush. I'm late for school, he said. Nobody woke me.

Barnabas stood with his hands on the sink. How old are you now? Can you not wake yourself up?

Billy walked to the stove and saw no porridge had been made. Where's me breakfast? he said.

You'll have to go without. The stove's just been lit. Barnabas looked about the kitchen. Here, he said. There's a heel of bread.

Where's Ma?

She's upstairs in bed.

The boy took the bread and stuffed it into the pocket of his coat and he grabbed his schoolbag. I'm going up the town after school, he said. He went out the back door and slammed it. Barnabas knocked on the window and motioned for him to come back. Come here, son, he said. Billy stopped sullen and then he turned and came back to the door. What? he said.

Will we see about getting you a new dog this week?

Aye. Whatever.

What radiance was held in those white clouds faded to grey and the sun stole behind it a stealthy animal. He went into the stable and spoke hello to the horse and he mucked out the stall, put feed and water before the animal. When he stepped back in a while later he saw she had eaten her feed. He praised the horse and led her outside to the field and as he walked alongside the animal a strange feeling of loneliness came over him and he fought against its intrusion. When he turned from the horse he saw part of the wire fencing by the side of the house was sagging as if somebody had fallen over it. He went back to the stable and fetched the wire tightener. Walked the perimeter of the field and tested the wire for slack and tightened it until rain began to stipple his shirt. As he walked back to the house he saw there were sheets out on the washing line, walked over to take them in. They billowed softly as if forms of small children were shaping them into ghosts. Something about them bothered him and as he came close he saw they were the fire-ruined sheets he had found in the press upstairs. They were hung neatly pegged and taking rain grey as the day they were ruined. What the fuck is she doing? he said. He yanked the sheets off the line and pegs sprung into the air like small birds. He balled the dirt sheets and stormed with them in his arms towards the house, stood in front of the stove and looked at them again to make sure. Saw they still bore the smoke marks of that day and he stood there thinking of all that happened since the fire, opened the stove in a rush and stuffed the sheets in with the poker. He stood a moment shaking his head, saw in the wall's scalloped mirror the distant shape of the horse under a tree.

It was only later that he saw it. He made tea and sawed bread and took the paper and sat down to the deal table. Had moved it aside with a sweep of his arm before it registered. A letter. What caught his eye was the handwriting – an envelope addressed to him with Eskra's handwriting on it. He felt then something tremor inside him, dull earth falling loose into the pit of his stomach, ran his thumb over the neat handwriting. The letter was a single white page of black script with no address on top. He read the letter twice, read it slowly, heard clearly her voice, circled over each sentence as if to test each line for solidity and meaning, and when he was finished reading he held the letter on his lap before him. He sat in the chair by the window and let the day die slowly around him, twilight casting buckled shapes of the world and a trapezoid of light on the deal table slowly retreating from him. A shadow forming at the table's edge and it began to swell and make towards him, travelled tentative across the wood, a sprawling ivy shape until it took slowly in its grasp the hands of Barnabas, began to creep up his arms, and when he finally stood he was entangled, the dark of the room and the cold and the fire gone out and a shadow made of that darkness had entered inside him. He left the letter on the table and began slowly up the stairs, went into the bedroom and closed the door, drew the curtains. He sat on the bed and kicked off his shoes, swung his legs under the blankets and pulled them up to his neck. What broke inside him was what breaks in a man and he lay there stiller than the night that crept around him a hunter of dusk, stealthy and relentless as it beat its dark void wing upon the ceiling, devoured the entire room.

When Billy returned home after dark Barnabas did not hear him come into the room. The lamp he held put pale fire on the ceiling as the boy leaned over him. He whispered, what's going on? Why are ye in bed? When Barnabas did not talk, he spoke again, a rising tremor in his voice. Are ye sick? Where's Ma? Barnabas lying there silent with his back to the boy and Billy crossed the room and stood over the other side of the bed and saw his father's eyes wide open to the dark but taking nothing in. He shook his father and Barnabas blinked.

The next morning Billy came into the room holding his mother's letter. His eyes were red from crying. He stood before Barnabas and prodded him with his finger until the man stirred and heaved his eyes up like heavy stones. What does

Mammy mean? Billy said. What does Mammy mean when she says she's going home? That you are to look after me until she's better?

Barnabas eyed the boy coldly and he spoke in a low monotone.

Your mammy's left, he said. Gone back to where she came from. She says she couldna take any more of it, son. All this. That her nerves are shot. That she canny look after you like this. She won't be back. She never liked this place anyway. Says she is gonna send for you when she is able but you'll not be going nowhere. You'll be staying here so you will. She can come back here, so she can, if she wants to be your mammy again.

Billy silent for a while, his face white. Is she not my mammy any more?

She is still your mammy. She hasn't been herself this last while. That's all there is to it. Now, please. Leave me alone.

The words of his father let flee something loose in the boy like storm-startled animals and he walked to the window and half opened the curtains and looked out. The view as he had always known it charged now with something different, as if the components of this world had come to hold an entirely different meaning. He turned around. Why didn't you go after her? he said.

I didn't know she'd gone only until later.

You coulda stopped her so you could.

Can't you see the car's gone? She went and took it.

His voice fell away for a moment and then he spoke. I don't have any energy for this. I'm done in. Please leave me alone.

Billy stood there and his face bittered towards his father and his eyes became slits and he reached towards the man and let loose his fists upon him, shouted all the while. Why didn't you go for her? Why didn't you go? You could have gone for her.

His father took the blows without moving, stared up at him a dumb beast.

He fell out of time, went to the deepest place. Days spent like nights and awake through nights like days. Where he lay was a stone room in his mind that shut out the dim day, the frowning night, the hours circling around him like prowling dogs unwanted and wary. He lay awake in that cold room cancelled from living things, nameless in his own void and when he slept it was a fitful sleep and he saw in that shapeless space leering faces of all those he loved and could not reach. She hovered like a wraith in his dreams with her spirit broken and he reached for her, saw her indifferent towards him, her eyes cold like she did not know him – like she had unlearned her love – left him with a feeling of pure hurt that carried through into his waking being. How he loved her. An ache of love. He dreamed he was walking along a road and he met a procession coming towards him and in that parade he saw every person he ever knew and as they walked past him weary in old clothes and sad faces he knew that every one of them was dead. He did not know if it meant anything. In his waking hours, the years of his life had taken on such weight he felt he could no longer lift himself from bed, lift himself into the world, felt like he had been tumbled out of his life. Images flickered and memories roamed unbidden, wild animals set loose to move about dangerously and each had their own distinct reek. It came to him how strange this place was to her when she first saw it, that it was no place she could call home. How she hated it but endured and he denied to himself that the vast and mythic place he held it to be in his mind was but a dream, that it was scant and cold and wild and it did not care for them. How he loved her. How he loved.

In the hours of day he could hear Billy making noise downstairs, the boy trying to keep the house going. The pump in the yard made its bird squeak and he could hear every few hours the opening and closing of the stove door, sometimes noises of cooking. The boy kept the radio on and let it run all day and every few hours he would appear with food speaking kindly, slices of buttered bread and tea, and the boy attempted to make soup and he cooked spuds and brought them up to the room steaming but the plates and bowls piled up beside the bed and the food went barely eaten. In the evenings Billy skulked softly in the room watching his father, afraid to open the curtains and when the man was sleeping he drew the covers over him. In the thin lamplight he saw himself a spectral figure upon the wall, did not know what it was like to watch a man dying but thought it might be something like this. Wondered if a grown man could die from hurt. He urged his father to drink some tea, to sup on water and after a while Barnabas would put his mouth to a cup. The lost child eyes of his father. The boy tried to talk about his mother but Barnabas guarded his silence as if his mouth had been bouldered up to keep in the dead and he did not hear how the certainty of being that was held in the boy's voice began to escape out of him. The boy hovering unlit amongst the shadows of the room, fear gnawing deeper into him.

The days swung loose around the house and then a night beamed a full moon oblivious, beamed again half hid in cloud and less the figure of what it was. He could hear the boy's breathing as he stood behind the door, hear the soft moan of wood as Billy stood at the top of the stairs, holding still in the dark afraid to make noise or take what was circling in his mind and let it speak. And when Billy went into the room later and spoke to Barnabas he did so quietly, spoke as if he were afraid his words would shatter what was left of the man. After he spoke he heard not a sound and he shook his father's shoulder with both hate and affection and he saw then that his father was asleep and the words that passed his lips went unheard, the shapes sounded by his voice uncoupling into silence.

Barnabas dreamed he was working again at great heights, stood on high steel and in each and every such dream he faltered, fell the long fall. Three times he had that dream and awoke from it sodden and helpless. And then he awoke and heard the drum of rain on the roof, noticed that his mouth was arid. He sat up and listened to the rain, heard when it stopped the house fill with silence and he spoke to himself. I'm not dying. The radio was off and he heard no sound of Billy and he reached for his water and saw it was finished, stuck his tongue up into the glass. He swung out of bed and stood on weak legs, began to walk as if his legs were new to him, padded downstairs in bare feet. Every room silent in the hand of the cold while his breath rode the air before him. Into the kitchen. Saw the place distressed as if a fight had occurred, a chair lying broken on the floor and an empty bottle of whiskey sideways on the table. He righted the bottle and called out to the boy. When he opened the fire he saw it had long gone out, saw on the table beside the whiskey a plate with food beginning to moulder. Called out to the boy again but was met with no answer. He went to the water jug and shook it and saw it was empty and he called out again, heard his own voice faltering, cleared his throat. Billy. Where are you? He went outside with the jug. Lost to whatever it was the time of day.

He found fuel for the fire and lit it, watched how it danced newborn upon the wood and held his hands over it. I hope that boy's not gone after her. How far will he get like that? We'll go together and bring her back. That is what we will do. The room began to spread with heat. Afternoon and he found only the dust of tea leaves in the tin so he drank hot water instead. A stale heel of bread to chew on. He tidied away the pieces of the broken chair and fed them to the fire save for the chair's seat that was too large to fit into the stove. He went upstairs to the room and went to the drawer in the dresser where all their money lay hid in a biscuit tin but when he opened up the box he saw all of the money was gone. His voice a whisper. Eskra. He sat down on the bed and held his head in his hands, stood again and began to look through Eskra's things, saw she had taken little with her but that her valise in the press was gone. He sat back down upon the edge of the bed. Wept.

Downstairs and he put on his hat and he went out to look for Billy. That boy lying some place silly drunk. He called about the yard and walked down the road until he came close to McDaid's and then he turned back. Billy. He went to the chicken coop and saw the birds had fled, had not been fed in days, one lone chicken wandering the far edge of the field, went over and rescued it. He felt about for eggs, found one and then another, stomped back towards the house. The eggs stood on end in water but he was too hungry to care, watched the water foam over the top of them, stood at the window peeling the shells. The albumin white rubber in his mouth. Through the window he saw the horse waggling its head up the side field. That animal unfed and how long. He put on his welly boots and went back out, walked through the dim day up the field. Billy. The horse came towards him and shook its head with welcome and he took it by the halter, began to walk it to the stable. How long you out here, horse? Eh? What is a horse to do? The horse sounded brightly upon the flagstones and he saw how the byre stood bare to the day in its shape of rough stone, roofless, waiting for him to return and finish it, and he walked the horse into the barn door and stopped. Held in that gloom of horse dung and web and must and a faintly reaching daylight was something else, the sensation that came to him of a person, and as soon as he was aware of it he turned and saw, let the horse's halter drop, saw held in a shell of grey light the limp hands of Billy as he hung lifeless from the roof, and something collapsed in Barnabas's mind for he turned then and walked the horse back out, walked it towards the field, let it loose, watched it roam towards the trough unfilled but for what rain had fallen into it and he stood watching the sky his mind darker than all things made of weather and anything else that stood under the sun.

McDaid was on his haunches unrolling wire when he looked up and saw the form of Barnabas taking shape through the trees, the man staggering down the road, coming near to his house. He stood quietly and backfooted into the wood. Lambs spangled snow-white around him and his left foot began to itch in his welly boot. He leaned against a tree, pulled out his foot to scratch it, saw Barnabas disappear and appear again at the edge of the field. The way he stood like he had a heap of drink in him, his hands making dumb fists and calling out to McDaid, squinting, could not see him. McDaid watching him, saw Queenie watching Barnabas, hope to fuck that dog will not give me away. How it seemed that Barnabas could barely speak. Heard in his voice a desolation that reached into the sky and fell silent and it was then that he wanted to go to him but would not, not until that man addresses the misunderstanding between us, watched as Barnabas turned and stumbled away.

Out of the house plodfoot he came with an old milking stool in his hand. Stood outside the stable and looked at the sky. Strange clouds. They stood over the land shaped in clusters of near-hexagonal cells, each cloud heavy at the centre with dark. Their outer parts were fringed with an electric light. He saw blue sky hovering behind the parts that did not touch as if waiting to break through.

He did not want to go in.

Upon the flagstones he watched a devil-wind whip together a vortex union of grass and leaves, a moment of pure concentric energy that rushed them into violent being, a dancing circle that danced and danced until the circle fell broken, grass and leaves blowing in different directions away. He puzzled on it for a moment as if he could read some meaning from it. He ground down on his teeth and went into the stable and stood the stool in front of the boy's bare bluing legs. He laid his coat out upon the floor for him. When he stood on the stool he saw the rope behind the throat, a goddamn double granny knot did the thing. He closed his eyes as he reached with a knife to cut the rope. What came from his own throat as he cut was a freak animal sound and he opened his eyes to catch the falling dead weight, laid the boy gently on his coat. He cut the noose free from his neck, bent to the ground and lifted him. He carried the body out into the day and stood grim in the shadow of the byre, the body's stiffness having passed so that the body fell loose in his arms. My dear boy. He could not stop his mind becoming vivid, pictures and smells of Billy as a young child feather-light in his arms, carrying him up to bed, a sick child a few years later, worn out from fever all hot skin and his small hands curling and clutching at him tightly never wanting his father to leave him. My dear boy. What he carried now in his arms was as heavy as all the clay of the earth and his heart the equal of it.

He did not know what to do so he laid him out on the deal table, made a pillow for the boy with his coat. His breath stalled into a terrible silence and then he let it out, his breath a cold and haunted face. Could feel against the flat of his hand Billy's cold skin, could feel the rough texture of his hair, smoothed with his thumb the boy's blue eyelids. The diagonal rope burn on each side of the boy's neck and soft light pressing through the window caressed his face, made him seem serenely beautiful, the bluing lavender of his skin, such lightness an unjust beauty. Barnabas stood over the boy and wanted to speak but his mouth was filled as if he had opened it to a scarp of loosed earth that pitched into him, clumped his tongue, stuck to his teeth, began to fill up the insides of him.

He lifted his boy up and held him longer than any time he held him alive since he was an infant, his tears warm on the boy's cold cheek.

He kicked something skidding under the table and he bent down to retrieve it. A black notebook. When he opened the cover he saw Billy's scrawl on it. Wondered why it was on the floor and then he knew what it was, the boy drunk beyond caring. He took it to the stove and opened the door, saw the fire reduced to a depressed red slump. He fed the fire turf and threw the diary in on top of it, closed the door and sat broken on the range chair. Suddenly he snapped back up. He opened the stove door and reached in and took hold of the notebook through smoke, saw it was not yet burnt. He collapsed into the range chair and opened it, the boy's scrawl a strange mix of small and capital letters, saw the notebook was filled with a confusion of entries and stories. He began to read and in his heart he feared it was a violation but could not stop. What he read placed Billy's voice into his mind in the purest form. He heard him in a way he had not heard him while he was alive and the strength of the boy's voice through each word struck him weighted with the full of the boy's being.

Hours passed. Flies began to appear around the table and he stood up and batted at them with his fists. When he looked again from the range chair their number had multiplied. He looked at them appalled for what they were wont to do, how they moved in black flits around the room, arced and alighted, flew away again to fill the space with their sickly buzzing. He saw them gather at the window nosing at the pane as if they could see a path out into the wider daylight, the drizzling rain, buzzing their way frantic at the glass without knowing it was the limit of their nature to be able to see outside but not to be able to pass through the window. He began to see a different picture of what had caused the fire as he read the boy's words, saw it puzzle together, keeping that Masher boy hid, that's what was going on, and it seemed to him a perfect picture.

An evening of two suns. Those strange cellular clouds had been scattered west by a wind that left the sky with what seemed like blue smoke. Upon it rolled a penny moon magnified and aflame. It made a fool of the waning sun and its flames sent filigrees of light into the sky, cast everything around it with a magnificent burnt-orange. There was within him now a rage, an anger basic and fundamental to the nature of what it was that made him, and he let himself ride its fierce energy. Walked through the rear gate and left it lying open. Behind him the gate finally gave up and slumped towards the earth. Through barren back fields he walked with his fists balled watching inward dark visions that came to him unbidden and he let them roam, those animals of a fiercer nature, his vision narrowing down so that he ceased to see what direction he took, ceased to see the land before him or what was underfoot, ten thousand wet tongues of grass reaching for his ankles, thistles spiking at the sky. The vanishing shape in the grass of his foot. Overhead a skim of dark birds passed with a great whoosh. He walked down a triangular field that narrowed to a rope-tied gate and he entered now into one of Fran Glacken's fields, the soaking bottoms of his trousers cold against his leg as he swung himself over the gate. Marched through a long slanting field shaped like a sickle, the earth freshly ploughed, stomped the soil under him slow and heavy like sand under his boots. The land leaning down and baywater a short distance away reflecting that smoke-blue evening light and what seemed like those two suns shimmering on its surface. Over the water a lone gull sobbed and jooked sharp for a flint horizon. Down the sloping land till he saw the isolate shape of Pat the Masher's house.

He walked in the door, stood in the man's kitchen, saw it was empty, took in the deepening strange smell, boiled cabbage and meat and other things he could not name, the unique smells of another. What was in him now needed letting out and he walked into the other room, saw Pat the Masher asleep on a chair, his hands shaped into useless fists on his lap, his jaw hung loose. There was serenity in his being and it slipped off him like a mask when he awoke, Barnabas standing over him with a fist balled the diviner of all malice. What Barnabas saw alight the man's eyes when he awoke was puzzlement, his brow lowering to thicken over his eyes, and then the wide startle of fear. Barnabas's voice coming at him sea-tidal and what he saw in Barnabas's eyes made him speechless, the animal shape of the man over him. Where is that fucking bastard son of yours? Where are you hiding him?

As Barnabas spoke he wavered a red fist before the man and The Masher opened his mouth but no words would come out. Barnabas pulled him out of the chair by his shirt but the mechanics that brought The Masher to standing ceased to work and he fell limp like a rag doll. Barnabas grabbed him by a ruck of his shirting and dragged the man out of the house, dropped him in the yard beside an old potato digger livered with rust, its giant wheels lying useless like discarded Grecian suns. He leaned down into him so close he could almost see the other man's thinking.

Where is he, Masher? You fucking hid him, didn't you? Oh yes you did. Now tell me where he is. He burnt down my byre and took away my farm and now he's kilt my son.

The man's face puzzled and he went to speak but he could not find the words and Barnabas beat him twice with his fist in the forehead. The man took the beating uselessly and his head fell loose to the floor and then Barnabas lifted him up again. Tell me, he said. Something then in The Masher came to life and he began to struggle and they turned about and he swung a fist up that made a perfect blow to the side of Barnabas's head. Barnabas staggered rearwards, lost his footing, fell in a helpless slow fashion upon the potato digger. The old metal rang from the bang of his skull and for a moment there opened up a terrible silence, Barnabas lying there stupid and mute, his eyes stunned,

The Masher standing over him in horror with his hands to his head, watching the dark blood come.

You stupid man, he said. See what you done to yerself.

The Masher turned and paced about the yard and he came back to Barnabas and leaned in again. His eyes shaking. That boy of mine, he said. His voice broke and his mouth fell loose but the power to speak was propelled by some last wind within him. He shook his head at Barnabas again. That boy of mine, Barnabas. He was kilt. Died weeks ago at the hospital. Took a bad beating at the asylum though they say he took a fall. Buried him in the asylum graveyard before I even got to hear. Twas the priest drove me up.

Barnabas trying to stand, his mind faltering, his hand to the soft and bloody part of his head, his body a tree riven in two places so that he began to see in double. He could not see where The Masher had gone. Could see hardly anything at all but for snatches of the evening light as he stood bent against it, the sensorium of his mind coming undone to a dazzling dark that sought to spread like ink within and consume him. He tried to speak, could taste himself in his mouth in new ways, clump of tongue-flesh rolling loose in his mouth, and a stumbling then towards the fence. Fell over it, began to move a wambling pack beast up the field, a mountain rill in the back of his mouth trickling iron blood. Back-bent and heaving. Blinking against the unseen light. His mind become animal instinct, a place of pure survival.

He made his way slow up that hill, the world an unearthly sloping while he tongued his wet blood mouth. Colding fingers. He found his way into the sickle field, walked till the nausea defeated him and he bent over and vomited food and blood, and when he stood back up he saw in his split vision his handprints as they had pressed into the earth.

An almost sparkling white hotness.

Shivering when his shadow fell in the door.

He made his way through the kitchen blind and past the point of grief. Did not stop to take in the shape of his son, took the stairs hands and knees drooling blood upon the boards towards the bedroom dark. Grasped off the chair a towel and when he lay down on the bed he put the towel under his head roughly folded. Lay there shivering in the long shadow of the bed while the night opened like a mouth from a dream.

Drifting then into a tangle of strangeness and what came to him was a talking in dream tongues, crazed stranger faces, a howling wind of pain. The nausea in his belly rose again and he awoke and was sick all over himself and when he lay his head back to rest and put his hand to his head he could feel his hair cotted with blood, the softness at his skull quietly weeping. He did not understand. He wanted to apologize.

The burning moon turned a cold bone. What light it cast fell weakly into the room, laid a shellacked shawl upon the dresser, glanced off the mirror onto the wall. And then the room became dark as the moon was fought back by clouds and it lay so until hours later. His hands so cold now, could not feel his feet, adrift into an oozy darkness, drifting and then slipping deeper into those dreams. Their faces. The pair of their faces before him. Dreamed the coming sound of a car.

He awakes to a room without moon, a void of pure dark and he hears an echo in his chest where his heart is. What lies behind his eyes is a pulsing hurt that drifts like the tidal sea, a soothing and crash, and he spreads himself starfish, drifts further down, drifts into the deepening sea, can feel himself letting go down into a benthic deep. Just his breathing now, so delicate a thing like an animal sensing the air before the rush of being born. So cold. So cold. And he lies there drifting down until something stirs in the room and his mind comes up out of that dark. Someone else. He senses in the room a person. A small stone of heat begins to burn in a place he has thought burned out and he pulls his hands free of the blankets, slowly sits up, blinks to see. Sees his own starlight first and then out of that sparkling dark at the far side of the room he sees a lamp's low glimmer. The yellow flame casts the silhouette of a figure in the chair and the stone inside him burns brighter now for he knows in his heart she has come. Love. The purest light. He climbs slowly out of bed, stands unsteady, begins to walk towards the shape of her and as he nears then he sees that the other person is not Eskra at all.

He sees before him Matthew Peoples.

The old man with his eyes upon Barnabas, so tired a face he has looking up at him, and then he rests his hands on his lap and stands up. He leaves the lamp upon the floor and tightens his blue rope-belt and lifts it up again, takes a look at Barnabas, shakes his head sadly for him. He turns and begins towards the door and Barnabas begins to follow, out of the room, slowly down the stairs he follows the lamplight of Matthew Peoples, shadows melting on the walls. In the hall he sees the moon is gone and he follows him into the kitchen, peace in his mind, peace in his heart, and Matthew Peoples pulls out a chair and sits down at the table. Barnabas sits beside him and they survey each other for a moment, and he can see now in Matthew Peoples the man's eyes so clearly, the pure look of them. The look of a man's sadness. And then Matthew Peoples stands and leaves the lamp upon the table, begins towards the back door, the room pooled to dark, and Barnabas stands slowly and starts to follow, so cold, so very cold now, and as he follows the night is without sound so still, his feet cold on the chill floor, and he can see the outline of Matthew Peoples open the back door, and then he is beside him and he stands looking at Matthew Peoples' face, old man face of wind and rain and rivers, and then Barnabas speaks, his voice a bare whisper.

I didn't know how to do it any better.

His voice falls away and there is silence and Matthew Peoples reaches towards Barnabas and he lays a hand to his cheek, smiles at him, and then he turns, the bulk shape of him moving out the door, the night that is starless.

In the field the horse stood and nickered softly, turned from the wobbled reflection of herself in the trough, began west towards the wooden fence. The day bright as crystal and the hills stood everlast in that wind that blew soft, soft through that land invisible like the harrying hand of time itself. It tipped the wilding grass in the fields that lay barren, shook dust over the hush of the farm house, shook dust from the byre's bare stones, the building as it lay roofless to the elements. A grand silence but for the hum of the world that came to the horse the same ever in all its sounding.

Epilogue

It were Stephen's Day morning and I'm trying to eat me porridge and the auld doll was over by the stove telling me about something to do with when she was a wee girl la la la and I'm watching through the window and I see the strangest thing, Cyclop standing in the front yard with his tail swung up and he's trying to snatch at a magpie. No chance though because them birds are too smart and there's two of them and they take up either side of him and one of them comes in at him daringly close and Cyclop turns around for him but as soon as he does that bird skips back and then the other jigs forward behind him and bites at his tail. It was like they were tryin to confuse and torment him and this went on with the birds snappin at his rear and the dog getting more frustrated. Me laughin me head off, come here Ma and look at this, and when the auld doll didn't turn I shouted at her, what, she says, and I motion towards the window, and then she comes to the window and watches, and at this point the dog is chasing his own tail in circles and she starts laughing too and outside Cyclop starts woofing and then the auld boy is coming down the stairs and he starts shouting, what is all the fuss about, and the auld doll points him to the window to watch, and he stands there between us with his arms resting upon each of our shoulders, the weight of him, and then the big sound of him, filling the room with his laughter.